Donna

Highlander The Dark Dragon

Cover art
Kim Killion Group

Ebook Design
A Thirsty Mind

Visit Donna's Web site
www.donnafletcher.com
http://www.facebook.com/donna.fletcher.author

Highlander The Dark Dragon

by

Donna Fletcher

Chapter One

Heather woke with a start, her heart beating wildly and her body chilled. It took her a moment to realize that she was home in the safety of her bedchamber and tucked comfortably in her bed. It had been two days since her return home and she had yet to feel completely safe and protected. She had woken the last two mornings, thinking she was still hiding in the woods from the ghost warriors while trying to make her way home. Her biggest fear had been that she would come face-to-face with her abductor—the Dark Dragon.

She shivered at the mere thought of his name and pulled the soft wool blanket up to her neck. Why the infamous warrior had had her abducted was still a question that haunted Heather and perhaps continued to be the cause of her unease. He abducted her once, would he not try again?

Heather shook her head. Lying abed would not solve her problems or ease her worries. However, her chores would provide a good reprieve from both. She hurried out of bed and slipped on her pale yellow linen shift, followed by her drab green tunic, and snatched up her brown leather boots near the fireplace to pull on and strap quickly. She ran her fingers through her soft blond hair, letting the natural waves fall where they may until she collected her four bone combs off the chest by the bed and with deft hands secured her long strands atop her head, though a few stubborn ones broke free and fell along the back of her neck.

After snatching her cloak off the peg by the door, she sighed as she rested her hand on the latch. She was home and she was safe, nothing would change that. She had her family to protect her. She could return to her daily life and everything would be fine.

Heather opened the door and as she stepped out of the room a little voice whispered in her head, "*nothing is the same nor ever will be again.*"

Another shiver ran through her and she hurried down the stairs and into the Great Hall. It was so early that the servants were yet about. It did not matter to her, for she was not hungry. What she wanted most was to walk through the village while it stirred awake and feel its peacefulness like she had done endless times before. Maybe then she would finally feel that all was well.

She draped her cloak over her shoulders and stepped outside. The sky was just beginning to glow with the first light of dawn and Heather was thrilled that she had not missed the sunrise. She hurried along to reach her favorite spot on a small rise and watched as the sun rose like a fiery magic ball from the depths of the earth.

Heather's smile grew as the sun inched its way up, spreading its glorious light across the land. She recalled all the mornings she had stood here watching the sunrise and how happy she had been then, and she wished she could feel that same happiness now.

Patience, Emma, and she had finally been reunited, and she was so very pleased that her sisters were both wed to two men they loved and who loved them. And even more exciting news was that she was to be an aunt. Emma was with child and when the time came Heather would be right there to deliver the babe and see her sister safe. She was also thrilled that her da was feeling much better and looked far better than he had in months. And though there was a chance of war with Patience's husband's family, the Clan McLaud, they would face the threat together as they had done before when a clan war loomed on the horizon.

With lightness in her heart, she had not felt since being abducted, Heather turned to walk down the small rise, eager to start the day and eager to begin life anew. She stopped when something caught at the corner of her eye and she turned to look out on the rise just beyond the village.

Her heart slammed in her chest and fear froze her in place.

There, spread across the rise, atop their horses were the Dark Dragon's infamous ghost warriors, their faces painted white, and in the lead draped in black and astride a black horse was the notorious Dark Dragon.

Heather shuddered at the sight. With the ghost warriors faces painted white, it meant they were ready for battle. She had to warn her family.

This was no time to hesitate. She turned and, yanking the hem of her shift up, ran down the rise like the devil himself chased after her. The sudden toll of the bell, warning the village of approaching danger, tore through the quiet morning. Her heart pounded harder and her feet ran faster and she wondered— how did one outrun the devil?

Heather reached the keep's steps just as her sister Patience came barreling down them, sword in hand.

Her eyes turned wide as she reached out and grabbed Heather's arm. "Get in the keep and stay there."

Heather was well aware of her sister's extraordinary skill as a warrior but even she was no match for the Dark Dragon, and it worried Heather that Patience would attempt to protect her against the notorious warrior. And what of her clan? They would fight to protect her as well and how many lives would be lost? The troubling thoughts sent her stomach roiling, but she would not let her sister know her worries. She kept her concerns mostly to herself ever since the day her mother died. She had been barely seven when she was thrust into the role of being a mother to her two younger sisters. She had stood by her mother's grave, an arm around Patience, hugging her tightly as an endless stream of tears ran down her small rosy cheeks. In her other arm she held Emma, the young child crying, though not understanding why. And her ashen-faced father stood staring in disbelief as earth was shoveled onto to his beloved wife. She had made a silent promise to her mum then and there that she would stay strong and would take care of them all. And she had and always would.

"Come inside, Patience, we must speak to Father," Heather said and slipped her hand in her sister's.

"I will not let him take you," Patience said with such conviction that Heather feared blood would flow this day.

Emma came rushing down the steps, her husband Rogan trailing behind her and Hunter, Patience's husband, flew past them to his wife's side.

Emma paled when she caught sight of the Dark Dragon and his men on the rise. "Oh my God, he has come for Heather."

"Over my dead body will the Dark Dragon take her from us," Patience said, gripping her sword tighter.

Hunter shook his head and slipped his arm around his wife's waist, ready to stop her from doing anything foolish.

Heather released her sister's hand and left her to her husband. Since her return home, she had seen how good Hunter was for Patience. They made a perfect pair. He was a handsome one and her sister beautiful. He also possessed a charming tongue and a good heart, and Heather was amazed to see how much he loved Patience and more importantly that he had the patience to deal with her sister's impatience.

"They sit waiting rather than attacking," Rogan said, placing a protective arm around his wife.

"Waiting for what?" Emma asked anxiously.

"That is what we need to find out," Rogan said. "We need to speak with your father."

"First, I will see that our warriors are at their posts and that the village is prepared for battle," Patience said.

"Or to greet a guest," Hunter chimed in.

"The Dark Dragon is no guest of ours," Patience said and looked to her sisters. "Tell Da to wait until I return to discuss this matter. I will not be long." With that she hurried off.

Rogan looked to Hunter. "See that she does not do anything foolish."

Hunter grinned. "I do not perform miracles."

Heather smiled as he hurried after his wife. His humor, patience, and thoughtfulness continued to confirm what a good husband he was for Patience.

Emma walked over to Heather and gave her a hug, though Heather sensed it was Emma who needed the hug just as she had when she was a child. Emma did not remember their mother, having been barely two years when she died. To Emma, Heather was not only her sister but mother as well.

"I will do whatever is necessary to keep you from the Dark Dragon," Emma said with the same conviction that Patience had.

Heather caught the fear that rose in Rogan's eyes at his wife's declaration. While Rogan could intimidate with his large size, striking features, and authoritative manner, he treated her sister like a man who truly loved his wife. And she was pleased that Emma was his wife instead of her, which had been her father's intention. Emma and Rogan were well-suited and Heather had been surprised upon her return to see how her plain-featured sister had blossomed into an attractive woman.

Rogan reached out for his wife's hand. "I think it would be wise to let your father know how upset Patience is."

Emma smiled. "Trust me, he already knows."

Rogan and Emma headed up the stairs, Heather following, having politely declined Rogan's hand. She had spent too many years alone, being strong, to rely on anyone now. A twinge to her heart had her steps faulting for a moment.

Quinn.

He was forever in her mind and heart. He was gone almost ten years now, but her love for him had never died nor would it.

She hurried after Emma and Rogan and into the Great Hall, chaotic with activity. Everyone was rushing around and Heather could see the fear on most of their faces. It was simple to understand why—no one was ever victorious against the Dark Dragon.

Emma rushed away from her husband and over to her father. He looked more like a mighty warrior than he had in months when an illness had struck and incapacitated him. He was quite the powerful chieftain in his plaid, his long white hair braided on one side and his stance one of strength.

"It is the Dark Dragon and we cannot let him take Heather," Emma said, gripping her father's arm.

Donald Macinnes patted his daughter's hand. "We will see this matter settled well."

His soothing voice and strong reassurance had Emma's shoulders sagging with relief. However, Heather was not as relieved. The only way this matter could be settled well was to give the Dark Dragon what he wanted. The question remained—why did he want her?

"Sit and do not worry yourself," Donald ordered Emma. "You have the babe to think about."

Rogan approached his wife. "Your father is right."

Emma shook her head. "I am fine and so is the babe. It is Heather who concerns me now." She went to her sister's side and slipped her arm around her. "Da will see to this. All will be well."

"With the Dark Dragon nearly at our door, how will all go well?" Patience demanded, entering the Great Hall with her husband and hearing her sister's reassuring words.

Donald Macinnes spoke up before anyone else could. “Please all of you take a seat.” He pointed to the trestle table in front of the massive hearth where many a night he would find his daughters deep in conversation, laughter, and sometimes tears.

“There is no time to sit,” Patience insisted. “The Dark Dragon has not stopped by to pay us a visit. He has come with his ghost warriors ready to fight for what he wants. And this time he is going to be vastly disappointed when he learns he will leave empty-handed.”

“The Dark Dragon is here at my invitation,” Donald Macinnes said with a ring of authority that could not be denied.

Everyone was too shocked to say a word.

Donald Macinnes continued. “War brews around us and clans that once were loyal allies are now questioning if they should remain so, especially if the McLauds ally with the infamous Dark Dragon. They fear the mighty warrior’s revenge if they should dare take up arms against him.”

Patience’s brow narrowed. “What are you saying, Father?”

“Sometimes unfavorable agreements must be made in order to avoid senseless deaths and endless bloodshed.”

“Do not tell me that you bargained with the devil himself,” Patience said her bold green eyes ablaze with anger.

"As chieftain of the Clan Macinnes, I do what is necessary to save countless lives and to secure our land," Donald said with a firm lift of his chin.

"What did you do, Father?" Patience demanded accusingly.

Donald turned to Heather. "I have wanted your happiness above all else, and there is nothing I would not do to see that come true. But I also know there is nothing you would not do to see your sisters and your clan safe."

"Father, no!" Emma cried out and Rogan was quick to slip his arm around his wife.

Donald stepped closer to Heather and reached out to take firm hold of her hands.

Heather was grateful for his strong grip, for it meant he had healed well and she was pleased to feel how warm they were when his illness had turned them so cold. But she was also reminded of how he had taken her hands in this familiar way on another day.

He had woken her and taken her to his solar. It was there he had taken her small hands in his just as he did now and had told her that her mum had died and that it was necessary, and her duty, to be brave and strong for her sisters and the clan. With just a few words she had gone from a carefree, young lass to a lass with responsibilities far beyond her barely seven years.

The weight of her father's words had placed a heavy burden on her that day and she feared that his words this day would be more terrifying than burdensome.

"You are a most precious daughter to me, Heather, and know that I love you dearly and that I did what had to be done." Donald took a strong breath, squeezed his daughter's trembling hands and with tears threatening his aging eyes said, "I wed you to the Dark Dragon."

Chapter Two

Shock froze Heather while chaos seemed to reign around her. Her sisters' raised voices rang in her ears as they endlessly berated their father. He, however, ignored them. His eyes remained focused on Heather and his hands continued to hold hers firmly, as if he did not want to let her go.

It was funny that she just noticed how the few wrinkles around his eyes had multiplied, spread wider, and deepened. It had not only been age and illness that had taken a toll on him, but concern for his daughters and clan whose care and protection fell solely on him. And her heart felt heavy with his burdens.

"This cannot be allowed," Patience screamed her fist pounding the table.

Donald released Heather's hands after giving them a gentle squeeze and stepped to her side to face Patience, and in a commanding tone said, "It is done and cannot be undone."

Patience opened her mouth to argue.

Her father raised his hand, silencing her before she could speak. "Do not bother to waste your breath, Patience. The deed is done and the Dark Dragon is here to collect his bride."

Tears ran down Emma's cheeks. "You cannot mean to sacrifice Heather to that monster."

Rogan took his wife's hand. "As dreadful as it sounds, I must agree with your father."

Emma yanked her hand out of her husband's and stepped away from him. "You cannot be serious."

"I too agree with him," Hunter said and looked to Patience. "And you, who hope one day to lead your clan, must see the necessity, yet the great difficulty of his decision."

Patience shook her head and dropped down to sit on the edge of the bench behind her. "I could not do this."

"Of course not," Heather said, walking over to her. "And I would not make you. I would make the choice myself, for I could not live knowing that my selfishness would be the death of many, least of all my sisters."

Emma joined them, her tears continuing to fall. "It is not fair."

Heather heard her father's words from all those years ago, reminding her and they slipped from her lips. "It is necessary and it is my duty." She looked down at Patience. "Did you not tell me that you wed Hunter out of duty?"

Patience stood. "Aye, I did, but Hunter is a good man with a kind soul." She shivered as she said, "The Dark Dragon has no soul, and we still do not know why he abducted you."

"I refused most vehemently his first marriage proposal," their father informed them all. "His second one warned me of the consequences if I did not agree. My concerns grew when our allies began to warn me of whispers that the Dark Dragon planned to join forces with the Clan McLaud."

"Is that why our neighbors the Clan MacTavish never sent help when I asked for a troop of their warriors to meet us at their border?" Patience asked, recalling their dangerous journey home from McLaud land.

Donald nodded. "They feared showing their allegiance to us with word spreading that Greer McLaud was about to sign a pact with—"

"The devil," Patience finished.

"So you signed with the devil instead," Emma said, shaking her head.

"Did he at least give his word that he would treat her well?" Patience asked.

"What good is the word of such a vile man?" Emma said frustrated.

Heather wanted to reassure the two that she would be fine, but she was not fine; she was scared to death. Actually death seemed preferable to what she was about to face. Tales of the Dark Dragon spread far and wide. Recently a traveler had passed through their village and she had overheard him talking with a Macinnes warrior. He had told the warrior that it was known that the only use the Dark Dragon had for women was to appease his lust for rutting which was as ferocious as his lust for battle.

The awful thought sent her stomach roiling and her heart pounding. How was she ever going to survive?

"Did you try to negotiate with him, Da? Something—anything—that would benefit Heather?" Patience asked with concern.

"There was nothing to negotiate. All the power was in his hands and when I realized that in the end he would have Heather one way or the other, I knew I had no choice. By agreeing to the marriage, it would avoid needless bloodshed and put us in good stead with the Dark Dragon, thus protecting everyone and suffering no casualties."

"Except Heather," Emma said.

Heather needed time to digest the startling news. A soothing brew would help as would a few moments alone to prepare, though how one prepared to meet the devil she did not know.

"We must make ready for our guests," Heather said, taking charge. "Food and drink will be needed and—" She was about to say a guest bedchamber prepared, but it would not be a guest bedchamber he would sleep in tonight. It would be hers. Her bedchamber no longer belonged to her alone. It belonged to her husband—the Dark Dragon.

Her father sent her a look that had Heather realizing there was more unsettling news yet to be delivered.

Her father was quick to tell her. "You will be leaving today with your husband."

His announcement brought utter silence.

Tears sprang to Heather's eyes. "I must prepare for my departure." She hurried out of the room, Patience and Emma following close behind.

Donald Macinnes dropped down on the bench afraid his legs would no longer hold him.

Hunter hurried to fill a tankard with ale and handed it to him.

Rogan laid a reassuring hand on his shoulder. "You did what was best for your family and clan."

"So I have told myself," Donald said. "I only pray it is so."

~~~

Heather collapsed on her bed, tears streaming down her cheeks. She wanted to be alone to try and accept her fate. But when her sisters entered the room and flung themselves at her, hugging her tightly, she was glad they were there, especially since she would be bidding them farewell today.

They stretched out on the bed side by side, Patience's hand clinging tightly to one of Heather's and Emma's hand almost choking the other, as though neither of them intended to let go of her.

"There must be something—"

"Do not say it, Patience," Heather begged. "The deed is done and I must face my fate and you two must help me."
~~~

Patience popped up and looked down at her two sisters. "How do I do that? How do I let such evil lay hands on my sister?"

Heather eased her hand out of Patience's hand to lay it on her rumbling stomach.

Emma hopped off the bed. "Your stomach troubles you. I will fetch a soothing brew to calm it and you should try to eat a little something."

"The brew would help," Heather agreed, laying her arm across her eyes.

Emma nodded to Patience and she followed her to stand just outside the door.

"She is upset enough, and rightfully so, do not upset her any further," Emma ordered sternly.

"How do we stop this travesty?" Patience asked tersely.

"I do not think we can. As father said, it is done."

"And what if he treats her poorly or how do we even know if he does treat her poorly, what then?"

"You are right. We cannot just let him take her away never to know what becomes of her," Emma said, growing teary-eyed. She swiped at the unshed tears. "Ever since I have gotten with child, tears come much too easily."

"A woman's tears usually turn men pliable, men that have hearts. It would be good to put the Dark Dragon to the test. At least then, we would have some idea of how he might treat our sister."

"And if it fails?" Emma asked.

"Then we make another plan."

After forming a hasty plan, Patience returned to Heather. She was still lying on the bed, her arm draped over her eyes, and Patience did not want to disturb her. A bit of rest would do her good. Patience sat in the chair by the fire where she had often found her sister through the years, working on her embroidery. Her heart turned heavy to think she would never see her sitting there again and as she glanced around the room she could not imagine it stripped of all of Heather's belongings, the room empty, and her sister gone from her life. The upsetting thought sent a shudder through her.

The door suddenly burst open, sending Patience flying out her chair and Heather popping up off the bed.

A breathless Emma stood, fighting to balance a wooden tray with a pitcher, tankard, and slices of bread and cheese on it. Her cheeks were flushed and she took a moment to catch her breath as Patience hurried to take the tray from her and place it on the small table near the hearth.

With a deep breath, the words rushed from Emma's lips. "The Dark Dragon sends word for you to be in the Great Hall to receive him. Father says to hurry, for the Dark Dragon is impatient to take his leave with his new wife."

"He does not want to take time to meet my family or rest and feed his men?" Heather asked. "And will he not give me time to pack my belongings?"

"The Dark Dragon has informed Da that he will leave some of his men behind to collect whatever you instruct your servants to pack and be delivered to you. He also instructed that you are to bring whatever you need until then."

Heather stared at her sister in disbelief. "He intends to just whisk me away?"

Tears clouded Emma's eyes. "It would seem so."

Heather stood there not knowing what to do or perhaps knowing and not wanting to do what she must. She had woken this morning relieved to find herself in her own bed after the ordeal of her abduction, escape, and dangerous journey to return home. And now the man she had managed to avoid was here to take her away and to make matters worse, he had all the right to do so since he was now her husband.

It was the terrified expressions on her sisters' faces that finally got Heather moving. The longer she delayed this, the more she allowed her fear to show, the more difficult it would be for them, and seeing them suffer would hurt her terribly.

She had two garments reserved for special occasions, one a red winter wool and the other a soft blue, linen shift with a pale yellow tunic draped over it, which she hurried to change into. She left her blonde hair pinned up, making certain the combs were secure. She had only bathed the night before, the rose-scented soap still lingering in her hair and on her skin.

Patience had insisted that she and Emma always keep a small dirk in their boots since you never know when one might be needed and so she tucked hers in her boot. The last thing she did was slip a blue ribbon through the ring that was forever with her and tie it around her neck, then tuck it beneath her clothes to lie against her chest. The ring meant everything to her. It had been given to her by the man she loved and would always love. It had given her strength through the years when she thought she had had none left. And at the moment, she could use as much strength as she could get.

She gathered up a few of her garments and items to tie securely in a plaid, knowing her sisters would see to the rest for her and without giving her bedchamber a second glance, she hurriedly left the room, closing the door behind her and on the safe and loving life she had always known.

~~~

The Great Hall had filled with Macinnes and MacClennan warriors. Rogan and Hunter wore their swords at their sides, their hands not far from the hilts. Patience had tucked two, unsheathed dirks, behind her leather girdle that held her sword to the right of her waist. She was prepared to draw a weapon quickly if necessary and that frightened Heather. She wanted no one dying here today because of her.
~~~

Tears still lingered in Emma's eyes, though she too had a dirk at her waist, though only one and it was sheathed. Her father was the only one who wore no weapons.

With a tempered smile, her father stretched his hand out to Heather.

A servant took the bundle with her few possessions from her with a nod and Heather noticed tears pooling in her eyes. Giving a glance about as she approached her father, she noticed most of the servants appeared ready to shed tears for her and her heart swelled with how much they cared for her.

It made it that more difficult to leave her loving home and yet made it somewhat easier, knowing her sacrifice would save the lives of those who loved her. She held her chin high and kept her shoulders back and walked with false bravado when truly she was more frightened than she had ever been.

She was certain her wobbling legs would betray her and give way or that the tremor she felt inside would suddenly break free and she would tremble all over with fear for everyone to see.

Her father reached out when she drew near him and slipped a sturdy arm around her waist to rest her against him. She was never so grateful for his support and never prayed so hard for a miracle that would allow her to remain there beside him forever.

The two large doors to the Great Hall opened and two Macinnes warriors entered and stood to the sides of each door. Other Macinnes warriors followed suit until twenty warriors formed two lines, ten on each side. Ghost warriors entered after that, not one wearing a weapon, and ten joined the two lines of Macinnes warriors, five at the end of each line.

The room turned completely silent and breathes were held in anticipation of the Dark Dragon's entrance.

Darkness suddenly filled the doorway, spreading as the black draped figure stepped through.

The Dark Dragon had arrived.

Chapter Three

Heather felt her legs give way and if it was not for her father's firm hold around her waist, she would have collapsed as she watched the Dark Dragon—her husband—walk toward her.

He was draped in black, from the black metal helmet that concealed all but his mouth, a portion of his jaw and his eyes, eyes that seemed as dark as his garments, all the way down to his black leather boots. He walked with such powerful strides that his black cloak bellowed out behind him or perhaps it was the pointed, stiff leather spikes that ran along his shoulders and down the upper arms of his leather tunic that kept the cloak a flight.

He seemed to grow in size the closer he got and Heather's fear grew with each step he took. It was no wonder he was called the Dark Dragon. He was a size taller than most men and broad with thick muscles that left no doubt as to his potent strength.

Fear reached up from deep inside Heather and gripped at her stomach. He had to weigh eighteen or more stones where she barely weighed eight stones and her head reached only to his shoulder. There was no possible way for her to defend herself against this man. Her only way to survive this marriage was to submit to him and that thought terrified her.

"Welcome to our home," Donald Macinnes said with a respectful nod when the Dark Dragon came to a stop in front of him.

"I came for what is mine. I will collect my wife and take my leave." His strong voice added to the force of his commanding tone.

"Drink and food first, to celebrate the uniting of our people," Donald offered.

"We leave now." He stretched his black glove-covered hand out to Heather.

She kept her hand tucked firmly against her stomach, knowing once she took his hand— she was his forever.

Emma hurried to her sister's side. "Please, share a drink with us. It will give us time to bid our sister farewell. We will miss her terribly." Tears began to roll down her cheeks. "Please do not deprive us of a little more time with her."

Heather turned from her father to comfort her sister as she had done so many times throughout the years.

The Dark Dragon glared at Emma. "Tears are wasted on me. Say your good-byes and be done with it."

Both women were stunned by his heartless words, and Emma sent a quick look to Patience. Their plan had worked. They now knew that the Dark Dragon had no soul. The only question was— how did they protect their sister against the heartless beast?

Patience went to step forward, ready to try another plan she had given thought to and before she could speak the Dark Dragon's powerful voice rang out.

"See that your wife holds her tongue, Hunter, or I will see it cut from her mouth."

Patience's green eyes blazed with fury and Hunter caught her firmly around the waist before she charged for the Dark Dragon.

"Now is not the time," he whispered as she struggled to free herself.

Heather paled. Would he truly cut her sister's tongue from her mouth? Could he be that monstrous?

Donald Macinnes stepped forward. "I will know where you take my daughter, and my family and I will know the face of her husband before you leave here."

The Dark Dragon took a quick step forward and his voice turned to an angry growl. "You will make no demands of me, Macinnes."

Patience jabbed her husband so hard in the ribs that his arms fell away from her and she charged at the Dark Dragon, her dirk drawn when she stopped in front of him.

"You will respect my father and his wishes or we can go to war now," she shouted, shaking the dirk in his face.

Hunter quickly stepped forward, his heart pounding in his chest, fearful of what the Dark Dragon would do before he could reach his impetuous wife and calm the situation. His heart slammed against his chest when in an instant the Dark Dragon's hand snapped out, grabbed Patience's wrist, spun her around, and slammed her back against his chest, forcing her dirk against her throat.

Hunter stopped where he was and Rogan stepped up beside him, both men keeping their hands off the hilt of their swords, not wanting to make the dire situation worse.

Heather never knew any fear when it came to defending and protecting her sisters and it was the same for her now. She stepped forward, her only thought to save her sister, and said, "You have won. I am your obedient wife. I will go with you willingly. I only ask that you do not mar this day that I take leave from my family with bloodshed. And I ask my husband if he would be so generous as to respect my father's wishes and do as he asks so he does not needlessly worry about his daughter. I also beg your forgiveness for my sister's impulsive actions."

Complete silence filled the Great Hall as breathes were held, waiting to see what the Dark Dragon would do. He did not make a move and there was not a flicker or hint in his dark, soulless eyes to her heartfelt words.

Suddenly he swung Patience away from him, snatching her dirk from her hand as he did. Hunter quickly stepped forward to grab her and steady her and to hold her in a way she could not escape him again.

The Dark Dragon threw the dirk, landing it in the wood floor close to Patience's boot. "Turn it on me again and nothing will save you."

To Hunter's relief Patience did not reach to retrieve it. His wife was wise enough to understand not only the foolishness of her rash actions, but what it had cost her sister.

The Dark Dragon glared at Heather for a moment, and then once again silence filled the Great Hall as ever so slowly he raised his hands to his helmet.

Heather held her breath and thought to close her eyes fearful of what she would see but too fearful to look away. A gasp caught in her throat when he fully removed his helmet while several gasps circled the room. Heather's one and only thought was—only evil could be that stunningly handsome.

His features were so strikingly defined that she was reminded of the painting her father had had done of her mum about a year before she died. The artist had captured her features to perfection and that too was true of the Dark Dragon. It was as if an artist had painted him to perfection, for all his lines and angles blended perfectly. He wore his dark hair severely drawn back and tethered at the nape of his neck and not one scar marred his sun-kissed skin.

There was something in his captivating dark eyes that held Heather's attention and would not let her look away. What it was, she could not say, but it nagged at her and refused to let go, and she silently reminded herself not to let evil rob her of her good senses.

She should be relieved that he was not difficult to look upon, but she was not. She was upset, for at first glance she had felt a twinge of attraction and that had not pleased her at all.

He kept his eyes on Heather for a moment as if with his helmet removed he could take the whole of her in, and she shivered at his close scrutiny.

He turned his head abruptly away from her and looked to her father. "With the Clans McLaud and McDolan hungry for war, I will remain close. I have land, a small keep with a few crofts surrounding it. It is but an hour's journey from here. I will settle with my wife there to help avert this brewing war."

"The small McCombs holdings belong to you now?" Donald asked.

The Dark Dragon confirmed with a nod.

"I am grateful you will remain nearby for the time being," Donald said.

"What choice do I have when the murdered body of Greer McLaud's wife has been found on your land? Greer is sure to accuse you of killing her, giving him the excuse he has been looking for to start a war with the Clan Macinnes."

"This marriage will change many a clan's mind of whose side they will fight on and hopefully prevent a war from starting and countless lives from being lost," Donald said.

"Make no mistake, Macinnes, lives are lost well before clans declare war. It is the way of greedy men."

Heather was impressed by his wise words, perhaps he was not the barbarian many claimed him to be.

The Dark Dragon turned to Heather with a look that could wither the staunchest of souls and said, "I have granted you this one favor. Do not ask for another. We leave now."

Hope sank with his words. He would command and she must obey. It would be the way of things from this moment on.

He slipped his helmet back on, and then held out his glove-covered hand to her.

Once she placed her hand in his that would be it, she would belong to him. There would be no escaping him. She wanted to run screaming from the keep, but knew she could not. Fate had dealt her another heavy blow. She was a fool. She should have realized by now that life was harsh and would always be so, but she had hoped—how she had hoped with all her heart that true love would conquer all. But it was not to be.

She reached out and accepted her fate. His hand grasped hers not firmly, but possessively, the strength of his grip letting her know that she belonged to him and that he would never let her go.

Emma cried out as the Dark Dragon led her sister out of the Great Hall, "We will visit soon."

The Dark Dragon stopped and turned. "You will visit your sister only when I give permission."

His words sent a chill through Heather. She was not his wife; she was his prisoner. He rushed her along so fast that she felt as if her feet barely touched the ground. That was when she realized that he had slipped his arm around her waist and lifted her ever so slightly as they walked. Another chill sent a shiver through her. If his one arm held such strength, how strong actually was he?

The thought turned her legs weak and she feared they would no longer hold her. His arm suddenly tightened around her waist and she was lifted, the ground gone from beneath her feet, though her feet continued to move as if she could still feel it.

The sun blinded her eyes as they stepped out of the keep and though the sun's warmth settled over her, it did not chase the chill that continued to run through her.

His ghost warriors had formed a circle around them and only parted when they neared his stallion.

Heather could not help but feel helpless just as she had that moment the ghost warriors had abducted her. Only this time it was much worse. Then she had hope of being rescued, for she knew her sisters would come for her. No one would come for her now. The frightening thought sent her stomach roiling.

His hands went to her waist and with one lift he hoisted her onto his black stallion and mounted behind her. His arms circled her as he took the reins to turn his horse and she had only a moment to catch sight of her family on the top steps of the keep, her sisters waving frantically to her before they disappeared from view.

With a gallop they rode through the village, his men on either side of them and before she knew it they had crested the rise. Her home would be out of view soon and she longed for one last look. Not thinking, only aching to catch one last look of her family, she took hold of his forearm and pulled herself forward, careful not to lean too far forward since she sat sideways in front of him and could easily slip off.

She could not see passed the leather spikes on the leather armor strapped to his upper arm, so she gripped his forearm tighter and leaned out a bit farther.

Heather yelped when he yanked her back and shoved her in the crook of his arm.

"Stay put. You will fall."

"I only wished to see my home one more time."

"It is no longer your home. Wherever I am is your home now."

His remark disturbed her. How could he be her home? Home was where there was love, caring, laughter, so that when tears and hardship came, love and caring, and even laughter, saw you through it. Was the Dark Dragon even capable of loving?

She chased the disturbing thought away and instead attempted to focus on the land in its rich summer growth. The trees, the grass, the wild flowers all eagerly stretched up to the bright sun, as if begging for their attention. Her eyes began to grow heavy and her head bobbed now and again. The pace they kept coupled with being snug in his arms gave the impression of being lovingly rocked and after fighting to keep herself erect, she capitulated and laid her head on his leather-clad chest. The muscles beneath were hard as were the muscles that ran along his arms. He was thick with muscles all over and her breath caught a moment when a vision of him naked came unbidden. She tried to chase the wicked thought away, but the startlingly image refused to dissipate.

She had never seen a man aroused, though she had felt an arousal pressed against her. Her heart plummeted. It had been years since she allowed herself to think of that moment with Quinn. Every time she had, she had grown aroused herself and had ached for the man she loved more than life itself. He had gone away and never returned, though he had promised to come back to her. And there could be only one reason he had not returned—death.

Death would have been the only thing that kept Quinn from returning to her. He had sworn to her the day he had left that he would return. That nothing—absolutely nothing—would keep him from her. He had told her that his heart belonged to her. That she was to keep it safe until he returned, and then they would join their two hearts as one. She kept her head bowed so that the Dark Dragon could not see the single tear that slipped down her cheek.

Now she was wed to another and she doubted their hearts would ever join as one. She wondered what kind of marriage she would have with this warrior who was feared like the devil himself? How would he treat her? Would he beat her if she displeased him? And what of intimacy with him?

She silently scolded herself for thinking of that now. It would do her little good to think on things that would only add to her distress. She raised her head and almost lost the courage she had gathered to speak when she met his dark eyes through the holes of his metal helmet. They struck her as soulless the darkness so deep, though there was something else about them that oddly enough touched her heart.

Her sister Patience had often warned her about feeling sorry for others. She could hear her saying, *not everyone is who they seem to be, and in the end, you will suffer for your kindness.* But how could she not be kind to her husband? What kind of marriage would she have if there was always cross words between them or worse, they rarely spoke at all?

The thought bolstered her courage and she asked, “May I know your name?”

“Rhys.”

She was not daunted by his curt response. She had found through the years that gruff men could be softened with a smile and thoughtful words. Patience had disagreed and once again warned that it was her beauty that softened the brusque men. But Heather was no fool when it came to men. She was well aware of their proclivity toward women and had never placed herself in a position that could prove compromising.

She did not have to force a smile. It came easily to her as she asked, “And are you a McCuil like your Uncle Ewan?”

“No.”

“Then what clan do I now belong to?” His dark eyes intimidated, peering through the holes of his metal helmet as he settled them on her, and to her concern it was the first time she ever had to force herself to maintain a smile.

“You belong to *me*—now and always.”

His response silenced her, for it was not delivered in a loving or caring tone and once again she felt a prisoner rather than a bride.

“There is one thing you must remember as my wife.”

His strong, imposing voice sent a tingle of fear racing through her or perhaps it was the anticipation of the command he was about to deliver that disturbed her more.

"*Never, ever* disobey me, otherwise things could prove difficult for you."

Her innocent thought turned to words before she could stop it. "Is it even possible for things to prove more difficult than they already are?"

He leaned his head down closer to hers. "I assure you, wife, it is very possible."

In the next instant, the truth of his words proved true. Suddenly, a ghost warrior rode up alongside Rhys and spoke anxiously in a language foreign to her. And the next thing she knew arrows whistled in the air, descending on them.

Chapter Four

Rhys wrapped his arms around his wife and draped himself over her just as arrows pinged off his helmet and bounced off his leather armor. He did not shout to his warriors, for they were well-trained for such a surprise attack. He hastily brought his stallion to a halt and dropped off him, his body wrapped tightly around his wife as he took her with him. His stallion fled to do what he was trained to do—hide until the attack was over and to let no one take him.

He hit the ground hard, taking as much of the blunt force as he could, then he quickly got them to their feet and hurried her to a large boulder. He pressed his palm to her chest and ordered, "Do not move from this spot."

He flung his black cloak off and drew his sword as he turned and faced the onslaught of warriors pouring out of the surrounding woods.

Heather's heart pounded with fear. It was as if she had been plunged back to the day she had been abducted. Only this time the warriors who attacked did not wear the white face paint of the ghost warriors. These warriors' faces were smeared with dirt and their fierce screams echoed through the woods as they attacked.

She did as her husband ordered and braced herself up against the boulder, terrified she would be taken captive once again. Her eyes grew wider as she watched her husband battle the warriors that came at him. Never had she seen a man fight with the ferocity and power that her husband displayed. He felled warrior after warrior. It was as if he grew in strength and determination with each deadly blow he inflicted.

When he suddenly turned around, his sword in the air, she cringed, thinking for a moment he meant to use it on her, but it caught a warrior perched on top of the boulder, slicing into his neck, his lifeless body dropping off to the side.

Heather looked to her husband, but he had already turned to battle another enclave of warriors advancing on him. Her eyes darted anxiously, watching as the ghost warriors fought the attacking horde, bodies dropping like swatted flies. She wrapped her arms around herself, frightened beyond belief.

Get a weapon! Protect yourself! Her sister's voice resonated in her head so loudly that she cast a quick look to see if Patience was actually there and was disappointed when she saw that she was nowhere to be seen. Patience had trained her and Emma in the use of various weapons. She had warned that fear would be the greatest enemy in such an attack. Turn that fear to anger, Patience had told them and do not go down without a fight.

Heather rarely got angry, but what did spur her into action was watching a wounded ghost warrior trying to crawl off the battlefield to safety.

Without hesitation or care for her own safety, she quickly slipped behind the boulder and made her way along the outskirts of the fighting. When she reached the wounded warrior, she ducked down by him. He had suffered a serious wound to his leg, making crawling difficult. She reached out and grabbed his hands and when he saw who had latched onto to him, he grabbed her hands tightly. With strength born of determination, she pulled him into the woods and behind an enormous bush. It provided a modicum of safety for the time being.

One look at his injured leg told her it was serious. Such a sizeable gash often proved difficult if not impossible to heal, but Heather did not intend to let that stop her. She slipped off her tunic, tore it in half at the shoulders and wrapped his leg with one of the pieces. Once done, she helped him sit, bracing his back against a tree trunk.

"Hopefully, you will be safe here while I go and see if other wounded warriors require my help."

He grabbed her wrist. "I cannot let you go, my lady. The Dragon would want you kept safe."

Heather twisted free, his strength having waned from the injury or else she would never have been able to escape his grip. "I will be fine. I will stay on the outskirts of the fighting." She turned and took off, ignoring his pleas.

Crouching down to remain as inconspicuous as possible, Heather made her way along the fringes of the battle. She managed to pull another warrior to safety and, with him leaning heavily on her shoulder, got him to where she had left the other warrior. He had taken a sword to his side and from what she could see it had gone straight through, giving him a better chance to survive. She wrapped the other half of her tunic around him and ignored his warning for her to remain with them.

It was too late to help the next two wounded she came across—they were dead. The two that followed she was able to help to safety, their wounds preventing them from fighting, but she doubted they would prove fatal. She tore the hem of her shift to make more bandages and once finished tending the warriors, she went in search of more wounded.

The next ghost warrior she came upon could not be helped, he lay dying. She dragged him away from the battle that seemed to be dying itself and sat on the ground beside him, taking his hand in hers. One thing she had learned about dying was that no one wanted to die alone. Those she had seen through death had gripped her hand tightly, as if by holding onto her death could not take them.

She offered the warrior what she had offered all those she had seen through dying, soothing words and her presence. She had often wondered if someone had been with Quinn when he died or if he had faced death alone. She hoped someone had been there for him as she was now for this warrior. She held his hand firmly, caressed his brow, and offered comforting words.

Before he took his last breath, he barely got out a whisper. "Thank you for...kindness."

A tear slipped down her cheek at the senselessness of his death. She closed his eyes with a tender hand and left him to, hopefully, help the wounded who could be saved. When she came upon the battle once again, she crouched down so no one could see her. She was horrified by the amount of men who lay dead or dying.

From the looks of it, there seemed to be more of the warriors who had attacked dead on the ground than ghost warriors. The few left fighting remained determined, though outnumbered and would soon meet their fate. When she saw that, Heather hurried further out onto the battlefield to see who she could help.

~~~

Rhys tore through the last few attacking warriors, wanting this done and Heather safely deposited at the McComb keep. He swung his sword with a heavy hand, easily slicing down those who dared to challenge him. The area around him was littered with bodies and the few left fighting stepped over them to get to him and certain death.

Battle always fired his blood and he grew stronger with each thrust of his sword, taking life after life. Until one last frenzied warrior lunged at him and with one mighty blow of his sword, his body crumpled to the ground, blood pooling out from beneath him.
~~~

With no more warriors left to fight him, Rhys turned to Heather only to find her gone. He hurried behind the boulder to see if she had taken shelter there from the mayhem, but did not find her. Had someone snatched her or had she fled on her own? Either way, how could he have not heard? The question left only one possibility. Heather was lighter on her feet than he realized and had fled on her own. If not, she would have screamed and fought her attacker and he would have heard.

He yanked his helmet off his head as he made his way back around the boulder to cast a glance over the battlefield littered with fallen warriors. More of the attacking warriors lay dead than his men, though several of his men appeared injured. He let his glance wander over every inch of the area and it was at the far end, near a copse of trees that he spotted her, though if she had not stood, he would have missed her. She brushed loose strands of hair out of her face, though they stubbornly returned. Her tunic was gone and the hem of her shift was ripped in several places as was one sleeve.

He watched as his wife gave a yank to the other sleeve and pulled it off her arm, then she hunched down and began wrapping the sleeve around the fallen warrior's arm. She spoke with him while she did, all the while maintaining a smile. When she finished, she rested her hand to his chest, gave him a nod, and moved on to the next fallen ghost warrior.

That she braved the battle to tend his injured warriors spoke of her courage, but she had also disobeyed him and that he would not tolerate. He slipped his helmet on, knowing full well he appeared more frightening with it on. Perhaps when she saw his true nature, she would think twice of disobeying him.

As he approached, he heard her give orders to a few of his warriors who had survived the battle unscathed. They hurried off without question, while she returned to tending the fallen warrior, and he grew annoyed and hastened his step.

"No one orders my warriors but me."

Heather glanced up quickly from where she hunched over the injured warrior and gasped loudly when she saw her husband. Blood drenched his sword and was splattered across his helmet and much of his leather armor.

She hurried to her feet. "Are you wounded?"

Was that concern he heard? He thought her gasp and rounded eyes were from fear, but were they?

"I am fine—"

"Thank God!"

"God had nothing to do with it. It was my skill that saved me."

Anger burned in his dark eyes and Heather wondered whether he was angry with her or God. "Your skill may have saved you, but only God can save some of your men."

Rhys removed his helmet. "My men have been trained to tend wounds."

"Good. The more hands to help tend, the better chance the wounded will survive. Carriers will need to be made for some of the injured."

"It will be seen to," Rhys said and held his hand out to her.

Heather noticed that several ghost warriors had gathered behind him and it suddenly struck her. "You cannot mean to send me on to McComb keep."

Not only light on her feet, but a quick wit as well. There was much more to his wife than he had realized. "You will be safe there."

"I am safe here and I am needed here."

Rhys dropped his hand to his side and took a step toward her. "It is not a request. You will do as I command."

A ghost warrior came running toward them and Rhys stepped forward to meet him. They spoke in whispers and when Rhys turned, he said, "You will stay here until I return for you. My men will protect you."

He turned and was gone before Heather could say a word. She wondered what was going on, who the attacking warriors were and why had they been able to attack the Dark Dragon when his ghost warriors seemed to see and hear everything? But she had no time to dwell on the haunting questions. She had to tend the wounded. Once there was time she would pursue answers, for she feared that this battle was not over—it had just begun.

~~~

Heather rolled her shoulders back to ease the ache in her back. She did not know how long she had been working on the injured and with no sun it was difficult to tell how much time had passed. She did not even know when the clouds had moved in overhead, she had been so busy. She was relieved that most of the injured had not suffered severe wounds. With care, they would survive. A few others she was not so sure about.

She saw those who could not walk settled on carriers that were built so they could rest comfortably and would not be made to move when it was time to leave. She wished they were already on their way, the clouds gathering more heavily overhead in the last hour or so.

"You should rest, my lady," the young warrior she sat beside said.

She placed a comforting hand on his shoulder and smiled. "There will be time for that soon enough, Douglas."

"You have done more than your share and your garment proves it. There is barely anything left of it."

Heather startled when she saw how much of her garment she had torn apart. Both arms lay exposed and her legs up to her knees as well. She
~~~

had also torn a piece off by her chest, leaving the top of her one breast to appear as if it would spill out at any moment.

"I had not realized," she said softly, trying to pull the torn garment together.

"You thought of others' needs, not yourself, and for that we are all grateful." He coughed and winced as he did. "I fear I will not survive. Will you tell my wife, Bea that I love her and I am sorry I will not be here to see our child born?"

"That is nonsense, Douglas. You will live and see your babe and many more babes born."

"I pray that be so."

"Then fight and make it so," the deep voice snapped.

Heather jumped and Douglas struggled to raise himself in the presence of the Dark Dragon. His helmet was gone, his dark hair free to fall to his shoulders and his handsome face set in tight lines.

Rhys lowered himself to rest on his haunches and placed his hand firmly on Douglas's shoulder, stopping him from moving. "Stay as you are. As a fine warrior, you instinctively know what weapons prove the most useful in battle. The weapons you need for this battle are rest and determination to heal and I expect you to use both."

Douglas nodded. "As you say, my lord, though I surely would have died if Lady Heather had not pulled me off the battlefield and tended my wound shortly after I had fallen. She is a kind and brave woman."

Rhys looked at his wife, his eyes going directly to her partially exposed breasts, then her bare arms, and finally taking in her bare legs. He stood and walked around to her, slipping off his cloak, and draping it over her shoulders before gripping them and pulling her to her feet.

"Rest, Douglas, we will leave soon and you will ride in one of the carts and be home to Bea before you know it."

Before anymore could be said, Rhys hurried Heather off to a more secluded spot, and she rushed to speak before he could. "Forgive my improper appearance, my concern was for the injured and I did not realize how indecent I appeared."

"You will never again strip yourself as you did today," he ordered sternly.

"I cannot promise that," she said quickly, "for if needed, I would so the same again."

"So, you blatantly tell me you will disobey me?"

"I tell you the truth, something I hope will always pass between us."

He felt her words like a punch to his gut. She would always be honest with him. Unfortunately, he was unable to reciprocate. His response was terse and hasty. "It is time to go." He hurried her forward and without thinking she rushed away from him to tend the more severely injured as they were loaded into the cart.

Rhys almost reached out and stopped her, but at the last moment he let her be. Later he would lay down some rules and God help her if she did not obey them.

Heather took a look at Douglas's wound before she allowed them to place him in the cart. She had no choice. The wound had to be seared before he could travel and even then she was not sure if he would survive.

She ordered a fire built and the warriors were quick to summon Rhys.

"Before you argue with me," Heather said when he stopped in front of her, "please understand that if his wound is not seared shut, he will not survive the journey home."

"See it done," Rhys ordered his men and turned to walk away.

"I request that I be allowed to accompany him in the cart."

"No," Rhys said bluntly.

"But—"

"Do not question me on this," he snapped. "Be satisfied with what I have granted you." He turned and walked away.

Heather turned her attention to the task ahead to keep her mind from dwelling on the fact that she now had to seek permission from someone after years of doing as she pleased. It was not something she could or wanted to comprehend right now. At the moment, making certain Douglas survived the journey was what she needed to think on.

Everything was prepared quickly and the task performed just as hastily. Heather was glad Douglas had passed out from the pain of the searing. He could then be placed on the cart and not suffer more pain until he woke.

Once it was done, Heather was surprised to see that she would ride her own mare. She pressed her face to the mare's face and whispered, "It is good to see you Meadow. I will find you a nice field where you can enjoy your wild onions."

As if she understood, the mare nodded and Heather smiled. It vanished quickly, startled when hands caught at her waist and she was lifted with ease onto the horse. She looked down at her husband with wide eyes.

He placed his hand on her bare leg. "Do not grow so alarmed when touched, for the only hands you will ever feel on you—are mine." He mounted his horse that waited a short distance from them and guided the animal alongside hers.

Meadow snorted as if displeased with the stallion's presence and Heather reached out to calm her with a soothing hand.

"I have things I must see to. I will see you at the keep."

Heather wondered over his abrupt departure, but did not dwell on it. She was bone-tired and wanted nothing more than to reach the keep and have this day end. Or did she?

Tonight she would see her marriage to the Dark Dragon consummated.

Chapter Five

Heather stared bewildered as they entered the McComb village. She had visited here with her father over the years and with each visit the place had grown more neglected and the clans' people older with few young ones to replace them. She was amazed to see the changes in the village. The cottages had new thatched roofs, doors and window shutters were all new, and summer flower wreaths graced most of the doors. It appeared as if the village had come to life. Even the gloom of a cloudy day could not diminish the improvements to the village.

As Heather looked about, she recognized few of the clansmen. Many of the women were young, their stomachs swollen with babes. There were a few elderly, but not many she recognized. Where were those she was familiar with?

Rhys was not there to greet Heather and though she was directed to the keep, she ignored the ghost warrior's orders and saw to the care of the wounded. Many wives and mothers came to claim the injured and Heather spoke with each of them, advising them on specific care needed.

It was when Bea appeared, looking far more pregnant than four or five months, that Heather knew she would need help with her husband. It was also the same time that the Dark Dragon made his appearance, all moving out of his path as he approached his wife.

"It has been a long day and it is time for us to talk," Rhys said, holding is hand out to his wife.

Heather looked to her husband and then looked to Bea, crying over Douglas who clung to her as if for the last time. She turned to her husband and said, "I cannot desert someone in need of tending." She waited, seeing the anger in his eyes grow, but what else could she do. She could never abandon someone in need and Douglas and his wife were in dire need, perhaps if her husband understood that.

She stepped closer to him and laid a gentle hand on his arm as she whispered, "I fear he will not last the night. Please let me help them."

Rhys felt his anger dissipate. She thought not of herself, but those in need. There was a time he had known such kindness, though he could barely recall it, but the memories it did invoke were better left buried.

Rhys brought is face close to hers. "You have asked many favors of me today. What do I get in return?"

"What do you want?" she asked without hesitation.

"A willing wife in my bed tonight."

Heather braced for the fear that clenched at her stomach. How did she submit willingly when she wanted no part of this marriage? But what choice did she have? The agreement had been made. She belonged to the Dark Dragon and could not refuse him. So, what else was there for her to do but submit?

She spoke truthfully. "I will come willing to you, but know little of what is expected of me, so I beg your tolerance of my ignorance."

Her words stabbed at him. She had known no other and would know no other but him. His touch would be the first she ever felt. She would truly be his and his alone. The thought turned him hard.

"Fear not Heather, I will not harm you." He brushed his lips over hers.

Heather shivered from the faint kiss. It stirred her, sparked her, ignited something deep inside her that had lain dormant far too long, and she leaned against him as if she suddenly needed to be close to him.

Rhys arms drifted around her and held her firmly. She leaned against him as if she wanted to be there, wanted his arms around her, wanted to feel him against her, wanted to be near him and he relished her closeness.

He brushed is cheek against hers and whispered, "You are mine."

She moved her lips to whisper softly in his ear, "Are you mine?"

"Forever," he said and his mouth drifted to hers and settled a soft kiss on it.

Heather closed her eyes and let her senses take hold. His kiss tempted, excited, and sparked a stirring in her, and she found she was disappointed when he abruptly ended the kiss.

Rhys rested his brow to hers. “Do what is necessary, but if you are not finished by nightfall I will come for you. Tonight is for us and I will let nothing stand in its way.”

Heather did not turn and watch him walk away, her legs too weak from his kiss to move. It had been ten years since she had last been kissed and the memory still lingered. She had been so young and in love and the kiss had stirred her wet. She had so wanted to make love with Quinn that day, but he had remained honorable, telling her that he would claim her properly when she became his wife. She had promised him then and there that she would not give herself to another or never feel for another man as she did for him. She would wait no matter how long it took for him to return to her.

Tonight she would break that promise.

With tears she refused to shed, she turned and hurried to the cart to help Douglas and his wife.

~~~

Rhys approached the keep steps, his lips still pulsing from the kiss. He had not expected his wife to so eagerly return his kiss or be so hungry for it, but then it had been some time since she had last been kissed. He knew her past well, knew more of it than she did, though he would not let her know that. Some things were better left unspoken.
~~~

Tonight he would seal their vows, forever uniting them, and hopefully he would plant a seed and a babe would grow, one of many. But that was later this evening. Now he must keep his thoughts focused on the matter at hand.

He reached the bottom of the keep steps as his top warrior Pitt was coming down them. He was almost as tall as Rhys, his body lean and hard from constant training. He kept his shoulder length auburn hair tucked behind his ears and his deep blue eyes drew the lasses to him like bees to honey. He had been with Rhys for five years now and the many difficult times they had faced together had made them more brothers than friends.

"You have news?" Rhys asked, remaining where he was.

Pitt shook his head. "Nothing. We can find nothing. Perhaps they left the area."

"Have the men keep searching. Something may turn up." He paused before asking, "How many men did we lose?"

"Five," Pitt said. "Too many, but minor compared to the twenty-five dead enemy warriors."

One warrior was too many for Rhys, but lost lives were inevitable in battle and there was no telling who would be claimed.

"Tell the sentries to keep alert. This is not over; it has just begun."

~~~
~~~

As soon as Heather saw Douglas settled in bed in his cottage, the area around his wound cleansed and redressed with clean bandages, she got busy brewing a mixture of herbs to give him in hopes of preventing a fever from settling in or the wound turning putrid. She also readied a soothing brew for Bea. It had taken time for the young woman to stop crying after seeing how badly her husband had been injured. And she had asked Heather several times if Douglas would be all right.

Heather had hopes he would survive, especially since the journey home had not claimed him. So, it was with more confidence that she told Bea that with care, time, and rest he should be fine.

Once Douglas was asleep, Heather insisted that Bea sit and enjoy the brew she had made for them. Bea did not argue, she sat at the table in front of the hearth and let Heather serve her.

It was when Bea was about to take a sip of the brew that her eyes rounded and she hurried to get out of the chair. "Forgive me, my lady, it is I who should be serving you."

Heather placed a firm hand on her shoulder and eased her down on the chair. "At the moment, I am simply a friend." Heather did not give her a chance to say anymore on the matter. She asked, "When is the babe due?"

Bea smiled and caressed her stomach. "As winter falls upon us." She looked over at her sleeping husband, her smile fading. "Tell me he will be here to see our babe born." She turned back around, tears pooling in her eyes.

Heather reached out and rested her hand on Bea's. "I cannot say whether your husband will live or die. I can tell you with care and rest, he has a good chance. And he fights to live, another good sign. I will keep a close watch on him and do what I can to help him."

"That is kind of you, my lady, and I am ever so grateful to you for your generosity."

A moan from the bed drew their attention and Heather reached Douglas before his wife. One touch of his brow confirmed a fever had set in and she was unable to hide her concern.

Tears started rolling down Bea's cheeks after caressing her husband's brow and seeing the worry in Heather's eyes. "Few survive fevers after suffering a bad wound."

"But there are those that do," Heather said. "Now let's get this blanket off him and a cool cloth on his brow."

A soft rap at the door had Bea going to it and opening it to find two women there, offering their help. They obviously were friends since they hugged Bea and tears filled all their eyes.

Heather was so pleased they were there, worried that it would be too much for Bea to handle once she took her leave, having to be at the keep by nightfall. After explaining to the women what needed to be done and making Bea promise to send for her if a problem should arise, Heather bid them good day.

She was no more than a few steps out of the cottage when an old woman approached her and she wondered if perhaps she was a McComb and could tell her about the changes that had taken place here.

"My lady," the woman said with a bob of her head. "I wanted to thank you for what you did for my nephew. Several warriors told me how you remained with Oran while he lay dying with no thought to your own safety." Tears clouded her eyes. "You do not know how grateful I am that Oran did not lay there on the battlefield dying alone. You are not only brave, but so very kind."

"He held tight to my hand and passed without great pain," Heather said tears filling her eyes. "I am so sorry for your loss."

"He had an honorable soul and was so very proud of being one of the Dark Dragon's warriors. He was all I had and I will miss him greatly."

Heather reached out and hugged the woman and when she stepped away from her, she saw the surprised look on the old woman's face. She often forgot that a chieftain's daughter or wife did not hug those beneath them, but Heather never thought that anyone was beneath her. It did not matter what station in life one held. Everyone hurt, bled, or suffered in some way. People were more alike than different, though few saw it that way.

"You are a very special woman, my lady," the older woman said. "I can see by your torn garment that you gave much of yourself to help the injured. I am glad the Dragon chose you for his wife. You will be good for him." She bobbed her head once again and walked away.

Heather had been so engrossed in making sure all the injured had been seen to that she had forgotten about her appearance. Disheveled and her garment torn, was not the way for her to be introduced to Rhys' people. She hurried along anxious to make herself presentable. She took only a few steps when she was stopped once again.

"Forgive me, my lady, for disturbing you, but I fear my husband's wound has worsened and I hear that the wounds you tended are doing well."

The woman was taller than Heather and thick in body, though it was a firm thickness. Her brown hair was sprinkled with gray, though her round face held few age lines. Her dark eyes held a note of worry and she gripped her hands anxiously.

"Let me have a look, and I will see what can be done to help him."

"Thank you, my lady. I am Belle and my husband is Henry. He can be a surly and stubborn one. He let one of the warriors tend his leg, no doubt thinking they knew more than you, not that they do not know how to tend a wound. Most have learned out of necessity. But I hear you have a tender and kind touch that helps heal well."

"It is my sister Emma I owe my knowledge of healing to," Heather said as she walked alongside the woman.

Belle shook her head. "I think not. Your mum had the healing touch, God rest her kind soul. You are much like her."

Heather almost stumbled over her own feet, she got so excited. "You knew my mum?"

Belle nodded. "Lady Enis saved my life. I am my mum's only child, she being older than most women when she had me. It was not an easy birth. I gave no cry when I was born and my mum told me that her heart broke at the deafening silence. But Lady Enis worked her healing touch on me and suddenly I was crying as loud as a banshee." Belle laughed. "And as my mum liked to remind me, I never stopped."

Heather had no time to respond, having reached Belle's cottage. There were questions she wished to ask Belle, to talk with her mum if possible, and to find out about the changes here, but that would have to wait.

"I warned you, woman," came the gruff shout when Belle entered the cottage and announced Lady Heather's presence. "There is no reason to be bothering Lady Heather. I am fine."

"Then you will not mind if I have a look so that I may see what a fine job your warriors have done in tending you," Heather said with a smile, though she could see from the soiled bandaged on his leg that the wound was far from fine.

"It's a scratch, nothing more," Henry insisted.

He was a sizeable man, thick in body like his wife, though age lines clung to the corners of his eyes and his hair was more gray than brown. And where his wife kept a smile on her face, he wore a frown, except when he looked at his wife. His whole face softened even when he spoke gruffly to her.

"Then it will be a quick glance I take," Heather assured him.

Henry looked to Belle. "You do not listen, wife."

Belle laughed. "What wife does?"

"Bah," Henry said frustrated, "have a look and be done with it."

"Henry, your manners," Belle scolded.

Henry shook his head before giving Heather a nod. "Forgive me, my lady, I am a rude, old fool."

Belle walked over to him and draped her arm around his wide shoulder. "You are my old fool and I love you dearly, and I will not let your stubbornness take you from me."

Henry slipped his arm around his wife's waist. "You can be a chore, woman, but I do love you."

Heather watched the couple with envy. She had thought that she and Quinn would be like them, growing old together and more in love each day.

"A peek and I will be gone," Heather said as she hunched down to unpeel the dirty bandage off his leg.

Belle hurried and got a small stool to rest her husband's foot on, making it easier for Heather to examine the wound.

One look at the wound and Heather knew it needed immediate tending or it would turn putrid. She looked to Henry. "It needs some cleaning and a clean bandage applied."

"I will fetch what you need," Belle said, then pointed a finger at her husband. "And you will sit there and say nothing."

Henry grumbled, but did as his wife ordered.

Once the wound was cleaned, Heather saw the problem. "You have a splinter of some sort embedded in the wound. It needs to be removed, and then you should heal fine, for the wound is not deep." She turned to Belle. "Though, you must change the bandage often."

"Bah," Henry snorted, "a waste of time and good cloth."

"You will mind your manners, Henry and do what Lady Heather says," Belle ordered.

"Sorry, my lady," Henry grumbled.

Heather bowed her head to hide her smile. He might be a gruff man, but he gave no guff to his wife when she gave him an order.

It did not take long to remove the sliver of wood with Belle's bone needle and apply a fresh bandage to the leg. After all was done, Heather stood and looked to Belle. "He should stay off that leg for at least the remainder of the day, two if possible, to give the wound time to close some. And change the bandage in two days. If the wound has a bad odor or reddens, let me know right away. In the meantime, I will leave some leaves for you to brew and have Henry drink."

Belle shot her husband a warning look before he could complain and he grumbled beneath his breath.

Heather left the cottage, her stomach grumbling, reminding her that the day was winding on and she had barely eaten. She also needed to change her garments, her appearance not at all presentable. She final made it inside the keep without being stopped and was delighted to see a familiar and friendly face.

Nessa was a few years younger than her. She was petite and plump with long red hair that she wore in a single braid. She had the prettiest face and the loveliest dark eyes and a smile that never faltered. She had worked, since young, alongside her mum in the keep. Her mum had passed on a couple of years ago and last Heather knew, Nessa had continued her duties in the keep. There was no one who knew the place like she did and Heather was glad to see her.

"Lady Heather," Nessa cried and hurried to her.

The two hugged, neither noticing the stares from the few warriors and servants in the Great Hall.

"It is good to see you," Heather said.

"I am so pleased to see you, though when I learned you were the Dark Dragon's wife, I prayed for you."

"The union was necessary," Heather said.

"So I learned."

"Tell me what has happened here," Heather said. "I recognize few villagers."

Nessa kept her voice low. "They are gone—disappeared—swallowed whole by the Dark Dragon."

Before Heather could ask what she meant, Nessa's face paled and her eyes turned wide. Heather turned to see the Dark Dragon standing a few feet away, raindrops running down his dark garments.

Chapter Six

Heather did not wait to be summoned. From the look on her husband's face, he was there for her. She went to him, leaving Nessa frozen in place.

Her stomach chose the moment she reached him to grumble in hunger.

Rhys did not say a word. He took her hand and called out, "Nessa, food and drink in my solar."

Nessa nodded and hurried off.

Heather followed along, his strides quick and powerful, as if leaving his mark wherever his footfalls fell. He shut the door behind them, slipped off her cloak, and taking her hand seated her in a chair by the cold fire. He turned his attention to the fireplace and in moments flames leaped off the logs and warmth drifted out to stroke Heather's bare legs. She hugged herself and shivered from the delicious warmth.

Rhys returned to her side with a soft wool blanket and draped it over her lap to cover her legs.

She closed her eyes and rested her head back against the chair. She had not realized how tired she was until this moment.

He placed his hands on her shoulders and squeezed, her tender muscles protesting. His fingers took charge, digging into the muscles and they screamed with soreness while she sighed aloud and his fingers dug harder, relieving the ache little by little. She almost cried out in disappointment when a knock sounded at the door and his hands fell away.

Food and drink were arranged on a small table without a word from the servants and when Heather heard the click of the door, she hoped she would feel his soothing touch on her shoulders again.

"Your stomach begs for food, eat," he ordered.

He was right; she was hungry. She reluctantly moved away from the fire, regretting the distance from its warmth with only a few steps. She quickly took some bread and cheese and hurried back to the chair, draping the blanket over her legs and settling once again by the fire's warmth.

She jumped when lightning struck just outside the window, turning the room bright followed by a crack of thunder that rumbled like the roar of a mighty giant. The rain began to slash angrily against the windows, and she was relieved to be tucked away safe and warm from the harsh downpour.

Rhys drew a chair up beside her and she saw that he had removed his leather armor. He did not appear as ominous without it, though one look in his dark eyes had her thinking otherwise.

"You disobeyed me," he said, handing her a goblet of wine.

She took it with a questioning look. "When?"

"During battle, when I ordered you to remain behind me against the boulder," he reminded.

His voice was not harsh or demanding, but more curious and amiable. Or was she hearing what she wanted to hear? She took another sip of wine, enjoying the warmth of it spreading through her body, easing aches that had crept up on her.

"The injured needed tending," she said as if it explained it all.

"That is no excuse for disobeying me."

"Your men—"

"Never disobey me again."

She stared at him, thinking she had heard concern in his harsh command and for some unexplainable reason she felt the need to reach out and rest her hand to his cheek. "I meant no disrespect," she whispered her glance falling on his lips and recalling how his kiss had tasted. The memory sent a tingle through her, stirring her senses and she suddenly got the urge to kiss him.

Her thought troubled her, for there had been only one man she had ever wanted to kiss. The urge grew stronger and her lips drifted closer to his. He did not stir, but his eyes lit with a touch of passion, flaring hers and made her wonder what it was about this man that seemed to draw her to him.

Just as she was about to rest her lips on his, a knock sounded at the door.

"Go away," Rhys shouted.

"It cannot wait," came the reply.

Rhys stormed over to the door and swung it open.

Pitt spoke before the Dragon could breathe fire. “Two of our sentinels have been found dead.”

Rhys turned to Heather. “Do not leave the keep and God help you if do not obey me on this.” The door closed abruptly behind him.

Heather stared at the door that trembled in the Dragon’s wake. He was angry and why not? His troop had been attacked without the slightest warning, a shocking revelation for warriors known for their exceptional skills of seeing and hearing everything, and now two of his sentinels had been killed. How could that be? How could anyone slip past such highly trained warriors? They could not unless their skills equaled or surpassed the ghost warriors.

With heavy thoughts and slow steps, Heather snatched up some meat and bread off the table before returning to the chair by the fire. She wondered if the McLauds or McDolans were somehow involved. Though the question begged, why would they be? Her marriage had yet to be announced. And the two clans certainly had no such skills as those she saw today. So who then was skilled enough to best the Dragon? And why would anyone want to?

She was just finishing her wine when a knock sounded at the door and she bid the person enter.

Nessa stepped in. "The Dragon ordered a bath prepared for you. It is being readied now."

Of course he would, Heather thought. It would see that she remained in the keep, and also see that she was presentable for their wedding night. The reason mattered not though, for she longed to bathe and wash away not only the grime but her aches as well.

"How thoughtful of him," Heather said, for she would not speak ill of her husband to anyone. She followed Nessa to the bedchamber and stepped into the room and around the servants who were busy filling a metal tub that had been placed before the hearth.

Heather's eyes were caught by the substantial bed dressed with fresh bedding that dominated the room. The pillows were fluffed and the blanket drawn back in anticipation of the night ahead.

Her hand went to her stomach at the thought of climbing into bed tonight, for she would be doing more than simply sleeping there.

"All ready, my lady," Nessa announced.

Heather turned to see that all the servants were gone, but Nessa. She waited by the tub. Heather went over to her and though she used no servant at home when she bathed or dressed, she knew it was expected of her here. She let Nessa help her undress, eager to get in the tub and soak her aches away. She stopped Nessa when she went to touch the blue ribbon that held the metal ring Quinn had made for her.

"I will see to this," she said and slipped it off, rolling the ribbon up carefully and placing it in her healing pouch to keep it safe. It would not do for her husband to see it. It was for her and her alone and she would seek its comfort when necessary.

Once done, she sunk down into the hot water with a sigh.

Nessa got busy pouring water on her hair and then scrubbing it with a slab of soap Heather had instructed her to find amongst her belongings.

"Lavender," Nessa said with a smile as she scrubbed Heather's hair.

"It is grown in my garden at home," Heather said and closed her eyes as Nessa's fingers massaged her head. She let herself enjoy the moment, but as soon as Nessa rinsed her hair and was about to wash her, Heather stopped her and took the cloth from her. "I will see to scrubbing myself. What I want from you, Nessa, is to tell me what you meant when you said that many of the villager folk had disappeared—swallowed whole by the Dark Dragon."

Nessa shook her head as she moved off her knees to sit cross-legged beside the tub. "The ghost warriors arrived here shortly after Fane McComb died with documents that showed the Dark Dragon now owned the land and all on it. Repairs began to be made and suddenly older clan's people started disappearing. No one saw them take their leave. They just disappeared along with their belongings. There was nothing left of them. Then young women began arriving, wives to the ghost warriors who were already here and they settled in the abandoned cottages."

"No one heard or saw anything?" Heather asked, feeling a chill, though the water remained warm.

"Nothing," Nessa whispered as if frightened that someone would hear. "Not a trace of them, it was as if they were never here."

"Have all the aged-folk disappeared? None of the young ones?"

"Some older ones still remain, though they fear one day they will be snatched away like the others." She leaned closer to Heather. "A few young lasses have vanished, though some say they have heard screams coming from the upper floor of the keep and that the Dark Dragon keeps them as slaves to satisfy his endless lust. It is forbidden for anyone to go to the upper floor." Nessa crossed herself, as if protecting herself from evil, as she stood. "You best not linger, my lady, the water will chill soon."

Heather finished and was soon dried and wearing a pale yellow nightdress, the hem falling to cover her feet, the sleeves hugging her wrists, and ties keeping the low neckline drawn tightly together. It was a favorite of hers, soft and comfortable.

She sat combing her wet hair while Nessa directed the servants in clearing the tub from the room. Once that was done, Nessa saw that a pitcher of wine was left for her, presumably to help her face the night ahead.

Once alone, Heather found herself restless. Her thoughts continued to drift to what Nessa had told her about the Dragon keeping young women prisoners in a room on the upper floor. Somehow she did not think it was true, but it could be that she did not want it to be true. The only way to settle her worries was to see for herself.

Heather hurried out of the room, closing the door gently behind her, not wanting to alert anyone to her nightly excursion, especially to forbidden territory. But if caught, she could feign ignorance. After all, she had only arrived and knew little of the keep's workings and rules.

She took the stairs quickly and once she stepped off the top step, she had second thoughts. The small area was dimly lit, one wall sconce holding a torch that barely flickered. There were three doors, one to the left and the other to the right and the third door sat between the other two.

Something told Heather that that was the room in question, but to be thorough or perhaps out of fear, she decided to explore that room last. With cautious steps, she proceeded to the room on the left and slowly opened the door. She had to open it all the way to allow light from the torch sconce to fill the room, if only partially.

It was not necessary to explore the whole room. One glance told Heather it was once the lady of the keep's solar. Here was where the lady of the keep could spend time for herself with her embroidery or simply seeking some solace. A fine covering of dust alerted her to the fact that it had not been used in some time.

Heather closed the door behind her and went to the door on the right, opening that one slowly as well. It appeared a room where unwanted furniture was stored and as Heather went to close the door, her eyes caught on the cradle stuck beneath some chairs.

Dusty and forever childless the piece appeared forlorn, discarded along with other furniture that had been of no use. She closed the door, feeling sorry for the empty cradle and for the woman who had had such hope of filling it.

She went to close the door when a wind whipped it out of her hand, slamming it shut in her face. She jumped back startled, her heart pounding in her chest. The wind no doubt came from an open window in the room, but she decided against confirming her suspicion and hurried over to the other door. The shadows seemed darker in this space, almost as if they were embracing her or were they trying to imprison her?

Heather almost reconsidered exploring what lay beyond the door. She could always return another time, preferably during the day when the sun shined bright. A loud crack of thunder caused her to jump in fright and her heart to continue to pound.

Once she reached the door, she turned her head and placed her ear closer to it to see if she could hear any sounds coming from inside. She wondered then what she would do if she found women being kept as slaves in the room. An answer came easily. She would free them and send them home to her sisters.

She shook her head at the nonsensical thought. How could there be prisoners when there was no lock on the door. And why would Rhys keep women as slaves to satisfy his lust when he was bringing a wife home? Unless...could he be that insatiable when it came to coupling? Did he require more than one woman to satisfy him?

She would find out tonight or would she find out when she opened this door?

The torch in the sconce flickered, sending shadows dancing across the wood door as if they dared her to enter the den of iniquity. She raised her hand slowly, telling herself this was necessary, she had to do it. She had to discover what lay beyond the door.

Ever so slowly, she brought her hand down on the metal latch.

A large shadow suddenly loomed over her, spreading around her, consuming her, swallowing her whole while a strong hand fell across hers, gripping it tightly.

Chapter Seven

"Never, ever, enter this room."

Heather's gasp caught in her throat and her legs turned weak. She did not know whether to be relieved that her husband was behind her or frightened that it was him.

He took firm hold of her hand resting on the latch and spun her around to face him. Her body fell against his and he held her there against him. He wore no armor over his black shirt so her breasts were planted firmly against his hard chest and she felt every taut muscle.

"What are you doing up here?"

"Exploring," she said, though did not sound convincing to her own ears.

"In your nightdress on your wedding night?"

"I got restless." This time the truth rang true in her voice. She was restless to know what was going on, not only in the forbidden room but about the surprise attack.

The torch sconce suddenly flickered low and then, as if a strong breath blew at it, it snuffed out completely, leaving her and Rhys engulfed in total darkness.

Heather reacted instinctively, her arms went around her husband and she held on tight.

The scent of lavender from her freshly washed hair drifted up and wrapped around him as strongly as her arms wrapped around his waist. "There is nothing to fear when I am with you," he said, feeling her body tremble against him.

His words soothed and so did the strength of him coiled protectively around her, but what of the darkness. Heather voiced her fear. "The darkness does not let us see."

"Fear stops you from seeing, not the darkness." He lifted her just enough so that her feet did not touch the floor and began walking.

Heather was amazed that he walked as if he could clearly see every step he took. She kept her arms firm around him, not that it was necessary she held on to him, the strength of his one arm alone was enough to hold her with ease.

She was relieved to see a flicker of light ahead as Rhys confidently proceeded down the stairs. And she did not mind that he did not place her on her feet until they were in their bedchamber.

Hundreds of questions wanted to spill from her lips, but she chose silence, waiting to see what he would say to her.

"Do not venture from this room."

Heather stood staring at the door as it closed shut behind him. Why had he returned if only to leave again? The question got her thinking. How had he known she was on the upper floor or had he? Had he come to the upper floor to retrieve something or in search of her? And why was she never to go into that room?

With questions continuing to grow, Heather began to pace. He had left her just as he had in his solar, which could only mean that he had not returned for her. What had brought him back to the keep and what had brought him to the upper floor?

She raised her hand to cover a yawn and realized that the long, eventful day was fast taking its toll on her. Finding out she was wed to the Dark Dragon, being taken away from her home and family, getting attacked by warriors with similar skills to the ghost warriors, tending the fallen and injured warriors, learning that many of the McComb clan had disappeared without a trace, and then being ordered never to enter a particular room made her wonder if she could possibly be caught in a nightmare. Perhaps if she went to sleep, she would wake at home with her loving family around her.

Though, what if it was not a dream? Her husband would certainly expect her to be waiting for him. Another yawn had her approaching the bed. She could rest, not sleep, though if sleep claimed her then perhaps she would wake and find herself home.

Home is wherever I am.

A shiver ran through her recalling her husband's words, and she quickly got in bed and pulled the soft blanket up over her. The bed was much larger than her one at home, but then this bed was meant for more than one person. She had shared her bed with her two sisters when they were young and needed her close, but that had been years ago. She was accustomed to sleeping alone now and wondered if she would easily adapt to sharing a bed with her husband or if it would become a chore.

She sighed and turned on her side, wanting to grab the other pillow and hug it to her as she did when she slept alone, but the pillow was not hers to hug. It belonged to her husband. Another yawn eased out of her and she snuggled in the softness of the bedding, her eyes closing and sleep settling in on her.

~~~

Rhys entered his bedchamber much later than he had planned to. The day had not gone as expected and the attack troubled him more than he would let anyone know. He had kept the secret well, only he and one other knew of it. But then he had known the risk he was taking at the time and not once had he doubted that the risk was worth it. Now it had returned to haunt him, but he had known it would. It had been only a matter of time and had he not wanted this, looked forward to it, and planned on it?

The problem was that now his wife's life was in more danger than anyone could ever imagine.

Rhys went to the hearth to add more wood to the fire, a chill having settled in the room, no doubt from the rainstorm that continued to pound
~~~

the keep. Once done, he stripped off his garments as he approached the bed.

Standing completely naked, he stared down at his wife tucked snug and warm beneath the covers and hugging his pillow. He gently brushed a strand of blond hair off her cheek. He had wondered if she would wait up for him, but was not surprised to see that she had not. It had been a long, tiring day for her, not to mention an upsetting one.

He wanted desperately to make love to her, had since he laid eyes on her, but after the day's events and seeing her sleeping so peacefully, he could not bring himself to wake her. Tomorrow would be soon enough and all the days to follow.

Rhys walked around to the other side of the bed and climbed in. He slipped into her embrace as he eased the pillow from her hands. She settled around him quite nicely, her head going to rest on his chest and her leg draping over his. He wished she was naked so that he could feel her soft skin against his, but then thought better of it. If she was naked, he would not be able to keep his hands off her.

He closed his eyes, not expecting to fall asleep, his thoughts much too busy. She stirred in his arms, wrapping herself more tightly around him, as if she could not get close enough to him, and his arms tightened around her.

The last thing he recalled as he fell asleep was the scent of lavender drifting around him.

~~~

Heather woke with a slow stretch and a wide yawn that turned to a smile. She had not slept so soundly or comfortably in years. Her eyes sprang open and she sprang up, recalling where she was, and found herself alone in bed and alone in the room. She cast a glance at the rumpled spot beside her and knew her husband had slept there.

She lifted the top of her nightdress to take a sniff and her breath caught when the scent of him stung her nostrils. Her cheeks burned red. She had to have slept nearly on top of him to have his scent so strong upon her. She sniffed again, finding the scent appealing. It was a mixture of earth, pine, and man. It was similar to Quinn's scent and she was troubled by the thought that she found Rhys' scent more intoxicating.

A light knock sounded at the door and Heather was glad for the interruption and just as pleased to find it was Nessa and she had a tray of food with her.

"I thought you might prefer to have your meal in some privacy after last night," Nessa said, placing the tray on the table next to the chair by the hearth. "Tongues have been busy all morning, especially since you have yet to be seen."

It took a minute for Heather to understand what Nessa was referring to and when she realized it, her cheeks tinged pink. Oddly enough, she felt embarrassed that her vows had yet to be
~~~

consummated. Could Rhys have possibly found her unappealing? Surely if anyone knew, she would be blamed and not the Dragon, since rumors had him having an unquenchable appetite for coupling.

"I am fine," Heather said with a forced smile.

"I am glad to see it," Nessa said and lowered her voice to a whisper. "One of the servants claims to have seen the Dragon go to the upper floor and not come down for a while before going to his bedchamber. She thinks he had his slaves satisfy him, so that he would not be too demanding of his bride."

He had returned to the upper floor last night after leaving her in their bedchamber? She had to find out what was in that room. Heather hopped out of bed and went to the tray of food. She rarely ate when she woke, but Nessa had been kind enough to bring her some food so she ate sparingly of the salted whiting and bread. There was a pitcher of wine, but she much preferred the soothing brew she made from herbs and would have to instruct Nessa on how to prepare it for her.

She turned to Nessa to do just that and found her staring at the bed linen.

Heather realized right away what the young woman was staring at. Heather's virgin blood should be on the bed linen and it was not. If word spread about this, it would not be in her favor. She doubted anyone would believe that the Dragon had not consummated their vows.

"I beg your silence on this, Nessa."

Nessa turned wide eyes on her.

"The time will come when you will find what you expected to find there this morning. Until then, I beg you not to speak of it to anyone."

Nessa stared at her a moment before shaking her head and saying, "I would never speak of anything I see here. You can trust me to keep a tight lip, my lady."

"I am relieved to know that, Nessa."

"I will make certain blood is seen on the sheets," Nessa said, gathering them up, "for inevitably there will be those nosey ones looking for it and ready to gossip if not found."

"I do appreciate your loyalty."

"Always, my lady," Nessa assured her with a bob of her head. "I know you like to tend yourself, but if there is anything you wish me to do, I would be pleased to serve you."

"Thank you, Nessa." Heather dropped the piece of bread in her hand back on the tray. Curious about the two sentinels that had been found dead, but not sure if Rhys allowed the news to be known, Heather asked cautiously, "By the way, has there been any word about the two sentinels that were found last night."

Nessa was quick to share what she knew. "A shame it is that one rushed to help defend the other against a wild beast only to have them both lose their lives. A troop has gone out to hunt the animal down. I hear tell it was a wolf." Nessa shook her head. "The bodies were so badly torn that the Dragon will not let anyone see them. A guard stands watch over them outside the barn until they are buried."

"That is a shame," Heather said, though wondered over it. Why would Rhys be summoned immediately if two of his men were mauled by a wolf? Naturally, he would be informed of it, but to disturb him when he was with his bride? Somehow that did not make sense.

She had to get a look at those bodies and satisfy her curiosity and she had to find out what was behind that door on the upper floor. She also wanted to look in on the warriors she had tended and see how they were doing. With so much to do, she hurried to dress.

Her usual daily attire was a plain skirt and blouse and she quickly retrieved them from the chest Nessa had placed her belongings in. She took a comb to her hair, running it through the soft strands, then quickly braided it. After slipping on her boots, she went to the door, swinging it open and ran right into her husband. Stunned by the impact of his solid body, she stumbled back and his hand snapped out to quickly take hold of her.

"Are you rushing from our bedchambers to avoid me?" he asked, taking her along with him as he stepped into the room and shut the door behind him.

"I am eager to see how the injured warriors are faring."

"But not eager to see me?"

Heather stepped away from him, his hand falling off her as she went. "I could easily make an excuse that would satisfy you, but as I have said, it is important to me that we be truthful with each other. I had not thought of seeking you out—"

"You are that adverse to my presence?"

Did she imagine a hint of concern in his voice or again was it simply wishful thinking? She smiled as she said, "Surprisingly, I am not as adverse to your company as I thought I would be, though there are times I still fear you."

"And well you should?"

"Why?" Heather shook her head. "Why would you want your wife to fear you?"

"So that she will obey me without question."

"You must give me time to adapt," she said softly.

He stepped toward her. "You do not command here, I do."

She stared at his handsome face, though it was his lips her eyes settled on and oddly, she got the overwhelming urge to kiss him. So much so that she stepped forward, went up on her toes and pressed her lips to his.

Her innocent, sweet kiss felt more like passionate hunger to Rhys and his body reacted—he grew aroused. His arms went around her and drew her closer as her lips continued to tempt his. He took over then, his tongue playing across her lips, urging them apart and slipping in so that their tongues could mate.

Passion caught and spiraled through Heather and when Rhys placed his hand on her backside and urged her against him, she found herself complying most willingly. She settled against him, his hardness poking at her, letting her know how much he wanted her. And she could not quite grasp why, but she wanted him.

Heather was shocked and disappointed when he brought their kiss to an end and stepped away from her.

"I have things that require my attention," he said and turned toward the door.

"Why?"

Rhys turned back around and asked with a brusque tone. "Why what?"

"Why did you not wake me last night when you came to bed?"

He walked over to her and grabbed hold of her chin. "When I want... I will bed you."

Heather wondered how many times she would watch the door close behind him and be left feeling perplexed. He had wanted her. She had felt his need. So why did he not seal their vows? He was becoming ever more curious to her, making her want to know more about him. And she would start her search on the upper floor.

With light footfalls, she made her way to the upper floor, stopping every now and then to listen and hear if anyone else was about. When she reached the top floor, she peered around to make sure no one was there.

Darkness greeted her, the lone torch sconce that had gone out last night still not lit. She went and retrieved the torch from one of the sconces along the stairway and made her way back to the unlit torch, intimidated by the shadows that danced around her. It was as if they were eager to reach out and capture her.

She thought to light the torch in the sconce, but then thought better of it. No one was permitted up here and if she lit the torch, Rhys would know someone had been here and, not wanting a servant punished for her misdeed, she left the torch unlit.

When she was a few feet from the door, she stopped abruptly, shocked to see that the door had been bolted with a heavy metal lock. Disappointment filled her. Now she would never find out what secrets the room harbored nor would she? There had to be a way to find out.

She turned to leave, more determined than ever to find a way into the room, and stopped when she thought she heard a noise. She listened and sure enough she heard it again and it came from the locked room.

With her stomach tightening in knots, she took a step closer to the door and listened. She jumped back when she thought she heard someone cry out and when the latch on the door began to rattle, her heart almost stopped beating.

Was someone trying to get out?

Now she had no choice. She had to find out what was in the room and if necessary set whoever was inside free.

Chapter Eight

Rhys sat, with heavy thoughts, in his solar. He knew all too well how kind his wife was, having proven it yesterday with how unselfishly she had helped those in need. He had not, however, realized the extent of her determination or curiosity. She let nothing stop her when either took flight and she had proven that not only with her questions but with the way she had kissed him.

The passion that had flared in her green eyes had surprised him as had her kiss. She had not been shy at all. It was almost as if she kissed someone familiar to her, and he wondered if he reminded her of the man she once loved.

Her father had made it quite clear to him that she loved another and always would and nothing would change that, but it had not mattered to him. He wanted Heather, ached for her gentle smile, her selflessness, her tender touch. If anyone could cope with the darkness that consumed him at every turn, she could.

Though, one question continued to plague him—was it fair to Heather? Would she truly be able to survive his darkness or would he pull her down into its dark depths?

A knock sounded at the door and it opened before he bid anyone to enter.

"I saw Heather talking with some of the villager folk, so I knew you would be alone," Pitt said, entering the room and closing the door behind him.

"Get us a drink and sit. There are things that need to be discussed," Rhys said.

Pitt filled two goblets with wine and handed one to Rhys before sitting in the chair across from him. "There has been no success with the hunt. If a wolf or some beast of the forest is not brought back, concern will grow."

Rhys swallowed a good portion of his wine before saying, "And if the villagers learn the truth of it, fear would spread like wildfire."

"The men will hold their tongues."

"But for how long? And do not tell me that tongues have not begun to wag about the warriors who attacked us. The ghost warriors that died were less seasoned ones. If it had not been for the experienced warriors with me, then no one would have survived. And with our warriors trained to pay attention to everything that goes on around them at all times, they will begin to see that I am relying more heavily on seasoned warriors. This will not be able to be contained for long, especially when this particular enemy will toy with us, instilling more and more fear in our people. Then, when he is ready, he will strike and strike hard, leaving nothing in his wake."

"What do we do?" Pitt asked.

"More men will be needed, but we also cannot leave our home vulnerable to an attack. Send Innis to me, he will deliver the necessary messages. Are the bodies wrapped and prepared for burial?"

"Henry's injury has delayed him, but he will be seeing to it shortly."

"Good. I do not want the bodies revealed to anyone, and Henry will make sure of it."

"When do you intend to make the men aware of the enemy they face?" Pitt asked.

"I have no doubt they are already aware of it. Their concern would be in how we deal with it."

~~~

It was a beautiful day with a warm breeze drifting across the land, but there were few smiles on peoples' faces. Heather easily understood why. With the attack on the troop yesterday, the numerous injuries suffered, and the two sentinels supposedly being killed by a wolf, the people did not feel safe. And she imagined that that was an unusual occurrence for those loyal to the Dark Dragon.

Heather followed her usual morning routine of walking through the village with a smile and kind greetings. At home, she would inquire of those who had not been feeling well or stop to speak with the women expecting babes. And if there was a minor complaint or dispute, she would settle it there and
~~~

then, so her father did not have to be disturbed with small matters. She had found it made for a more pleasant day for all.

But today she also had another reason to talk with all she met. She wanted to discover what she could about the mysterious things happening here and loose tongues or innocent remarks could often prove useful.

After having engaged three women in conversation and not finding out anything she did not already know, Heather spotted the barn and made her way over there toward the man who stood guard in front of the closed doors. He was one of the warriors she had treated yesterday. He had suffered a minor wound that would not even leave a scar on his arm, though it would be sore for a few days.

She smiled as she approached him. “All is well with your wound, Sim?”

He returned her smile. “Aye, thanks to you, my lady. Elma, my wife, changed the bandage today as you said I should. She looks forward to meeting you and thanking you for helping me.”

“I was only too glad to help. I only wish I could have helped the two poor souls you watch over.”

Sim shook his head slowly. “A shame it is. Hyatt and Neil were good men, but the Dragon will see the wolf that killed them caught and revenge their deaths. Henry and his men will be here soon to wrap them for burial.”

"Then I will say a silent prayer for them as I pick some flowers along the edge of the woods."

"Do not go into the woods, my lady. Danger lurks there until the beast is caught."

"I will not stray from the edge," she said with a cheerful smile. "You take care of that wound, Sim, and if it should trouble you let me know."

"Thank you, my lady, you are most kind."

Heather went to the edge of the woods and began picking the wildflowers that grew there, intending to take them to Bea when she went to see how Douglas was faring. Heather continued to drift along the edge of the woods, making her way behind the barn. When Sim's glance finally ceased following her, she knew other eyes had to be on her. With all that had happened, her husband probably had doubled or tripled the sentries so that there were eyes everywhere on the village.

It was when she spotted a lose board on the back of the barn that she got an idea. She looked at her handful of flowers and smiled, as if pleased with the bouquet. She walked without haste away from the woods, though stopped abruptly, staring down and shook her head.

She pretended that she had stepped in something unsavory and went to lean against the barn with one hand while wiping her boot along the grass as if cleaning it off. She only hoped that whoever had an eye on her tired of her actions after a few minutes and took his eyes off her.

Hoping she picked the right moment, she squeezed behind the loose board and slipped into the barn. Sunlight filtered through the numerous cracks and holes in the worn barn and it was easy to locate the two bodies. They lay on the ground in a stall, blankets covering each of them.

Heather knew she did not have much time. She had to take a quick look and be on her way and pray she did not get caught. She placed the flowers on a nearby barrel top and lifted the blanket covering one of the warriors. No claw marks marred his body. Her heart broke for him, for he was a young, strong warrior and the only wound she could see was a wound to his chest, no doubt made by an arrow. She said a silent prayer as she dropped the blanket over him.

Her free hand shot to her mouth to stifle her gasp when she raised the blanket on the other warrior. His eyes had been gorged from his head and his throat had been cut. This had been done on purpose. It was meant as a message, a clear one, and fear rushed up to grip her heart.

Heather heard voices approach and quickly dropped the blanket down, grabbed her flowers, and hurried to the broken board, slipping out with ease, only to turn and see her husband standing there with his arms folded across his chest and his dark eyes filled with anger.

"Do you truly think that I do not have eyes on you at all times?" he snapped. "What excuse do you have for your actions now? And do not tell me you were restless."

She spoke the truth. "I was curious."

"Of two dead warriors?"

"Of their deaths. I could not make sense of why you would be summoned away from your bride because two of your warriors had been mauled to death by a wolf. You could have been told of it in the morning."

"It is none of your concern," he said in a tone that warned. "And you will speak of this to no one. Now go to my solar and wait for me there." He raised his hand when she went to speak. "Not a word. Go!"

Heather had no choice but to obey. She hurried around the side of the barn and stopped when she saw Henry and two other men enter. They would wrap the bodies for burial and only a few would know the truth and whether a wolf was caught or not, a beast still remained on the loose.

"Go!" her husband said as he came up alongside her.

She bobbed her head and walked off, glancing back to see Rhys enter the barn, the doors closing behind him.

"My lady! My lady!"

The frantic voice had Heather turning around to see Bea running toward her.

"Douglas is beset with fever," Bea said with tears in her eyes and fear in her voice.

Heather did not hesitate; she hurried along with the desperate woman.

~~~

Rhys stood as the two murdered men were swathed in cloth, their graves ready and waiting to receive them. Their families consisted of the ghost warriors, both having arrived together and trained together three years now. They had met up on the road in hopes of joining and becoming one of the infamous ghost warriors. They were good warriors, filled with potential to be the best and Rhys hated losing them, especially in this fashion. Neither deserved to die, and certainly not to die in the manner the one had. Their deaths would be revenged and all the ones to follow, for his enemy was not done with him yet.

The village would turn out for the burial and pay tribute to these two brave souls. Rhys would go and collect his wife and they would stand side by side as the two were placed in the ground.

There was much he had to say to Heather, though he wondered what good it would do. She did as she pleased at every turn and thought nothing of it. Her father had warned him that Heather did not follow the path of others. She had forged her own out of necessity with such heavy responsibility having been placed on her since she was young. In other words, Donald Macinnes had been warning
~~~

him that it would be difficult for Heather to change her ways after all this time.

After only a day spent with his bride, Rhys was discovering how right her father was. But as difficult as it may be, his wife had to learn to follow his dictate whether she liked it or agreed with it or not. It was for her own good and for his sanity.

"Toll the bell when it is time for all to gather for the ceremony," Rhys instructed and left the men to finish their solemn task.

He took brisk steps to the keep, wanting to have this talk done with Heather and this burial behind them.

Pitt stopped him before he reached the keep. "Innis waits in your solar for you."

"Along with my wife?"

"Lady Heather is not in your solar. I saw her rush off with Douglas's wife and fear his wound has worsened."

Rhys rubbed his chin. He could not fault her for helping one of his warriors, but that he thought she was tucked safely away in his solar when she was not, irritated him. She was always someplace other than where he ordered her to be.

"She is not an easy one to keep eyes on; she moves around so much," Pitt said. "And with extra sentinels posted, I fear there may be times when she becomes like the ghost warriors...invisible."

"That is not what I want to hear."

"I know, but until more warriors arrive there is little that can be done about it, which is more of what you do not want to hear." Pitt hesitated a moment before he continued. "We could reach out to Macinnes—"

"No, I will not drag them into this hell and see them suffer for it. I will see my wife kept safe if I have to keep her by my side until this thing is done."

"I have come to know Lady Heather well since I spent much time observing her after I led the troop that abducted her, and believe me when I tell you that that will be an impossible task."

"I am beginning to realize that myself," Rhys said and climbed the stairs, shaking his head.

Rhys entered the Great Hall to find Innis sitting on the floor in front of the hearth with a tankard in his hand.

Nessa rushed toward Rhys and bobbed her head. "I am sorry, my lord, but he refused to remain waiting for you in your solar and I fear he is far into his cups, for he grumbles and speaks to the flames like some are friends and some are foes." Nessa wrinkled her nose. "He also has a foul order about him and grew upset with me when I asked if I could wash his garments for him."

"It is all right, Nessa, I will see to him, but keep the servants and anyone else from entering the Great Hall until I am done."

"Aye, my lord," she said and hurried off, wondering why the Dragon would speak to a drunkard alone.

While Rhys filled a goblet with wine, he cast a glance at the man on the floor. Many would turn away from the stench and his filthy appearance. His senseless utterings would also keep people at bay. It was a perfect disguise for slipping past the enemy or in some cases being right in the middle of them. A dangerous game, but one Innis always looked forward to playing.

Rhys joined Innis on the floor. "I have a mission for you."

Innis nodded. "I thought as much, after seeing what was done to the one warrior."

"How did you know that?" Rhys asked concerned that the news had somehow already gotten out.

"It was easy. I knew the two bodies would be taken to the barn, so I arrived before them and hid. I had a look, and then stumbled out of the barn as if I had just woken from a drunken stupor and, with my stench ripe, the guard waved me away and ordered me to stay out of the barn."

"And what do you have to say for what you saw?"

"It is a clear message. *I will cut your throat and you will never see me coming*." Innis took a hardy drink from his tankard.

"Then you know what needs to be done."

"I go east and north and gather the troops that lay patiently in wait for such a moment. Some I send to your land to protect those there and the others I send here, though not where they can be so easily seen."

Rhys stood. "Time is of the essence, Innis. Do not delay." Rhys turned away, then turned back again. "And stay safe, Innis. This enemy we deal with is not so easily fooled."

"And I am not a fool when it comes to such evil. I will send our warriors and we will defeat this evil before it can spread."

The bell tolled, letting the village know that it was time to gather for the burial ceremony. Rhys turned to ask if Innis wished to attend before he took his leave, knowing what a close knit band his warriors were, but the man was already gone.

Rhys went to collect his wife from Douglas's cottage and was not pleased when he saw her disheveled appearance and flushed face.

"I am needed here. I cannot leave," Heather said worried for Douglas. She could not get his fever to fade no matter how hard she tried. And if she did not succeed soon, she would lose him and Bea would give birth to a fatherless child. That was something she refused to see happen, knowing how difficult it had been for her sisters growing up without their mother.

"You are my wife and expected to stand by my side and show respect for such a solemn occasion," Rhys argued, thinking she was trying to do the impossible—save a warrior that could not be saved.

"Those brave warriors are already dead," Heather said with tears in her eyes. "Douglass is not. Give me the chance to save him."

How could he deny her the possibility of saving one of his warriors when they had lost too many already? Rhys reluctantly gave his nod of approval and took hold of his wife's hand to draw her close to him. "Do what you can, but know that you cannot save them all."

Heather pressed her cheek to his and whispered in his ear, "If I felt that powerless then I would not be able to save any of them, and I certainly would not be able to save the Dragon from himself."

Chapter Nine

The villagers made their feelings known for Lady Heather as they filed passed the Dragon after the burial ceremony.

"It is a fine thing Lady Heather does, giving her help to the living while the dead are buried."

"Lady Heather is a selfless woman."

"God bless, Lady Heather."

"She heals the sick and comforts the dying."

"Lady Heather has a healing touch."

One day and his wife had won the villagers hearts, would he ever win hers?

Rhys stood glancing down at the fresh graves long after the ceremony was over and the villagers had dispersed. He had much on his mind, mostly why his wife had thought she needed to save the Dragon from himself.

He was not sure what she had been alluding to and that troubled him even more. He harbored secrets he did not want anyone to ever uncover, since the knowledge could cost them their lives. And he would not lose his wife when he had just found her.

He recognized the footfalls that approached. They were light and slow, as if unsure as whether to approach him or not. He turned and stretched his hand out to his wife.

Heather hurried to take it. "Douglas is well, the fever broke. I came to pay my respects to the fallen warriors and to thank you for letting me stay and tend Douglas. I am pleased to have such a thoughtful husband."

Thoughtful? He was far from thoughtful and how could she ever be pleased to have him as a husband? He was not what she thought him to be and yet he felt a spark to his heart, a small sliver of something he had thought he would never feel again. Had his wife actually penetrated his icy heart?

Heather took his hand and stepped close, resting her tired body against his, wrapping her arm around his waist, and laying her head against his chest. She smiled when she felt his arms circle her and hold her tight. And she could not help but think that embraced in his arms like this made her feel as if she had finally come home. A strange feeling while being held by the Dragon, but one she could not ignore.

"I am glad Douglas does well. He is a fine warrior."

"And will make a fine da," Heather said, thinking what a comfortable pillow her husband's chest made. She smiled to herself. In just a day's time, she found the Dragon's chest more to her liking than she would have ever imagined possible.

Rhys cherished this moment with his wife. The comfort of their embrace had joined them more deeply than coupling ever could. They clung to each other as if neither wished to let go, as if they had just found each other and would never, ever part.

"My lord."

Rhys and Heather turned reluctantly, both wishing the moment was theirs alone yet to savor.

"I am sorry to disturb you, my lord," Pitt said, "but there is news of Greer McLaud."

Rhys nodded and looked at his wife, as he made ready to step away from her.

Heather grabbed his arm and moved closer to him, making it clear she intended to remain by his side. "You cannot mean to order me away when this news concerns my family."

"Considering what your curiosity had you doing in regards to the fallen warriors, I can only assume what it would have you do where your family is concerned. So, I will allow you to hear the news, but I will have your word that you will not let your inquisitive nature interfere," Rhys said.

"I may be curious but I am not foolish," Heather said.

"Curiosity and foolishness often go hand in hand." He turned to Pitt, letting his wife savor his words and pay heed to them. "What of Greer McLaud?"

"Greer has received word of his wife's death and is on his way to Macinnes keep with a sizeable troop."

"His land is a distance away to learn the news so fast. Something is not right," Heather said.

"And Hew McDolan?" Rhys asked.

"It will not long before he and his warriors arrive at Macinnes keep," Pitt said. "And Rab McLaud rides with him."

"He is coming for his wife Saundra," Heather said worry wrinkling her brow.

"And your family will have no choice but to return her to her husband," Pitt was quick to advise.

Heather squeezed her husband's arm. "We must do something. Rab means to see his wife dead. Something I doubt Hew McDolan knows. Perhaps there is another place where Saundra could hide?"

"If McLaud has eyes on the keep, it will not matter," Rhys said. "McDolan is no fool. He probably sent someone ahead to see what he could find out."

"That is good." Heather said. "Then he will learn of our union and know he will face more than just the Clan Macinnes."

"Our union has no bearing on this matter," Rhys said. "A wife cannot be kept from her husband. Saundra will have no choice but to return to her husband."

"How do we simply hand her over to a man who means to kill her?" Heather argued her concern growing and not only for Saundra. "Patience will never agree to return Saundra to her husband."

"That refusal coupled with Greer's wife being found dead on Macinnes land will surely start a war," Pitt said.

"Send two trackers out and see what they can find out," Rhys ordered.

Pitt appeared ready to speak, but hesitated.

"I will have a few moments alone with Pitt," Rhys said to his wife. "And do not bother to argue. I have been more than generous in granting your numerous requests."

She could not argue when he was right. She bobbed her head and stepped far enough away where she could not hear their conversation, though she wished she could. Pitt no doubt spoke to Rhys about their current enemy, a mysterious foe with far too many similarities to the ghost warriors. It had her more than curious.

Rhys approached her as Pitt went off to do his bidding.

His expression was stern and Heather could tell his thoughts were heavy and rightfully so.

Heather took hold of his arm, an instinctive action, she gave no thought to, but Rhys did. Any fear she had of him was rapidly dwindling and he wondered why. Was she simply accepting her fate and forcing herself to tolerate him or was she truly at ease with him?

"Do you often wear peasant garments," Rhys asked as they walked toward the village.

Heather took no offense to his remark, turning a smile on him. "Tending to the ill, seeing to the running of a keep, and tending a garden are all best served in peasant garments."

"My home has two healers and servants tend the gardens, peasant garments will not be necessary for the running of the keep. I will see that you have fine garments to wear."

Heather chuckled softly. "Fine garments will not keep me out of the garden or lending a hand to the healers. Besides, these garments suit me better than any other."

"They do not suit me and it appears that you need constant reminding that my word is law."

Heather stopped walking, forcing Rhys to do the same.

"I was frightened enough when I was abducted and you cannot imagine how my fear escalated when I found out that the infamous Dark Dragon had ordered my abduction. My fear soared beyond reason when my father told me he had given me in marriage to you. And when I met you for the first time and had to take my leave with you, I thought my legs would fail me."

"I well remember, since I all but carried you from your keep."

"In barely two days' time, and to my utter surprise, I find fear has been replaced, somewhat, with curiosity. The Dragon may spit fire on occasion, but his nature is not evil as most believe."

Rhys brought his face close to hers. "Do you not know that evil lies hidden until ready to strike?"

Heather rested her hand to his chest. "I do not believe evil resides in you."

Rhys placed his hand over hers. "Trust me, wife, when I tell you that evil is there and warn you to be wary that one day it does not strike at you."

Heather smiled and tugged him along as she started walking again. "Evil cannot touch a faithful soul, so I have no worry."

This time Rhys stopped, though abruptly and yanked her up against. "Evil can take the most faithful soul and rip it apart before it destroys it completely. No amount of faith can survive against pure evil."

Heather felt a tug at her heart. She did not know when or how it had happened, but Rhys had obviously suffered at the hands of someone vile. She wished somehow she could ease his pain, his memories that no doubt haunt him. So she did what instinct urged her to do— she kissed him.

Her kiss felt like a rope being tossed to a drowning man. Only it was not the sea, she was rescuing him from, but the horrendous darkness that forever consumed him. And he could not stop himself from holding on tight and not letting go.

Her lips were strong, demanding, and full of passion, but then Heather had a passion like no other. She had a passion for everything and it was contagious, drawing you in, making you want to smile even when you had no reason to, and making you believe she could save you from the devil himself.

Rhys felt the grip to his heart, the kick to his gut and he reached up, grabbed the hair at the back of her head and yanked her head back, reluctantly breaking the kiss. "Are you ready to sink into the darkness with me?"

She winced from the pain of his grip and once again rested her hand against his chest. "Are you ready for me to pull you from the dark?"

"You haven't the strength," he said, wishing differently.

"Perhaps, but I can try."

"And if you fail?"

"Then the Dragon will not be alone in the darkness anymore."

Rhys brought his mouth down on hers and kissed her with a fierceness that ran a shiver of fear through her. She could taste his ferocious hunger and she worried it could never be satiated.

He tore his mouth away from hers. "You quake in my arms from a mere kiss. What will you do when I plant myself inside you and ride you endlessly?"

The thought frightened and excited her at the same time and she wondered if she was already slipping into the darkness with him. "I do not know, for I have never lain with a man."

"And no other will ever touch you but me," he said and softened the grip at the back of her head as he kissed her again, his hunger tempered. He ended the kiss abruptly again and turned his head. "You better pray this interruption is important."

Heather looked to see Pitt standing there. She had not heard him approach, but then she had been too occupied with his kiss to hear anything.

"Your uncle awaits you in the Great Hall."

"I will be there shortly," Rhys said and turned to his wife.

She slipped out of his arms. "We must hurry. We do not want to keep your uncle waiting and I am eager to hear news of my family." A strong tug to her arm stopped her abruptly.

"He is not here to see you."

"But surely he will expect to see me if only to share news of my family. You would not deprive me of that, would you?"

"What possible news could there be with you gone barely two days?"

"There is my da's illness and Emma's pregnancy and with Patience's impatience there is no telling what she has gotten herself into. And there is the summer harvest that needs to be prepared for winter and—"

"Enough!" Rhys said with his hand raised. "I will grant you a few moments with him and then you will leave us."

He started walking and she hurried to keep step with him.

~~~

Rhys spotted the look of relief on his Uncle Ewan's face when he saw Heather. This was more than a visit to speak with his nephew. It was to see how Heather was faring.
~~~

"It is good to see you looking well, Heather," Ewan said, having stood as the couple approached the table.

"I am quite well, thank you, and adapting nicely to my marriage," Heather said with a smile. She was aware that Ewan would report all he saw to her sisters and she did not want them worrying about her. There were far too many other important things to concern themselves with.

"Your sisters send their regards and hope to visit soon," Ewan said with a glance to his nephew.

But it was Heather who answered. "Please tell them I look forward to their visit and will send an invite as soon as I settle in here."

Rhys admired his wife's intelligence and love for her family. She made it clear that her sisters were not to visit until she sent word and she did that not to obey his command, but to protect her family. She no doubt feared they could possibly be attacked as she had been on her journey here.

"I am sure they will be pleased to hear that," Ewan said, the news seeming to please him as well.

"Please sit and tell me how my father is faring and how my sister Emma is feeling." Heather summoned Nessa with a wave and instructed that more food and drink be brought. "And how is Patience."

That brought a laugh from Ewan. "She prepares to rescue you if necessary."

Heather smiled. "She would do that, but then I would do the same for her. Please make it clear that I am not in need of rescuing and that I am quite safe with my husband."

"That will be a message I will gladly deliver," Ewan said.

Conversation flowed as easily and steadily as the wine and after Heather learned what she wished about her family, she stood. "I will leave you gentlemen now so that you may discuss the matters of men. I am also pleased that my husband will be able to deliver an important message for my family to you in person instead of sending a messenger. Do take care, and I am sure we will see each other again soon."

"They say Emma is the most intelligent of the three Macinnes sisters, but I believe it is Heather," Ewan said as he watched her leave the room.

"Is that because you are just realizing she got more information out of you than you intended to share?" Rhys said a smile stirring, though it did not reach his lips.

"And that she made certain I know that she was well aware of this important news." Ewan turned to his nephew. "Does this mean you trust her enough to tell her who attacked your troop on the way here?"

"You received my message."

"I did and I did not share it with anyone as you ordered. Did you tell her?"

Rhys shook his head. "There is enough for her to think on. I will not burden her further."

"Heather is a strong woman and would not shy away from burdens."

"You are right about that, but I am her husband now and will carry the burdens," Rhys said.

"I doubt she will let you carry them alone, no matter what you command."

"Enough about my wife, did you know that Rab and McDolan are not far from the Macinnes keep?"

Ewan shook his head. "I did not. Macinnes will not be happy with this news and I do not see Patience agreeing to surrender Saundra to her husband. I myself would not want to. Rab means to see her dead."

"So I learned. I think little matters to McDolan and McLaud except their unquenchable hunger for power. Greer will not tolerate that his brother's marriage to Patience and mine to Heather align Hunter more closely with the Dark Dragon than with Greer himself. And no doubt Hew McDolan will be disappointed as well, for Greer and his plans would be for naught."

"That could prove dangerous, for I do not see either man accepting defeat easily. Greer planned the immediate demise of Hunter after he wed Patience and he intended to blame it on the Clan Macinnes. When that did not work, his wife's dead body was found on Macinnes land. And no doubt he intends to ask me, the Dark Dragon's uncle, for your help in his revenge on the Macinnes for supposedly killing his wife. When he learns that that is no longer possible, I do not know what he will do, but he will do something."

"I hope he does. It will give me a good reason to take his life and be done with him."

Chapter Ten

Heather decided to see if she could find Belle. She had been born here and yet she was wed to one of the ghost warriors. When and how that came about Heather was curious to find out. She also wondered if Belle knew of the whereabouts of the older clan members that had mysteriously disappeared.

She found Belle in her garden, pulling weeds and stopped her from getting to her feet. "No, please stay as you are, I do not wish to disturb you. I know how weeds thrive after a rainstorm, sprouting up everywhere."

Belle sat back on her legs, smiling. "You are much like your mum from what my mum told me about Lady Enis. My mum felt like she lost a friend when your mum passed. I wish my mum was still around so you could talk with her. She has passed three years now."

"I am sorry to hear that."

"My mum told me just before she died that she had been lucky. She had a good husband, a good daughter, a good clan and a good life. She had no complaints even when there were times she could have complained, she never did. I still miss her."

"I miss never having known my mum," Heather said and not wanting to linger in talk that only brought heartache, she asked one of the questions that had her curious. "Many changes have taken place here and there are many new faces. Where have the elders of the Clan McComb gone?"

"I imagine most have died, for there were few that I knew when I returned here. My da saw how the clan was declining many years ago and wisely moved us away. I met Henry when he passed through our village." She laughed. "He kept returning after that and we were wed. Unfortunately, I must be like my mum, struggling to conceive a child, though I hold out hope that I may still have one as my mum had me when she was older."

"A babe comes in its own good time," Heather encouraged.

"That is what my mum told me."

"How long have you and Henry been married?"

"Ten years now," Belle said with a smile.

"I am curious, Belle," Heather said, lowering her voice. "Was Henry a ghost warrior when you wed him?"

"Henry is a warrior no more, no less and you will hear the same from all the other wives."

Heather understood without actually being told that the ghost warriors would never be acknowledged by their wives as such, and she had a strong suspicion that it was a rule of the Dragon's that made it so.

"How is Henry's wound?" Heather asked. Belle smiled wide and Heather sensed she was relieved at the change of subject.

"I changed the bandage this morning, with much protesting from Henry, but I think he was relieved to see how well it looked. He drinks the brew you showed me how to make and though he will not admit it, he has grown partial to the taste. Though, it might be that the pain subsides some afterwards."

"I am glad to know he is doing well. Will you and Henry remain here when the Dragon takes his leave?"

"I am not sure, but either way I do not mind as long as Henry and I are together. I have fond memories of this place and it would not trouble me to remain here, but the Dragon's home is beautiful, the village lovely, and I do so love it there. But either place is home for Henry and me."

Heather and Belle talked a few minutes more, and then Heather took her leave. She stopped to see how Douglas was doing and was pleased to see that his wound looked good and that his fever had not returned.

She continued walking through the village, not sure what to do with herself. This would not be her permanent home, so she was not certain as to her duties here, and she certainly was not accustomed to being idle. She wished she could walk in the woods. She had done that often at home, sometimes to gather plants or wildflowers and other times it was simply to enjoy the solitary time it brought her.

Her eye caught a young lad busy polishing Rhys' helmet and she walked over to him.

He rose quickly, grasping the helmet in one hand as he did and gave her a respectful bob of his head.

"Please sit and continue your chore," Heather said. "You are charged with keeping the Dragon's helmet fit for him?"

"Aye, my lady. I polish it every day," the lad said with pride.

"And a fine job you do," Heather praised.

The lad smiled. "Thank you, my lady."

"Roy!"

The lad jumped up. "Pardon me, my lady, my da calls."

"Hurry then, you do not want to keep him waiting."

The lad bobbed his head again and ran off after placing the helmet on the bench where he had been sitting.

Heather's glance fell on the helmet and the odd symbols etched into the metal. She reached down and picked up the helmet. Holding it in one hand, she traced the unfamiliar symbols with her finger.

"Be careful, my lady, those symbols are evil."

Heather turned and stared a moment at the old man, stooped with age and leaning on a worn walking stick. He looked familiar and she smiled, recognizing him. "Seamus, is it not? I tended your arm injury a few years ago when I was here with my father."

"Aye, you did Lady Heather, and grateful I am for it. So I return the favor when I tell you those symbols are evil and better left alone." He hobbled forward, relying heavily on his walking stick, reached out, and slipped the helmet from her hand, then placed it on the bench.

"Why do you say they are evil?"

He stared at her as if he was not quite sure if he should speak or not.

Heather placed her hand on his arm. "I am a friend, Seamus."

He kept his voice low. "Evil protects evil. Those are witches' symbols and they protect the Dragon. The village looks better than it has in a long time. Cottages are being repaired and fields replenished along with the villager folk." His voice sunk to a whisper. "But the old people are disappearing and no one says a word." He looked around to see if anyone lingered nearby, then said, "One night I could not sleep. I heard a strange noise and peeked outside. I saw Harold and his wife Bethany being placed in a cart and carried away, never to be seen again." Seamus shook his head. "There is talk that the Dragon disposes of those who are no longer useful to him, just as he did to Glynnis."

Before Heather could inquire about Glynnis, Seamus's daughter called out for him.

"My Alaina keeps an eye on me. She will not admit it, but she fears me being carted off one night, never to see me again. I am old and nearly crippled and of no use to the Dragon. You be careful, my lady, do not become useless to the Dragon or you too will disappear."

She watched him shuffle off, leaning heavily on his walking stick. She did not believe her husband evil, though her sensible side warned that two days' time was not enough to truly know someone. Why then did she feel so strongly that evil did not reside in her husband? Her husband did, however, seem to be a man shrouded in mysteries and she was curious to solve them for her own peace of mind.

Roy returned and she left him to finish his chore.

Heather headed to the keep with thought of asking Nessa if she knew about Glynnis and what had happened to her. Her husband was bidding his uncle good-bye as she approached and she gave Ewan a wave as he rode by her.

Her husband walked down the steps to meet her and stretched out his hand. "Time for us to talk." One look at her soft pink lips and his thoughts were not on talking.

Eager to speak with him, Heather hurried to take his hand, though once he took hold of it, a gentle tingle rippled through her. And for an instant something warned her to never let go.

Rhys settled Heather in a chair in his solar and before he could say a word Heather spoke.

"I am curious about something," she said.

"Only one thing?" he asked.

Was that a slight smile she saw? Her own smile brightened at the thought that there was hope in getting the Dragon to smile. "One thing for now."

"Have your say, for there is much I have to say to you."

Heather did not let his chastising tone bother her. She continued on, though her heart thumped a bit harder as she asked, "Where have all the McCombs gone? I recognize so few faces."

"Who has been whispering in your ear?"

His curt response sent her heart thumping even harder. "What do you mean?"

He took a step closer to her. "Did you not say you wished for us to always be truthful with each other?"

She nodded.

"Then say what you will and be done with it."

He sounded as if it was an order, so this time she decided to obey him. "Why are the older McComb people disappearing?"

He took another step closer and leaned over her, planting his hands on the arms of her chair. "That is not your concern."

Was it her curiosity or foolishness that had her pursuing it? "It is everyone's concern when clan members vanish without explanation."

"How many times must I tell you that I rule here? My word is law. I need not explain myself to anyone. Your duty as my wife is to obey, without question. And that is what I expect you to do."

She inched forward in her seat, her heart racing wildly now as she brought her face closer to his. She could not pull her gaze from his dark eyes, for they seemed to invite her in. But the question was—what would she find there? And once there would she be lost forever?

She spoke softly in almost a whisper as she said, "Is that what you truly want, a meek wife who never questions. A wife with no thoughts of her own?"

Her breath was soft and sweet as it drifted across his lips like a faint kiss and the thought came fast and furious. *Kiss her*. Difficult as it was, he ignored the urge. "I want an obedient wife who will not anger me at every turn."

It struck her then like a great weight that surely had to be weighing him down, and she rested her hand to his cheek as she said, "What is it you fear?"

He stepped back quickly as if he had been struck. "I fear nothing."

She stood. "I do not believe you. You reminded me about speaking the truth, now I ask the same of you."

Rhys reached out, grabbing her by the shoulders. "Fear was beaten out of me a long time ago as was faith. Power is what matters. It controls. It rules. It is obeyed."

"Love matters more," Heather said and was shocked to hear him laugh, though it was no humorous laugh.

"You are foolish if you believe that. People do not follow and obey powerful Kings and Rulers or warriors out of love, they follow out of fear, they submit out of fear."

"So you would rather I fear you than love you?"

"Love?" he said on a laugh that rumbled deep in his chest. "You truly believe that you could love me?"

"Why not?"

"You will find out soon enough," he said and released her, turning away.

"Why is everything a mystery with you? What do you hide? What do you fear?"

Rhys swerved around. "I hide what is necessary and did I not make it clear that I fear nothing? Enough of this nonsense," he ordered with a wave of his hand. "There are other more important matters to discuss."

"There can be no matter more important than that of your wife one day possibly falling in love with you."

Rhys stepped closer to her. "I would prefer your obedience to love."

"I cannot promise you either one, but I believe one would be much easier than the other for me to give you."

Her voice was gentle, her words heartfelt, and her lips inviting.

Kiss her.

This time he did not ignore the urging. His arm hurried around her waist to pull her close and his lips settled eagerly on hers.

Heather let herself be swallowed not only by his powerful arms, but his kiss as well. She had been waiting for him to kiss her, wanted him to kiss her and did not waste time wondering over why she enjoyed his kisses. She simply allowed herself to do so, for in his kiss was a mystery she intended to solve.

He commanded well with words, but more so with his lips and she had no trouble obeying what he demanded of her, for she demanded of him as well. And the deeper the kiss delved the more she sensed she drew closer to uncovering the mystery.

When he tore his mouth away from hers, she felt as if he took her breath with him and she gasped momentarily for air.

Rhys lowered her to the chair and poured her some wine, handing her the goblet. "Drink."

She did not argue. She sipped at it as her breathing began to slowly return and the pleasurable tingle that had settled over her had begun to fade. She looked up at him at a loss for words.

"Drink," he ordered again, though this time with firmness that warned of any protest.

It was not his demand that had her taking another sip. She took it because it helped calm her, for calmness was her only shield in dealing with the fiery Dragon.

Rhys paced in front of her. *Love.* It had been foolish of her to have mentioned it and he let her know it. He stopped abruptly and pointed a finger at her. "There will be no more talk of love." With that he stormed out the room.

Heather jumped when the door slammed shut behind him. She took another sip of wine, wondering how she was ever going to manage being wed to the Dragon. She sat enjoying the solitude and quiet, and the wine.

Feeling quite calm after finishing the wine, she planned to go in search of Nessa in hope of finding out about Glynnis and hoping the answer would not disturb her.

The door opened abruptly and Rhys walked in. Shoving the door shut behind him, he walked over to her with a look on his face that for a moment frightened Heather. She was not sure if it was anger or passion she saw there. She took several anxious steps away from him, but he quickened his step and his arm shot out, coiling around her waist, yanking her forward, and slamming her against his hard chest.

"You want to see the beast you truly married?" he said, though did not give her a chance to respond. His mouth came down on hers so harshly that it stole her breath.

Chapter Eleven

Heather did not struggle against Rhys' overpowering kiss nor did she respond. She was too busy trying to breathe. It did not help with how tightly he held her against him with one arm or how roughly his other hand gripped the back of her head, forcing her mouth to remain on his. If his intentions were to show what a beast he could be, he need not have bothered. His size and strength alone had done that. She was not foolish enough to think that she could ever defend herself against him and hoped she would never have to. But now?

He hoisted her up, not taking his mouth off hers and walked her to the door, planting her back against it and pressing his body tightly against hers. She felt him then. He was hard, thick, and large. And the image of what he possibly intended to do to her right here and now sent a ripple of fear through her.

When he rubbed himself hard against her, his tongue drove deeper into her mouth and he stole the last bit of breath she was fighting to keep. She shoved at his shoulders, trying at least to push him away enough for her to breathe, but she met solid muscle and could not budge it.

Her next action was instinctive. She challenged his tongue with her gentler one and stroked the side of his face with her hand as she did.

He responded more quickly than she had expected and with his kiss easing she was able to slip her mouth off his, rest her brow to his, and take his face gently in her hands as she struggled to say, "You stole my breath."

He stared at her and she was caught in the depths of his dark eyes. They seemed to always mesmerize her. There was something there, something about them...

"Be wary, wife, of the beast unleashed, for he cannot be harnessed or tamed," he said as he lowered her so that her feet finally touched the floor.

She rested her hand on his arm and as her breathing calmed, she said, "I would never be so cruel as to try to harness or tame a beast that lives wild and free. But if he wished to befriend me, I would welcome his friendship wholeheartedly."

"It would be foolish to befriend a wild beast."

"Not as foolish as to think to tame one."

"He could harm you."

"Or not," she said softly.

"Do not trust the beast," Rhys warned.

"I will not—at least not until he trusts me." She brushed a kiss across his cheek and with quick steps left the solar, the door closing behind her this time.

Rhys stared a few moments at the closed door, then went and poured himself a generous goblet of wine. He had meant to make her see the truth of who he was and to teach her a lesson. It had not gone as planned, but nothing seemed to be going as planned.

Heather was so much more than he had imagined she would be. While she wisely feared, she also wisely did not let fear stop her. She was more of a courageous woman than she knew, for she had quieted the Dragon with a tender touch.

She had infuriated him with her talk of love. A beast could not be loved nor could it give love. She needed to understand that and accept it.

He went and sat in the chair near the hearth, stretching his long legs out, the flames leaping back as if fearful of him. He had fought to keep control of himself when he had kissed her, but his need had suddenly raged out of control when he covered her mouth with a kiss that was anything but gentle. She needed to see the consequences of irritating the Dragon. She needed to know what she would suffer and yet...

He stood and poured himself more wine, though he had yet to finish what he had. He downed a mouthful and shook his head. He had been the one to suffer, the taste of her igniting a slumbering need, but it had been the remembrance of her gentle touch, the brush of her lips across his cheek, the mention of friendship that had left him, still now, hard and aching.

There had been no one to call friend until he met Pitt and that had taken time to evolve into friendship and now the brotherhood they shared.

Pitt had trusted faster than he had, but then he had rescued him from a pit where he had been left to die a slow death. When Rhys had asked his name, he had said Pitt, claiming a new name, for the man the culprits had dumped in the pit had emerged a far different person, much like Rhys had.

Rhys was not who he once had been or ever would be again.

He could never let the beast inside him rest. *Never.* It was the beast—the Dragon—who rose up and did what was necessary and God help his wife when the Dragon truly touched her.

~~~

Heather slowed her steps as she approached the Great Hall. She wondered over her husband's actions. Why had he tried to frighten her? Surely he realized that she did not know him well enough not to be afraid of him and certainly not well enough to believe she could trust him completely. He was still a stranger to her and that seemed odd to admit since after only two days with him she felt comfortable enough to accept his kisses and return them, something she had never expected. She had thought with time perhaps she would grow accustomed to intimacy with him, but to her great surprise she was not adverse to his kisses or his arm around her. How further intimacy would be she could not say, though recalling how hard and large he had felt against her was a bit of concern. The rough encounter had
~~~

given her pause since before that she had enjoyed all encounters with him. But then he was a man of many mysteries of which needed solving.

"Nessa," Heather shouted as she entered the Great Hall and the servant hurried over to her. Before Nessa could say anything to her, Heather spoke. "I need to speak with you." She lowered her voice. "It is important."

Nessa nodded. "Aye, my lady, this way."

Heather followed the servant through the passageway to the kitchen, then straight through the kitchen and out a door. They wound their way past several cottages until Nessa stopped at a small, well-kept one, a lovely garden surrounding most of it.

"My home," Nessa said and opened the door for Heather to enter.

It was one room, neat and well-kept, what little furniture there was fitting nicely into the small space. Nessa offered her the one chair in the room while she sat on a small bench.

"How can I help you, my lady?"

"I was wondering if you knew what happened to Glynnis?"

Nessa gasped. "All that is left of the McCombs wonder what happened to poor Glynnis. She was a pretty one with long dark hair and such lovely blue eyes. All the young men favored her but she had eyes for only one." Nessa shook her head. "Sadly, he died. An accident, though many think otherwise."

"Why?"

"The Dragon had summoned Glynnis often after his arrival and many believe he had taken a fancy to her and wanted her for himself. Some believe the Dragon holds her captive in the room on the upper floor, a slave to his wickedness."

"I was up there. The room is bolted."

Nessa's eyes turned wide. "No one is allowed up there." Her eyes grew even wider. "Good lord, he has locked her in, never to get out."

"I do not believe that and I wish to prove it. Do you know of any other way into the room?"

Nessa turned silent for several minutes before saying, "I remember my mum telling me once that there was a secret way in and out of the keep from the upper floor. It was meant to help the laird's family escape if necessary, but it was never used." Nessa gasped. "That must be how he is able to get the women to the upper floor without anyone seeing them."

"The Dragon would have to have learned of the secret entrance to be able to use it. Who else knows of it?"

Nessa chewed on her lower lip as she thought. She finally shook her head. "I cannot say, for my mum never said how she learned of it."

"Then you cannot say for sure if a secret passage does exist."

"No, though I do remember my mum tapping and pushing against walls in the rooms on the upper floor when we would see to cleaning the rooms there. She would look at me and tell me she was searching for secrets."

"Then I will continue her search."

Nessa jumped up. "Do you forget that the Dragon forbids anyone to go to the upper floor?"

Heather stood, smiling. "I have no intention of disobeying my husband."

"Then wherever will you search?"

"Outside," she said, "and I can count on you not to breathe a word of this?"

"You have no worry there, my lady, and I would be pleased to help you anyway I can."

"I appreciate that, Nessa, but I will not see you suffer if caught helping me. I will do this on my own, for then I will be the only one answerable to the Dragon."

"As you wish, my lady, but I am willing if you should need me."

Nessa returned to her duties and Heather stood outside Nessa's cottage, glancing up at the keep. It was a fair size, though seeing how the tower narrowed as it stretched to the upper floor made Heather realize how small the space actually was. The top portion was usually left as one large room and often used for storage of linens and such, but this top had been divided into three small sections when finished and she wondered why. Did it have something to do with the secret passage?

Heather slowly made her way around the bottom of the keep toward the side she was most interested in. She was glad the area was not in view of the entire village. It was more secluded with no one about, a perfect place to make an escape.

Her glance went to the ground instead of the keep itself. She walked over and squatted down, her hand going to an area of grass that appeared to have been trampled. Why would grass so close to the keep wall be trampled?

"What are you doing there?"

Heather fell back on her bottom startled by her husband's stern voice.

His hands quickly slipped under her arms and he lifted her to her feet.

"I never hear you approach," Heather said with a shake of her head.

"And you never will, so do not think to hide anything from me."

"How did you learn to walk so that your footfalls were not heard?" she asked, taking his arm and leading him away from the keep and from her reason for being there.

"An exceptional warrior taught me the skill." There were times her beauty caught him unaware and this was one of those times. Her blonde hair glistened in the sunlight and her cheeks were tinged soft pink, her lips a deeper rose. Had his harsh kiss still lingered there, staining her lips? Her green eyes sparkled with almost as much pleasantness as her smile.

"Will you teach me the skill?"

Rhys stopped. "If I did that, I would never hear you approach and already your steps are faint."

He bit his tongue for allowing the words to slip from his lips. He had allowed her beauty to distract him just as he had allowed her words of love to anger him. Too easily, she slipped past his defenses and that had to stop.

She laughed softly. "I believe my light steps were born out of necessity. I found myself treading lightly when my sisters were mere babes and I had put them to nap or bed and did not want to wake them as I left the room. As they got older, I kept my steps light so I could sneak up on them and catch them doing things they should not have been doing. Other times it was so I could sneak off by myself for a few moments of peace and quiet. Not that it lasted very long. Patience learned how to track young and was forever finding me. Do you have siblings?"

"No," he answered and wanted to bite his tongue again. He did not want her knowing anything about him and here he was answering her. He grew more annoyed when he realized that he had gone in search of her to see that she was not upset over their recent encounter when truly it was because he favored her company. She was stirring things to life in him that he had thought long since dead.

"You do have cousins, your Uncle Ewan's four sons."

"I barely know them."

"Then you have been gone from the area a long time. I suppose few would remember you."

This time he wanted to rip his tongue from his mouth for letting her deduce something about him from his response. "You ask far too many questions and disobey far too often."

She looked at him and soft laughter again preceded her words. "You are getting to know me well."

He had to look away from her and suppress the smile that hurried to his mouth. He rarely, if ever, smiled and it shocked him that a smile had come so easily. Unlike others who trembled when he admonished them, she showed no fear, took no offense, and responded more often than not with a smile or gentle laughter that always managed to stir him in more ways than one.

"So I should expect more disobedience from you?"

"Not intentionally," Heather said.

"Perhaps a fitting punishment for your disobedience so far would have you think twice before disobeying me again."

"Perhaps a reprieve since I am doing my best to find my footing and adapt to an unexpected marriage and a new home."

"You negotiate with me?"

"I have done so before."

He remembered it well, for she had agreed to come to their bed willingly if he allowed her to tend Douglas instead of attending the burial of the two warriors. He had yet to take advantage of the bargain they had struck, not that he was not most eager to, but in a way he was also reluctant. She was so very innocent and kind, but would she be after he put his mark on her?

"I will see you wear, at supper tonight, the garment that waits for you in our bedchamber. Only then will I consider a reprieve."

"Only consider, not grant me the reprieve?"

"You are lucky I even consider it." Rhys turned his head just as Pitt came into view.

"Pardon, my lord, but possible wolf tracks have been spotted by one of our sentries," Pitt said.

Rhys turned to Heather. "Our agreement has been struck. I will see you dressed appropriately tonight." He reluctantly eased his arm away from her hand and walked over to Pitt, though called out as he did, "And you will also tell me what you found so interesting in the grass by the keep wall."

Heather watched the two men walk away. Her husband was much too observant, but then so was she. There was something more to the wolf tracks that had been spotted and she wondered over it. She wished her husband trusted her enough to talk with her on all matters, though given time perhaps he would.

One problem at a time, first she wanted to prove to herself and others that the Dragon did not keep young lassies locked away in the upper floor room. She hurried back to the spot where she had seen the trampled grass and noticed another spot where the grass had been trampled close to the keep. She worked her way along the area and saw two more similar spots. Was someone else also searching for an entrance to a secret room or had it been found and someone left these spots to misdirect?

Heather stepped back. Who else could possibly be aware of the secret passage? Had Fane McComb revealed its existence to someone before he passed? Could Rhys possibly know its whereabouts?

"Excuse me, my lady."

Heather turned to see Bea standing a few feet away from her. "Douglas?" she asked anxiously.

"It is probably nothing, but his wound appeared different to me when I went to change his bandage a short time ago. I hoped that you might have a moment to look at it."

"Of course," Heather said and went with Bea, leaving the mystery to solve for another time.

~~~

Supper was not far off when Heather returned to the keep. Bea's worry was for naught; Douglas's wound was healing nicely. She had taken the time to visit a few other wounded warriors to see how they were faring and was pleased that all except one was doing well.

Fife had suffered an arm wound that was not serious and looked to be healing well, though pain seemed to plague him enough that he could not hold
~~~

his sword for long. He worried that he would not be able to continue to serve the Dragon.

Heather tried to reassure him that with time and rest he would be fine, but he was eager to return to duty and no amount of reassurance could soothe him and no amount of consoling would appease him. She left him brooding over his situation. She wished there was something she could do for him, but some men simply did not listen and she would not be surprised if he returned to his duties before he was sufficiently healed and make matters worse for himself.

Heather hurried through the Great Hall surprised to see it dressed in such finery, a white linen tablecloth covering the long table on the dais with a silver nef placed in the middle holding several linen napkins. Four pitchers lined the front of the table and four pitchers sat upon each of the trestle tables in the room. It would be a fine feast that would be served this evening.

With quick steps, Heather climbed the stairs to her bedchamber. She was pleased to see a fresh bucket of water waiting for her and when her eye caught the dress on the bed she hurried over to it. The dress was lovely, soft blue with threads of gold running along the low cut neckline and crisscrossing in the middle and gracing the hem along the sleeves. But what caught her attention more was the sapphire necklace that lay on top of the dress. She had never seen anything like it. The single, large sapphire hung from an intricate silver chain and Heather was afraid to touch it.

She stared at it, the dark blue gem appearing to wink at her from the way the hearth's light reflected off it. There was no denying that the necklace was lovely, but she much preferred the simplicity of the metal ring Quinn had made for her. It had been forged with love.

Gently, she lifted the necklace. It held no warmth, no love. Once placed around the neck, it would feel more like a shackle than anything else. With reluctance, Heather prepared to fulfill her end of the bargain she had made with her husband, not looking forward to the time the sapphire necklace went around her neck.

Chapter Twelve

Rhys sat at the dais table with Pitt enjoying the wine as warriors filed in and began filling the many tables. Soon talk, accented with bouts of laughter, circled the room and shouts of joy rang out when platters heaped high with various foods were placed on each table.

"This small feast will be good for the men," Pitt said, glancing around the room slowly.

"And which lassie catches your fancy tonight?" Rhys asked.

Pitt shook his head. "I forget you see what others do not."

"You forget I have grown to know you well. You are rarely without a female companion for the night, though perhaps it is time for you to find a wife."

"I am not ready to be shackled to one woman."

"Well, you certainly have your pick, since most of the servant lasses have difficulty keeping their eyes off you, all except one that is."

Pitt's glance drifted to Nessa, speaking with one of the servants.

"Pretty as Nessa is, she is not what I favor in a woman. I prefer a lusty, confident woman. Nessa barely looks me in the eye when I speak with her. I have no use for shy women." Pitt turned a grin on him. "But if I remember correctly either do you."

Rhys cast a glance over his men, having noticed that all sound had ceased and Pitt joined him in looking to see why. His wife had entered the room, turning the men speechless.

Pitt's mouth dropped open at the sight of her and when he realized it hung open like a gaping hole, he quickly snapped it shut.

Rhys drank in every inch of his wife. She approached the table with a gentle grace and a beauty that could not be denied. Her long blonde hair was swept up with several strands falling down the back of her neck and a few wisps around her face. The soft blue dress she wore dipped low on her chest and that was where Rhys' eyes stopped. He stood and walked to the front of the dais to meet her.

"Thank you for the generous gifts, my lord," Heather said when she came to a stop in front of him.

Talk and laughter resumed as Rhys gave her a brief nod and offered his arm to her, then escorted her back up on the dais to sit between him and Pitt.

"Your beauty outshines the sapphire, my lady," Pitt said.

Heather smiled. "How gallant of you to say, Pitt." She turned to her husband. "I was rather astonished to see it laying there upon the dress. It is far too generous of you, my lord."

Heather was not sure if his eyes were enthralled with the sapphire or her full breasts, since the gem rested just above the valley between her breasts.

Rhys turned away to pour her a goblet of wine. "I wished for you to have proper garments befitting my wife."

"The dress is most proper, but the necklace is not necessary," she said, accepting the goblet from him. "It belongs more on one of nobility than on me."

"Not if I deem otherwise," Rhys said.

"Wherever did you come by such a lovely garment and such a stunning jewel?" she asked.

"In my travels," he said. "Come now you must eat and enjoy the evening."

It was a more pleasant evening than Heather had imagined. Pitt was quite the storyteller, though she wondered if some of his tales were more truths. Many of the warriors raised repeated toasts to the lord and his lady and a few warriors broke into song.

Later in the evening, Rhys ordered her to remain at the dais while he spoke with Pitt privately for a few moments. He told her they would retire when he returned and her stomach fluttered. She knew this time would come and she could not help but grow more nervous as she watched him leave the room.

Rhys turned an angry voice on Pitt as soon as the door to his solar closed. "That bastard gained access to the castle, his message clear. He lets me know he is here and that he plans to take what I took from him. He gave that sapphire necklace to his wife the day they wed. I want you to find out how he gained access to the keep."

"There are sentries everywhere. He could not have gotten passed them."

Rhys shook his head as if suddenly realizing something. "He did not get passed them. He had someone else leave the message."

"He would have been seen and stopped," Pitt argued.

"Not if he was one of us."

"A spy among us?" Pitt said, questioning his own words.

"A spy," Rhys confirmed, "but more importantly, how long has he resided among us?"

"I cannot believe this. Each warrior seems so loyal to you. Who would be so foolish to think he would not be discovered and suffer for it?"

"The man is no fool. He has been taught to be a loyal servant to his master beyond anything else, even death."

"I do not understand how someone can follow so blindly," Pitt said.

"Only those who are blind follow blindly."

"It would explain how the death of our two warriors could happen under our very noses. They would have trusted one of their own. The problem now is...who can be trusted?"

"Some of our seasoned warriors who came to us after losing their land and their families would be the most loyal. It would be one of the ones who sought us out, whose backgrounds we know little of who would be more likely the culprit. What we need to find out is if any warrior has been seen in the keep beyond the Great Hall. He would have had to know how to get to my bedchamber."

"Nessa would be the one who could tell us that."

Rhys rested his hand on Pitt's shoulder. "That she could, which is why you are going to show her some favor and work your charm on her so that she does not shy away from talking with you."

"Why is that necessary? I can just question her and be done with it."

"And not get the answers we seek. If she feels she can trust you, she will be more forthcoming with all that goes on in the keep. Also find out who was on duty at the time of the two warriors' death. Confide in Henry what goes on, he and his wife can be trusted, and have him help you."

"What of Lady Heather? She believes the ghost warriors protect her. Will you confide in her and warn her not to trust any of them until this can be settled?"

"I do not want her knowing of this yet. I will order her not to go off with anyone but me, you, or Henry."

"And she will obey?" Pitt asked with concern.

"She will have no choice or I will shackle her to me until this is done."

~~~

Heather sat fingering the sapphire at her chest. She felt foolish wearing it and could not wait to take it off. She had met nobles who did not have such a fine gem and she wondered where in Rhys' travels he had come upon it.

"More wine, my lady?" Nessa asked and before Heather could refuse—her goblet still half full—Nessa leaned past her to pour the wine. As she did, she whispered, "Laird McComb believed Seamus his most trustworthy warrior."

"More bread, please," Heather said, giving Nessa an excuse to linger. "The laird could have confided in him."

"I thought it might be possible," Nessa agreed.

A shout went out and tankards were raised and the two women turned to see Rhys and Pitt enter the Great Hall. Nessa hurried off and Heather watched as Pitt stopped her, his arm going around her waist as he leaned down to say something to her.
~~~

Nessa appeared uncomfortable with his closeness and eased away from him with a nod, then hurried off.

Rhys took his seat. "A few moments more and we shall retire."

Heather nodded, though her attention went to Pitt as he took the seat next to her. "I know Nessa well and she is not free with her favors, so do not force yourself upon her."

Pitt looked stunned by her blunt remark, his glance going past Heather to Rhys.

"You do not tell my men what they can and cannot do," Rhys said.

Heather turned to her husband. "Then you order him, for I will not see Nessa suffer such abuse."

Rhys placed his face close to his wife's. "Pitt has never forced a woman, he has no need to. They fall at his feet most willingly. And never ever think to order my men about."

"I cannot give my word on that, for there may come a time I have no choice. And I would not be able to adhere to your command. So I cannot in all honesty give you my word when I do not know if I will be able to keep it."

Rhys stared at her perplexed. How could he fault her when she was being so honest with him? And with the possibility of a spy being in their midst, there was a good chance she might not be able to keep her word, and he would not want her to.

"I mean no disrespect, my lord, I only mean to be honest with you," Heather said and was surprised to see a slight smile tease at the corner of his mouth.

"Then be honest, wife, and tell me what you were looking for when I found you at the wall of the keep today?"

He had played that hand well and backed her in a corner. Now she had no choice, though she was careful how she answered him. "I was searching for a secret way into the keep."

Rhys' brow went up and Pitt said, "There is a secret entrance?"

She sat back in her chair so that she could glance more easily from one man to the other. "Gossiping tongues say there is." She was not about to implicate Nessa.

"What is it they say?" Pitt asked.

"It seems that the old laird had a secret passage built in case he or his family ever needed to escape unnoticed."

"But no one knows where the secret entrance is or where it leads to?" Rhys asked.

Heather did not know if the entrance actually led to the upper floor room that had been bolted so she was honest in saying, "I do not believe so."

"So you went in search of it?" Rhys asked.

"How could I not, being as curious as I am?"

"And what had caught your eye earlier outside near the keep?" Rhys asked.

"Trampled grass far too close to the keep, though when I went to take another look after speaking with you I saw more spots of trampled grass. So, I wondered if someone else could also be searching for the entrance or if someone was trying to mislead others."

Rhys looked to Pitt. "Find out what you can." He shifted his glance to his wife. "You will search no more."

"It would be far better that more than one person searched for it, and I do love solving mysteries," Heather said, looking at her husband.

"Some mysteries are better left unsolved."

Heather smiled. "Not to the curious mind."

Rhys leaned close to whisper in her ear, "Since you are so curious let us retire and see what intimate mysteries we can solve."

Heather's breath caught, but she retained her smile and said, "As you wish, my lord."

Rhys pressed his cheek to hers and his whispered words faintly brushed her ear, sending a shiver through her. "My wish is about to come true, for I intend to strip you naked and taste every inch of you."

Flutters rushed throughout her entire body and settled between her legs and she caught the gasp in her throat before it could escape, not that it mattered, for she knew her husband felt it being so close to her.

Rhys stood, taking his wife's hand and helping her to her feet. "I expect no interruptions, Pitt."

"Aye, my lord," Pitt said.

Cheers went up as Rhys escorted his wife from the room and up the stairs to their bedchamber. They no soon as entered the room then Rhys removed the necklace from around her neck and placed it inside a small chest stacked on top of two others near the door.

Heather waited in the middle of the room unsure of what to do and apprehensive of what was to come. She had seen him gentle and not so gentle, a fiery demeanor lurking ever so close to the surface and that gave her reason to pause in worry.

She did not know if his steps were slow or if her concern saw it that way. But whichever it was, it made the wait for him to reach her all the more difficult since he seemed to grow more formidable with each step he took. He moved much like the animals in the forest did, when on alert or stalking, with purpose and strength, every muscle taut and ready to spring if necessary.

He stopped in front of her and brought his hand up to stroke her cheek with the back of his hand. She almost jumped at his touch not certain if his touch felt hot or cold, though it was gentle.

"You are so very beautiful, wife," he whispered and lowered his mouth to hers.

He did not demand, but rather invited her to join him in the kiss, encouraging her tongue to mate with his and she did. His one hand went to her backside and eased her up against him, while his other hand settled on her breast to squeeze it lightly.

He felt her slight surrender, her body resting less rigid against him. He let his hands roam more freely over her, though kept control of them. If he allowed his rugged passion to rule, she would be stripped bare by now, his mouth devouring every inch of her, not to mention what his hands would be doing. He did not want to frighten her from their bed, though he feared that it might be inevitable.

He eased his hand down to dip into her bodice and release one of her plump breasts and as she gasped, he bent his head and took the tightening bud in his mouth.

Heather gasped again, the sensation so new and pleasing that she startled and pulled away from him. He stopped her, his hand at her backside moving up to press against her back and hold her still. And as he continued to tease and suckle, her body began to awake as if from a long sleep. Sensations suddenly sharpened and she felt things like she never did before. And oh how she enjoyed his tongue at her breast, his hand at her back, and his manhood hard against her. This night would not be the night of horror that she had once feared and that thought had her relaxing in his arms.

The next thing she knew, he gave her a hard shove backwards. So hard that she felt herself sail through the air, her hands flailing and when she landed, the back of her head smacked against something hard and everything went black.

Chapter Thirteen

Rhys rounded on the man he heard approach from behind. He had no time to give thought to how the culprit had gotten into their bedchamber. The man's face was smeared with grime so as to be undistinguishable and to create fear. To anyone else he would appear a demon born of the earth, but to Rhys he was a man who had entered his private chambers and was about to suffer for it. The culprit danced like a string less puppet in front of him, taunting as he skillfully tossed a small dagger back and forth in his hands.

Rhys was well aware that he would get no information out of the man even if tortured. He would suffer whatever pain necessary before betraying his master. So, he decided to send a message of his own. He waited, watching how much the man was enjoying his little act and when the he least expected it—Rhys' hand shot out and grabbed the dagger and with one swift blow sent it through the man's throat.

As the man's body dropped to the floor, Rhys turned and ran to his wife's lifeless body and went down on one knee beside her, frightened to death that he had killed her. Carefully, he reached down and lifted her gently into his arms and just as gently laid her on the bed. To his great relief she was breathing, but when he ran his hand faintly along the back of her head, he felt a large bump and fear took hold of him again. He had seen too many warriors never wake up from such a bump and he would not have that with his wife... he would not lose her.

~~~

"Heather! Heather! Do you hear me?"

"Quinn!" Heather thought her heart would burst from her chest. Quinn had returned to her. "Quinn! Where are you?"

"Here."

She turned to find Quinn standing in front of her and she threw herself into his arms. He caught her and held her tight. She looked up at him. He was no longer the young lad that had left her. He was now a strong strapping man, though his smile was the same. She would never forget his smile. It always warmed her heart.

"You came back," she said, tears gathering in her eyes.

"I gave you my word I would return for you. Nothing. Absolutely nothing would stop me from coming back to you. Nothing will stop me from keeping you safe."

"My heart has ached for you; I have missed you so very much."

"And I you and I give you my word once more...we will never be parted again."
~~~

Heather let her tears fall. Quinn was home. He had come back to her and nothing else mattered. "I love you, Quinn. I love you so very much."

"And I love you, Heather, Now and alw..."

A strange sound vibrated in her head as his words faded along with him and with tears falling, Heather cried out, "Quinn, do not leave, not again. Quinn!"

"Heather! Heather, wake up!"

Heather fought to open her eyes, but it seemed with each flutter of her eyelids, the more her head pounded with pain. Finally, she managed to open them a sliver and she winced with pain.

"Open your eyes, Heather, now!"

She forced her eyes open, wanting desperately to see Quinn and know he was safe and had returned to her. She blinked several times to clear her vision, though it did little good, for her tears continued to fall and blur everything. Finally, when she could see clearly, it took a moment for her to realize that it was the Dark Dragon sitting beside her on the bed and all she could do was stare at him.

Fury gripped Rhys with a vengeance. It was his fault she shed tears and that was unacceptable to him.

Slowly Heather began to recall what had happened and her tears began to subside. "You shoved me away."

Rhys' explanation was brief. "We had an intruder."

Heather nodded, the movement bringing her pain and she scrunched her face against it.

"Your head hit the stone hearth and you have a large knot on the back of it," he explained.

"You shoved me to protect me." Her words were a bare whisper. "You shoved me away to keep me safe. Did you get him?"

Rhys leaned to the right so that she could see the man's body near the door, knowing his wife would not rest until she did.

Heather stared at the lifeless body and saw that the man wore the same grime on his face as those who had attacked them on their journey here. The Dark Dragon had an enemy, and he meant to see the Dragon dead.

Heather saw several of the Dragon's warriors roaming about the room. It appeared as if they searched for something while one stood guard over the body.

"Pitt," Rhys called out and the man hurried to his side.

"I am most pleased to see you awake, my lady," Pitt said

Heather grimaced as she turned her head, and said, "Thank you, Pitt."

"Do not move. You cause yourself pain every time you do," Rhys ordered.

"Aye, that I do," Heather said and let her eyes drift closed.

"And do not go to sleep," Rhys shouted at her. "I have seen too many men fall asleep after such a head wound never to wake again. You will keep your eyes open."

His caring words, though abrupt manner, brought a smile to her face that caused her to cringe again.

"No smiling," he warned.

"Then what am I allowed to do," she asked with a sigh.

"You are to do nothing but lie there and rest." Rhys turned to Pitt. "Dump the bastard in the woods and leave the dagger in his throat. And I expect you to find out before morning how he got into my bedchambers."

"Secret passage," Heather said. "Is not that what your men search for?"

Even after a blow to the head her attention was sharp and Rhys was impressed. His wife was a strong woman and while it might pose problems along the way, he was glad for it.

"They do," Rhys admitted, "but they have found nothing so far."

"They should be searching outside as wall," Heather said.

"They are," Pitt said and received a scowl from Rhys.

"You are not to concern yourself with this," Rhys ordered his wife, though knew his demand useless.

"I can help," Heather said, laying her hand over her husband's.

"No!" he said forcefully.

Heather had no want to argue with him in her present condition and she had no want to sit by and do nothing. And while she knew that Seamus might know something about the secret passage, she did not wish to share that information with her husband. Seamus did not trust Rhys and he would stay quiet if asked anything about a secret passage. She would wait until she was feeling better, and then ask the old man if he knew anything about this phantom way into and out of the keep.

Rhys took her hand. "You are to rest, nothing more."

She stared at him for a moment, not able to take her eyes off his face, then as if coming out of a fog, she said, "As you wish."

Rhys thought she acquiesced to his demand much too easily. He would have to keep a watchful eye on her. He looked to Pitt again. "The men have spent enough time here. Take them and search elsewhere, and leave two men outside the door for the night. And send Nessa up."

Pitt nodded and within minutes everyone was gone along with the dead body.

Rhys squeezed her hand lightly. "Nessa will help you into your nightdress while I go see to some things."

Heather grabbed onto his hand, not wanting to let go. "You will not be long? You will be coming back?"

He caught the sudden fear in her eyes and it tore at his gut. "You are safe. Warriors will be right outside the door and I will not leave until Nessa is here."

"But you will come back?" she asked anxiously.

"I will return," he said.

"Promise?"

"I promise," he said and raised her hand to his lips and kissed it softly.

A smile rose on her face, though a grimace robbed it fast enough and he grew angrier at himself for having hurt her.

This time she cast a slight smile and held his hand tighter. "Thank you for saving me."

He did not mean to say what rushed into his head. "I hurt you."

"Not intentionally. You did what had to be done and may have to do so again if the situation should arise, since this matter is not settled."

"No, it is not, but it will be and this time permanently."

Heather had no chance to ask what he meant by *this time*. Nessa entered the room and her husband called her over to him.

"You will see to getting Lady Heather settled for the night, though you will not let her fall asleep while I am gone and you will stay with her until I return," Rhys ordered.

"Aye, my lord, I will see to her every need," Nessa said, nodding repeatedly.

"Will you help me stand before you go so it will be easier for Nessa to assist in undressing me?" Heather asked.

Rhys reached down and slipped his arm gently beneath her back. "I will sit you up first and see if you grow faint." He spread his hand against her back to support her as he brought her up to sit.

Her head swam a bit, but she remained still once she sat up, giving it a chance to pass and it began to fade.

Rhys could see that the slow movement affected her and he was concerned she would not be able to remain on her feet. "Tell me when you wish to stand."

Heather took a deeper breath before reaching out to him and saying, "Now would be fine."

His arms went around her and he slowly helped her to her feet.

She looked up at him as he did, her eyes never leaving his face and she whispered, "Do not leave me."

It was a desperate whisper filled with fear and it felt like it all but tore him in two. He did not turn to Nessa when he said, "You may leave, Nessa, and tell Pitt I will see him in the morning."

"Aye, my lord," Nessa said and left the room.

Heather rested her head on her husband's chest, the strong, rapid beating of his heart echoing in her ear and sounding like a comforting melody to her.

"Let me get you out of your dress and into your nightdress so that you may rest more comfortably."

"Aye, I think that would be wise, though I do not know how much help I can be."

"I will see to it, do not worry," he said and went to sit her on the bed so he could fetch her nightdress.

She tightened her grip on him. "I fear I will not have the strength even with your help once I sit."

Rhys wanted to be able to slip her nightdress on as soon as he slipped her dress off, otherwise it was not going to be easy to hold her completely naked in his arms. He had waited impatiently for the first moment he would see her naked. He had not expected that when it came he would not be able to touch and kiss her lovely body, but rather he would be dressing her in her nightdress and tucking her into bed and that the whole ordeal would be his fault.

So with reluctance he said, "Then I will get your dress off first, then you can sit while I fetch your nightdress."

"I would be most grateful."

Grateful. He had never expected her to be grateful to him for stripping her naked or that he would be disappointed when he did. He pushed the annoying thought from his head. He needed to see this done and as fast as possible. He worked on the ties at the back of her dress, loosening them and hoped that she wore other garments beneath like some women did. Then he could leave them on her to save his sanity while he got her nightdress.

As soon as he freed the ties all the way, he could see she wore no top undercover. He had to be done with this and see his wife clothed shortly after stripping her or he might not be able to keep his hands off her once he got in bed with her.

He worked the dress down over her shoulders and then her breasts. It was impossible not to let his eyes feast on what his mouth could not. He shut his eyes for a moment, but the images of her lovely breasts followed behind his closed lids and, of course, he grew aroused. How could he not when looking on such enticing breasts.

Her soft moan had his eyes springing open.

"Bed," she whispered, "I need to get in bed."

He admonished himself for thinking of his own need when she was suffering. Keeping his thoughts focused on seeing her comfortably settled for the night, he hurried to rid her completely of the dress. And when he pushed the dress down over her curvy hips and it fell the rest of the way down at her feet, his eyes could not help but admire the thatch of blonde hair at the apex of her legs. How he ached to touch her, explore her, and bring her pleasure.

He shook his head.

"My body does not please you?"

"It pleases me too much. You are more beautiful than any woman I have ever known."

She moaned again. "My head...hurts."

Rhys eased her up into his arms, and then laid her down gently on the bed. He slipped off her shoes and pulled the blanket over her, though he would have loved to continue to feast his eyes on her enticing body. She was curved perfectly in all the right places and her skin was soft with not a single blemish on it. And she must have done much physical work for while her skin was soft to the touch there was tightness to her body that he rarely saw in a woman.

He was growing far too aroused and turned to walk away and not only fetch her nightdress, but take a moment to collect himself and calm his growing arousal.

She reached out, grabbing his hand. "Do not leave me."

"You need your nightdress," he said, knowing it was a necessity for his own sanity.

"I need you more."

Her desperate plea grabbed at his gut and turned his ache for her unbearable. But he would not deny her when she had been left frightened from the incident. He would, however, leave his garments on.

He went to climb in bed with her, but her words stopped him.

"Your garments...take them off or you will not sleep comfortably."

He never expected to hear his new wife tell him to take his garments off and at any other time he would be only too pleased to oblige her. But this night had been difficult enough without having to crawl into bed with her naked. Another thought he never believed he would ever have.

"Please hurry," she begged.

He did as she asked and got in bed carefully so as not to jostle her and cause her more pain. As soon as he stretched out beside her, she turned, pressed herself tight against him, placed her leg over his, her arm across his waist and rested her head on his chest, and sighed contentedly.

This was going to be an unbearable night and yet he cherished having her in his arms. He rested his arm around her shoulders and slipped his other hand in hers, locking her safely in his embrace.

"How many women?" she whispered.

He narrowed his brow, not understanding. "What is that you ask?"

"You said I was more beautiful than any woman you have ever known. How many women have you known?"

"More than I needed to."

"That is an odd answer."

"It is a complex matter."

"How so?" she asked.

"You need your rest."

"You told me not to sleep."

"You can sleep now. I will stir you now and again to make certain you are all right," he said, not wanting to discuss the matter with her now or possibly ever.

"My head hurts too much for me to sleep. If we talk, it may take my mind off the pain and allow me to sleep."

"Then talk...of something else."

"Have you ever truly loved anyone?" Heather listened as her question caused his heart to beat faster.

"I will not discuss love with you," he snapped.

"Why not? Does love frighten you?"

"Very little frightens me."

"Then what is it that does frighten you?"

"A wife who nags me with endless questions."

Her soft laughter turned to a yawn. "See I grow tired already, and I do not nag. Are you not curious about me?"

"I know all I need to know."

"And what do you know?"

"That you belong to me now and always," he said, declaring it so.

"You will never let me go?"

"Never."

"You will never leave me?"

"Never. You will remain by my side always whether you like it or not."

"You do not have to make it sound as if you must order me. Being wed to you is not the burden I imagined it would be."

"You say that now, but in time you may think differently," he said. "Now no more talk. Go to sleep."

Heather yawned again, finding their conversation had taken her mind off the pain that seemed to have faded. Her eyes grew heavy and began to drift close and just as she slipped into slumber she heard the whispered words that often filled her dreams.

I love you, Heather.

"I love you— always—Quinn," she whispered as sleep took hold.

Chapter Fourteen

Heather woke alone in bed the next morning and was glad of it. She needed time alone to think and to make sense of last night, to make sense of what she was thinking then and now. She shook her head and winced, the pain reminding her of the bump she had suffered to the back of her head. It also reminded her of the dream and Quinn and when she had woken from it to find...

She shook her head again, though more slowly this time.

It was her imagination, it had to be, and yet somewhere deep in her heart she knew it was the truth. She had seen it in his eyes, felt it wrapped in his arms, when he touched her, and most of all when he kissed her. She shook her head again. She was not mistaken about this.

The Dark Dragon was Quinn.

Her heart swelled with the thought while tears filled her eyes. What had happened to him that had him returning to her a different man and not just in name only? And why had he felt the need to keep his identity from her and force her to wed him?

A tear fell from her eye, for knowing Quinn as she did, he would be doing this to protect her, but from whom?

She wanted to rush off and find Rhys and let him know that she had discovered his secret, but his secret was meant for him to reveal. In the meantime, she would help him the only way she could...she would love him with all her heart and soul.

One thing that weighed heavily on her was what he had said in response to her asking him how many women he had known.

More women than I needed to.

Naturally, the thought of him with other women upset her. And it had sounded as if it also upset him, for she had heard regret and anger in his response. So why then had he been with more women that he needed to? She hoped one day to find out.

Heather felt at the bump on the back of her head and was relieved to feel that the swelling had gone down. It still pained her to touch it, but it was not as painful as last night. Her vision had not been impaired as she had seen happen with some severe blows to the head, and she felt hungry, so she deemed herself fit.

She gave a stretch while slowly working her way out of bed and was pleased that she suffered no adverse effects from the movement, nor did she grow faint when she stood. She actually felt wonderful, but then she could attribute that to finally being with Quinn again.

What if she was wrong?

Heather chased the doubting thought away. She was not wrong. She had spotted something familiar in the Dark Dragon's eyes when she had been up close to him. And now she knew what it was. It was a tiny spark of the love that had shone so brilliantly in his dark eyes before he had gone away. It had not died. It never could. He loved her too much. It may have gone dormant out of necessity, but it was still there and would always be.

She would ignite that spark and bring Quinn back to her.

A soft knock on the door sounded before it opened and Nessa walked in, balancing a tray on her arm. She stopped abruptly and looked about to say something, but quickly closed her mouth along with the door.

Nessa did not say a word until she stood in front of Heather. "The Dragon has ordered you to stay abed all day. He will be furious if he learns you are up and about. I was sent to see that you were awake, wake you if you were not, and see that you ate something."

There was no possible way she would stay abed all day. She wanted to spend every moment she could with... She thought about whom it was she would actually spend time with and a smile spread across her face when the answer came easily.

She would spend time with the man who loved her as much as she loved him.

Her smile remained firm as she said, "I feel fine. There is no reason for me to lie abed all day."

"The Dragon thinks differently and the guards will follow his command and not let you leave the room," Nessa said, placing the tray she held on the small table near the bed.

Heather reached for her skirt and blouse and Nessa was quick to help her.

"Let me, my lady. You really should rest after the bump you took to your head."

Heather allowed Nessa to help her slip into her clothes, seeing the concern on her pretty face. "I feel quite well and have less pain than last night. I will be sure not to exert myself today."

"Please sit and let me attend to your hair, my lady," Nessa offered. "I will comb it gently and braid it for you, for you surely do not want to pin it to your head with combs and disturb the bump that is healing."

Again Heather acquiesced to her suggestion and sat while she tended her hair. "You have a gentle touch about you, Nessa."

"Thank you, Lady Heather, my mum said the same about me and advised that it would be an asset when dealing with a husband."

"And is there anyone who you favor for a husband?"

Nessa smiled as she said, "Fife. He is plain in features and form. One would never expect him to be a ghost warrior. He is also kind and thoughtful." Her smile grew. "He picked a bunch of wildflowers and brought them to me. He is easy to talk with and feels the loneliness that I do, having lost his entire family like me." Her smile faded. "This morning Pitt attempted to engage me in conversation, turning that handsome smile of his on me. But I want nothing to do with the likes of him. A man as handsome as him would only bring a woman trouble. But I have no worries, the Dragon forbids his men from forcing themselves on the women here."

Heather was glad to hear that, though wondered why Rhys had not mentioned it last night when she had commented to Pitt about not forcing himself on Nessa. That mattered not now. What did was this news only helped to confirm even more that the Dark Dragon was Quinn, for he would never standby while a man forced himself on a woman.

"I am happy for you. You deserve a good man," Heather said.

"Thank you, my lady," Nessa said, resting the long braid over Heather's shoulder and glanced around the room. "Where are your boots, my lady?"

Heather stood and also cast a glance around and smiled. "I believe my husband took my boots and shoes."

"Oh dear, then you are stuck, for you cannot go barefoot."

"I will not let a small inconvenience stop me. I have gone barefoot before and I can do so again," Heather said.

"Before you do, you may want to fortify yourself with some food." Nessa handed Heather a piece of cheese and bread.

Heather took it and between munches said, "I made no mention that Seamus might possibly have some knowledge of the secret passage."

"That is good, for Seamus does not trust the Dragon and his warriors. He will tell them nothing. You, a Macinnes, he would trust."

"I thought the same from having spoken with him, and I do hope he can be of some help." Heather brushed her hands of any crumbs clinging to them, and wished she could brush away the problems at hand so easily.

"Shall we see what the guards will do when I attempt to leave?" Heather said.

"I would suggest a quick gait, my lady, since they will be expecting me and may not bother to look until too late. I will follow close behind and keep them from you if possible."

"I do not wish you punished because of me."

"What do I do but follow you out, nothing more," Nessa said with a shrug.

"Thank you, Nessa, I appreciate it, but promise me you will do nothing that will bring punishment down on you."

"As you wish, my lady," she said, picking up the tray.

Heather nodded, though knew full well that Nessa would do anything to help her and Heather would do anything to make sure the woman did not suffer because of it.

Heather went to the door, opened it, and rushed out past the guards before they realized it was her. She did not stop; she kept a fast pace, Nessa following behind her.

The two guards rushed after her. "My lady, the Dragon has ordered you to remain abed."

"I am going to speak with him about that," Heather called back to them, grateful that Nessa was blocking them from reaching out for her.

"You need to return to your room, my lady. We will fetch the Dragon for you."

Heather rushed down the stairs. "I will fetch him myself."

"Move out of the way, woman!"

Heather smiled, silently blessing Nessa for keeping the guards at bay, and then she heard a piercing screech that rang in her ears followed by the clatter of the tray and its contents falling and several oaths being shouted. Nessa had done well in stopping the guards.

Servants were the only ones in the Great Hall and Heather asked if any of them had seen the Dragon. They shook their heads and she wondered why they appeared so fearful. It struck her as she reached the door. Her husband had made it known that she was to remain abed and she was blatantly disobeying him. They feared for her punishment.

The sun and a warm breeze hit her as soon as she stepped outside and she drank both in happy she had escaped the confines of her bedchamber. She wished she could go find Seamus and see if he knew anything about a secret entrance to the keep, but now was not the time.

She looked around and spotting Belle near the edge of the woods called out to her as she approached.

"My lady, you are feeling better?" Belle asked with concern.

"I am fine, a bump is all. Have you seen the Dragon?"

Belle hesitated a moment before saying, "He made it known to all that you would spend the day abed."

"It is too fine a day to lie abed."

Belle hesitated once again. "Perhaps you should do as the Dragon says, my lady."

"You would be wise to follow Belle's advice, least I shackle you to me until I say otherwise."

Both women turned to see the Dragon and Pitt approach.

Belle gave a respectful nodded and stepped away.

Heather smiled at his remark, thinking it would be a good way of keeping him from ever leaving her again. "Promise?"

Pitt chuckled. Rhys did not.

Rhys turned to Pitt as they stopped not far from her. "Bring me those two fools who were supposed to be sure she remained in her room."

Pitt nodded and went to do as Rhys bid.

"It was not their fault," Heather said as she approached her husband."

"You escaped them. They should have stopped you and that means they did not do as ordered," Rhys said. His brow arched as his eyes went to her feet. "You are barefoot."

"You took my boots and shoes."

"And I see it was for naught."

Heather stopped in front of him, holding out her wrists. "I would rather be shackled to you than confined to our bedchamber all day."

He pushed her wrists down and brought his face close to hers. "And I would rather be confined to our bedchamber all day with you shackled to me." He paused before saying, "You took a sharp blow to your head last night. You need time to heal."

She heard the sincerity in his strong voice and saw the concern in his dark eyes and her heart swelled with joy once again. This was Quinn. Her Quinn. She was certain of it, though she would give no clue that she knew. "I am attending to my healing the best way I know how. The sun and its warmth would do far more to heal me than the confines of our bedchamber."

"You disobey me again, wife?" he whispered close to her lips.

Heather brought her lips to where they were almost touching his. "I missed you."

Her soft, sincere words punched at his heart and damn if he did not want to reach out and slam her against him while he devoured her lips in a kiss. She aroused him much too easily and with her still needing to heal, he took no chances...he stepped away from her. "You will remain by my side without question." He realized then what he had done. He had committed himself to a day of torture.

She felt his absence as soon as he stepped away from her, though he was not that far a distance from her, and she said quickly. "I will."

Rhys turned, seeing Pitt approach with the two warriors in tow. He cast a quick look to his wife. "Wait here." He walked to meet Pitt.

"It would seem your wife had some help," Pitt said as the two warriors stood off to the side until summoned.

"Nessa," Rhys said. "Have you befriended her yet?"

"She pays me no heed and keeps her distance as if I was diseased."

A smile played at Rhys' lips. "A woman who does not fancy you...that is unusual."

"And something I intend to rectify. I will have her talking with me soon enough."

"See that you do. We need to find who among us does not belong." He gave a nod to the two warriors and they stepped forward, neither offering a word.

He had chosen the two because they had been with him since almost the beginning and he knew their history. They were good, worthy men and he could see that they were upset over their failure to see successfully to their task.

"You both will be assigned a month's extra perimeter duty."

Both men appeared surprised by the light punishment.

"It would seem my wife has learned some of the ghost warriors' skills."

"Lady Heather is light and fast on her feet like us," the tall, slim one said with admiration.

"See that this does not happen again," Rhys said in a tone that had both men bowing their heads.

He dismissed them and saw that Pitt was staring at his wife who had gone to sit on a stump near the edge of the woods and appeared to be talking to a squirrel a short distance from her.

"She has much courage," Pitt said.

"She will need it for what she will face being my wife."

"I believe Lady Heather is up to the task," Pitt said, "And I should be up to mine. I go to speak with Nessa."

"Have her bring Heather her boots. You know where I had them put."

"I do, but I see that did not stop her." Pitt chuckled again and was gone before Rhys could admonish him for it.

Rhys stood watching his wife. The squirrel inched ever closer to the green leaf Heather held in her hand, though he wondered if it was her soft voice urging him to take the food that the animal found more appealing. A few more steps and the squirrel snatched it from her hand, though he did not run off with it. He sat beside her and munched on the leaf while Heather continued to talk to him.

Rhys shook his head as he approached and the squirrel hurried off as he drew near, running up a tree with his leaf.

Heather went to stand but Rhys said, "Stay as you are." He hunched down in front of her. "Tell me you feel well enough to be about."

She smiled, glancing over his face and seeing why she had not recognized him when she had first laid eyes on him. The faint lines around his eyes, the slight scrunch of his brow from frowning so often, the lack of a smile and the fullness of his face from the passing years, concealed the man she knew and loved. But he was there, she knew he was there and somehow, someway she would get him to reveal himself. "I feel good. I have a bit of pain now and then, and I will acknowledge if I do too much and if I am in need of rest."

"And you give me your word on this?"

"I do," she said and reached out to rest her hand on his arm, remembering the many times she had done just that while they walked, talked, and laughed. "Besides, I will be with you. What could happen?"

Rhys did not want to think about that, since the prospects would be far too terrifying. And the thought that he would fail to protect her was even more terrifying. Never, ever, would he let that happen. As he stood, he took her hand and she stood along with him.

Once on her feet, she slipped her arm around his and held tight. She intended to make sure she kept him close. "I want to thank you for being so tolerant of me last night. I felt safe with you close."

"I will not deny you when you need me. I will always be there for you."

Heather felt her stomach clench. Quinn had said those words to her before he knew he would be leaving. He had never intended to leave her, but things do not always go as wished.

They walked along slowly. "Tell me where you heard of the secret passage."

She did not want to implicate Nessa and have her subjected to endless questions, but she also wanted to be honest with her husband, so she said, "I believe it was a servant who made mention of hearing of it. Do you think that is how the intruder got into our bedchamber last night?"

"No, I heard the door open."

"That is why you shoved me aside?"

"It was his light footfalls that let me know he did not want to be detected."

"How could he have gotten into the keep with so many of your men keeping watch?" she asked. "And why do these men who smear their faces with grime chase after you?"

"I would tell you it is nothing you need to concern yourself with, but I know that would mean little to someone as inquisitive as you."

She laughed softly. "See you known me well already." Her laughter faded along with her smile. "Who are these men who want to harm you?"

"Old enemies and as you saw for yourself very dangerous ones. So it would be very wise of you to finally obey me. Is that all you know of the secret passage?"

Heather hesitated, knowing that Seamus would not be forthcoming to the Dragon and not knowing what the Dragon would do if the old man was not.

"What causes you to pause?"

What did cause her to pause? While he was the Dark Dragon, he was also Quinn and Quinn would never harm an old man. But he was a changed man, could she be so sure? In her heart, she felt she could. "I know of an old man who may know something, but he does not trust the Dragon or his men."

Rhys did not bother to ask her how she knew all this, he already knew. She had a kind soul. People saw it in her caring ways and her generous smile. They trusted her, were drawn to her, felt comfortable around her, and so they spoke openly with her.

"He would trust you," Rhys said.

"I believe he would."

"Do you feel well enough to speak with him now?"

"I do, and I am eager to speak with him and see what he knows, for I do not want another intruder interrupting us in our bedchamber."

"That I agree with," Rhys said, "Shall we go find him?"

"I would like that."

And he liked that they would be spending the day together. He could make certain she stayed safe that way and besides he wanted her no other place than by his side.

Chapter Fifteen

Heather sat on a bench while Nessa slipped her boots on. Heather could very well do it herself, but her husband had insisted. Rhys stood a distance away speaking with Pitt, and it was a good thing since Seamus saw her and wandered over to her.

"Your mum often went barefoot. You are the exact image of her. Beautiful and kind," Seamus said.

"You knew her well?" Heather asked just as Nessa finished and took her leave.

"Well enough."

"Please sit and tell me more." Heather patted the spot beside her on the bench.

Seamus sat. "She was a good friend to Mary McComb long before you were born. They would often spend time in Mary's solar stitching and talking. Your mum cried along with her with every babe Mary lost. Sometimes it is just not meant to be." Seamus nodded his head toward the Dragon. "Your mum would not be happy, you being married to the likes of him." He scrunched his brow. "Though, I do recall overhearing your mum telling Mary one day that you would marry a good man who loved you deeply and you and he would have many children and have a long and good life together. She had a knowing about her and I do not remember her ever being wrong. She had even mentioned to Mary that she would not be here to see it and that saddened her."

Heather remembered how her da always took his wife's warnings seriously. "I have a few good and happy memories of my mum, others have faded with time, though I wish they hadn't." Heather cast a glance toward her husband. "I believe my mum was right. My husband is a good man, though most do not believe him so."

Seamus snorted. "Do not be blind to the devil's ways, lass. The Dragon is not a man to trust and I have heard not a kind man to women. Your mum would not want you to suffer with a man such as him." He lowered his voice to a whisper. "Run if you get a chance."

Heather took the opportunity that presented itself. "How can I when he keeps an eye on my every move?"

Seamus shook his head and whispered. "There is a secret way out of the keep, but Fane never did tell me where it was. The only thing he mentioned to me was that Mary knew the way and that was all that mattered." Seamus scratched his head. "I would not be surprised if she confided in your mum, they were that close." Seamus shook his head again. "Here I am talking away when I should be asking how you are feeling."

"I am doing very well."

"The Dragon did not harm you, did he?" Seamus asked his voice remaining low.

"No, it was an intruder and the Dragon saved me from him."

"Intruder you say?" Seamus said questioningly. "How can an intruder sneak past all the ghost warriors without being seen? It would seem more likely that it was one of the Dragon's own that was the culprit."

"I never thought of that, but why ever would one of his warriors do such a thing?" Heather said.

Seamus shrugged. "My guess is a mighty sum of coin was involved. The Dragon does have more enemies than friends. You need to be careful, my lady. You should keep your distance from the Dragon. You do not want his fate to accidentally become yours."

"Daaaaaa!"

Seamus winced. "That daughter of mine never lets me be. I say if the Dragon is going to do me in, I will go down fighting like any honorable Highlander." He stood and bowed to Heather. "Lady Heather, it has been a joy talking with you. It reminds me of the days your mum would come and visit."

Heather smiled. "Until next time, Seamus."

He grinned. "I look forward to it."

Heather's smile faded as Seamus walked away. She may not have learned what she wanted to about the secret passage, but she did discover something she had not expected to and it would explain how the intruder got into their room. She could understand her husband not wanting anyone to know of this, for if it was made known the culprit would know his time was limited. The Dragon would find him and he would suffer dearly for it.

"Heather, are you all right?"

Heather looked up and it was not the Dragon she saw standing there...it was Quinn. How had she missed it? *Fear.* She had been so afraid of the prospect of being wed to the Dark Dragon that it had blinded her to what was right in front of her. Years, though, had seasoned him. He was no longer a young lad on the verge of manhood...he was now a man.

"Heather?"

Concern had grown heavy in her husband's voice and she was quick to smile, reach out, take his hand, and tug him down on the bench beside her. "Seamus spoke of my mum. It brought back memories."

He squeezed her hand. "Good memories."

It was not a question he asked, for he knew the answer. She had spoken often of her mum to Quinn, but she made no mention of that. "What few memories still linger in my mind of her are very good ones and Seamus gave me more good ones to enjoy."

"Then I am pleased for you."

"Unfortunately, he knew of the secret passage but not of its location."

"You believe he tells you the truth?"

"Without a doubt I do," she said. "He told me I should run from you if I get the chance and if he knew where the secret passage was he would tell me so I could do just that."

"I would find you. There is no place you could go that I would not find you." There was no anger in his words. He was simply stating the truth.

Heather rested her hand on his arm. "You would not need to find me, for I am where I want to be. You were good to me last night, Rhys, when I needed you. You will make a fine husband."

He tilted his head and narrowed his eyes, though a smile teased at the corners of his mouth. "I have not decided yet if you will make a good wife or not."

She grinned and patted his arm. "Good or not, I fear you are stuck with me, for we are wed and it cannot be undone."

Rhys leaned his face close to hers. "We have yet to seal our vows, wife, so I could give you back to your da if I so wish."

"Or you could see our vows sealed and keep me, for I will make a better wife than you think." Heather felt a chill take hold of her as his slight smile faded and a shadow fell over him, or had it stepped out of him?

"I have warned you before that there is darkness in me—"

She pressed her finger to his lips and whispered, "I will chase it away."

He captured her finger with his hand, moving it away from his mouth. "Be warned, wife, for it is an evil darkness and may consume you."

"Do not waste your breath in trying to frighten me," she said and stood, taking his hand to tug him to his feet. "Come, we should examine that trampled grass and see what we can discover."

Rhys tugged her back against him. "You do not give me orders, wife, or tug me along at your whim, or soon the villagers will think that you tamed the Dragon."

Heather laughed softly. "Those familiar with me already know I have a way with animals and probably expect no less from me."

"Never will you tame the Dragon," he said as if the task was impossible.

"My dear husband, do you not know that *love* can tame any creature?"

"Excuse me, my lady."

Rhys turned on the young man with anger in his voice. "You dare to interrupt when I am speaking with my wife?"

The young man quickly lowered his head. "I am sorry, my lord, but—"

"I will hear no excuse. Leave us be!"

The young man shivered in fear, but made no move to leave.

Rhys took a sharp step toward him, but Heather stepped in front of him, resting her hand to his chest. "Perhaps he is in need of help."

The young man did not wait, he spoke up and he spoke fast before he could be stopped. "My wife Jenny is having difficulty birthing our babe, and the women who are helping her do not know what more they can do. Can you please help her, Lady Heather? I know you suffered an injury last night and I have no right to ask you, but I fear for Jenny's life"

Rhys knew there would be no stopping his wife, so he snapped at the young man, "Show us the way."

Once again words rushed like a rapidly flowing stream from the young man's lips. "Aye, my lord. Thank you, my lord. I am most grateful, my lord."

Rhys waved him on and the young man turned and hurried off, leaving Rhys and Heather to follow.

Heather cast her husband a smile as she picked up her skirt and hurried along, Rhys keeping pace alongside her.

When they reached the small cottage, Rhys grabbed her arm and gently brought her to a halt. "I will wait out here and if you feel unwell you are to tell me, or so help me, Heather..."

"I will not cause myself undo harm." She kissed him on the cheek and whispered, "I wish to save all my strength for tonight when *we* seal our vows."

He stared after her as she disappeared into the cottage and wished it was night already. He turned to the young man who remained outside as well, though a distance from him. "Your name," Rhys demanded.

"Gillie, my lord."

"Gillie, you are going to pass the time with me by helping me decide on a fitting punishment for you, for daring to interrupt me when I was speaking with my wife."

Gillie lowered his head. "I care not what punishment you serve on me, my lord. I will suffer anything as long as my Jenny and our babe are well."

A piercing scream ripped through the air and Gillie winced, suffering along with his wife. And Rhys knew there was no punishment he could serve on the young man as bad as the one he now suffered.

Rhys turned when a few minutes later he heard rushing steps and saw Pitt hurrying toward him.

"There is a problem," he said.

"Get Henry and bring him here. I will not leave Heather without someone I can trust watching over her."

Pitt went to do as told and returned in a few moments with Henry in tow.

"Once my wife finishes take her to the keep and wait in the Great Hall with her until my return," Rhys ordered and as he walked off another piercing scream followed him.

~~~
~~~

Heather took account of the situation. One thing she had learned about births, after delivering so many babes, is that all are not alike. Each mother is more comfortable, more likely to birth her babe with ease, if no complications arise, when left to her instincts than those forced to do as others say.

"I have done it all as I have been told," Jenny cried, pacing the floor by the bed. "I have squatted, walked, knelt, sat and still the babe refuses to be born. I can do no more."

Heather turned to the two women who were helping Jenny. "We will need buckets of fresh, heated water.

The two women looked at her oddly wondering over her request, but neither of them asked. They simply went off to do as Heather bid.

Once Heather had the two out of her way, she went to Jenny. "What is it that you would like to do now?"

Jenny stared at her not sure what to say, then said, "I would like to rest, my lady. I am so very tired."

"Then that is what you shall do," Heather said and helped her into bed, making her as comfortable as possible and pressing along her stomach as she did.

Whcn thc pain camc again, Hcathcr talked her through it with a soothing voice. "You are doing wonderful, Jenny, and I am sure the babe will come soon now, so we must get you ready."

Jenny agreed with an eager nod and Heather quickly helped her to bring her knees up and push her nightdress back over them to drop on her stomach. She was soon urging Jenny to push, telling her how the babe was nearly there. With more eager coaxing from Heather, and Jenny anxious to be done with it, the babe came in no time.

"A fine lad," Heather cried out as the babe made himself known with his own cries.

The two women were shocked when they returned. The babe lay wrapped in a blanket in Jenny's arms while Heather saw to the aftermath of the delivery. Once Jenny was seen to, she saw to cleaning up the babe and wrapping him in a cleaner blanket that Jenny had recently finished stitching.

Heather turned to the two women who were fawning over the new babe in Jenny's arms. "If you both would go to the keep's kitchen and ask for Nessa and tell her that I sent you to collect food for Jenny and her husband, enough for two days, she will see it done."

The three women looked at her as if they could not quite believe what she said.

Jenny finally spoke up, "My lady, that is far too generous of you."

"A gift from the Dragon and his wife, and you know you cannot refuse the Dragon."

The three women simultaneously nodded their heads vigorously.

"I will wait with Jenny until you return," Heather said. "And please tell my husband I wish to speak with him."

The one woman stepped forward. "The Dragon left. Henry, Belle's husband, has been left to wait for you."

Heather would have liked to ask them if they knew where her husband had gone, but that would not be proper for her to do. She went to the door with the two women and stepped outside, calling out to Jenny's husband to come see his newborn son. He came running, a broad smile upon his face.

She closed the door behind him to give the couple time alone and walked over to Henry, standing a few feet away. "Henry, you are feeling well?"

"Very well, my lady," Henry said with a firm nod.

Heather cast a glance about, noticing that clouds now threatened the beautiful day. "Some rain I think."

"It feels it for sure."

"Do you know where my husband is off to?"

Henry shook his head. "No, my lady. I only know I am to take you to the Great Hall when you are done and I am to remain with you there until the Dragon returns."

Something had happened to take Rhys away. She had seen or perhaps had sensed that he had been just as eager to spend the rest of the day with her as she had been to spend it with him. Something urgent must have happened to take him away from her.

And she intended to find out what it was.

Chapter Sixteen

Rhys entered the camp with Pitt. He wore his leather armor, though no helmet. Most of the men in the camp stared at him in fear, some backed away, and a few would not look at him, too frightened that evil would touch them.

The warriors' reactions mattered not to Rhys. His interest was in the short, thick man who stood in the middle of the camp, his head hanging down, staring at the dead body at his feet.

Rhys dismounted as did Pitt, their horses remaining where left as the two approached the man.

"See what the Macinnes have done to my son-in-law when all he asked was for his wife—my daughter—to be returned to him?" Hew McDolan said, raising his head.

Rhys looked at the badly beaten body of Rab McLaud.

Hew choked on his words as he said, "They beat him unmercifully."

"How do you know it was the Macinnes that did this?" Pitt asked.

"Rab had insisted on going along to the Macinnes to retrieve his wife, but not trusting the Macinnes, I sent one of my warriors to follow him. He watched from a distance as Donald Macinnes had his warriors beat Rab to death." He shook his head.

"What of Hunter?" Rhys asked. "Did he stand there and watch his brother beaten to death?"

"He did," Hew confirmed with a snarl, "and said not a word or lifted a finger to stop it."

"What of Rona?" Pitt asked. "Rab did not ask for his sister-in-law's return as well?"

"The bastard took her captive too?" Hew spat.

"What concern of this is mine?" Rhys asked.

"I want my daughter returned to me and if they would not return her to her husband, I fear they also will refuse to return her to her father. I am asking for your help in freeing my daughter from the Macinnes. In return, I offer her to you in marriage. Saundra is a good lass and obeys well. She would make you a good wife. And with the uniting of our clans, I will pledge my allegiance to you."

"So what you ask for is revenge against those who had your son-in-law beaten to death," Rhys said.

"Aye, I do, but not without offering you something in return."

"So if I give you what you ask for, you will give me your daughter and pledge your allegiance to me; this I have your word on?"

"Aye, I give you my word here and now on it."

Rhys glanced at Pitt and gave him a barely visible nod before saying to Hew, "Bring me the warrior who witnessed the beating."

"John," Hew shouted.

A warrior stepped forward. His chin went up and his shoulders went back, expanding an already thick chest as he approached with a confident gait. He stopped beside Hew.

"You heard Donald Macinnes refuse to return Rab's wife to him?" Rhys asked.

"I did and I heard Rab tell them that they it would be war if Macinnes did not return her to him. That was when Donald Macinnes signaled his warriors and they descended on Rab like a pack of hungry wolves."

"Was Rab's brother Hunter there?"

"He was and lifted not a finger to help him. His wife Patience stood at his side and watched."

"And the two other sisters were they there as well?"

"Aye, and never turned their heads away as Rab was brutally beaten."

"How did you come by the body?" Rhys asked.

"Macinnes ordered it to be dumped in the woods for the animals to feed on. I followed and brought the body back to Laird McDolan."

"And that is how your hands suffered those cuts and bruises?"

John startled a moment before giving a quick answer. "Aye, it is."

Rhys stared at the man in silence and it did not take long for John to grow uncomfortable and Hew as well.

Hew finally spoke up with annoyance in his tone. "It is as I told you. Now will you help me get my revenge?"

"Against those who did this evil deed?"

"Aye, and an evil did it was, and we best see to resolving it and rescuing Greer's wife before he learns of it and a bloodbath ensues."

Rhys glared at John. "Who helped you beat Rab McLaud to death?"

"What nonsense is this?" Hew shouted. "Why do you accuse John when he told you what he saw?"

"He is lying."

Hew went to argue, and Rhys took a quick step toward him and Hew hastily shut his mouth. "You think to deceive me?"

"No, no," Hew said, "It is as John says."

"It is not as John says; he lies," Rhys said anger sparking in his dark eyes and voice. He turned his heated glare on John. "Tell me you saw the blonde-haired Macinnes sister there."

"Aye I saw her there," he answered with a grin. "Who could miss that beauty?"

"Evidently you, since she was not there."

"If John says she was there, then she was there," Hew argued.

"So it was by your order that John, and I would say one or two others, beat Rab McLaud to death?"

"You make no sense," Hew said, shaking his head. "Why would I have my own son-in-law beaten to death? This is complete nonsense. Will you keep your word to me or not?"

"Will you keep yours?" Rhys asked.

"I already gave you my word, now what of yours?" Hew demanded.

Rhys stepped forward and grabbed John by the throat so fast that neither man in front of him had time to react. He squeezed, his fingers digging into the man's neck. "I will have the truth from you now."

Hew was so shocked it took him a moment to speak up. "Let him go. John did nothing. It is Macinnes you should be after."

Rhys ignored him and squeezed a bit harder.

John's hands came up to grasp at Rhys hand, trying frantically to free himself, but it proved useless. The Dragon's grip was like a band of metal forged around his neck.

"Release him or I will have my men take the Dragon down here and now." Hew raised his hand and his warriors, some with reluctance, stepped forward.

Ghost warriors rushed from the woods and dropped from the trees completely surrounding the group and Hew paled along with several of his warriors.

Rhys' grip tightened. "It matters not to me if you die. I know the truth. That blonde-haired beauty you say was there could not have been there. Heather was with me; she is my wife."

~~~

Heather sat at one of the tables in the Great Hall wondering where her husband had gone off to. Henry had stood nearby until she had insisted that he sit and give his injured leg some rest. He had not argued; he sat.

On her walk to the keep, Heather had discovered that Henry would not be forthcoming with any information about her husband's whereabouts. She wished she could have spent more time walking through the village for surely someone would have heard something, though now that she had sat for a while she realized that she was tired and that her head ached a bit.

She silently admonished herself for not taking more care with her injury. She had ignored the fatigue that had crept up on her and the throb in her head.

"Your brew, my lady," Nessa said, placing a tankard with swirls of steam rising from it in front of her.

"Bless you, it is just what I need," Heather said, lifting the tankard to her lips to sip cautiously.

"I hope I made it to your liking."

Heather smiled after tasting it. "Perfect."

"You look tired, my lady, perhaps you should rest in your chambers."
~~~

The thought appealed to her, but before she could agree, Henry spoke up.

"My orders are for me to remain with Lady Heather in the Great Hall until the Dragon returns, and here is where she will be staying."

"But she needs rest," Nessa protested.

"I have my orders," Henry said.

"I will wait here," Heather said the pair's bickering causing the slight pain in her head to increase.

Nessa shook her head as she walked past Henry, saying, "It is her bed she needs."

Henry ignored her and after few moments, he said, "I am sure the Dragon will return soon."

Heather saw the concern in his eyes and reassured him. "It is all right, Henry. I will sip my brew and rest right here until my husband returns."

The brew soothed her as always and the pain in her head lessened, but her eyes grew heavy and by the time she finished the brew, her eyes were closing and her head felt too heavy to hold up. She folded her arms on the table and brought her head down on them to rest.

"My lady, are you all right?" Henry asked anxiously.

"Need a bit of rest," she said as her eyes drifted closed.

~~~
~~~

"You are wed to Heather Macinnes?" Hew asked as if he did not believe his words.

"I am. Now tell me why you had Rab McLaud beaten to death," Rhys demanded.

With his shoulders drooping in defeat, Hew said, "I discovered he intended to kill my daughter and that Greer knew and approved of it. I began to wonder what other things Greer had planned for me. I decided it would be wiser to free myself of one McLaud and in so doing free my daughter and make her available to wed you, thus joining forces with you and protecting myself against Greer." Hew shook his head. "Donald Macinnes beat me to it."

"You got part of what you wanted," Rhys said and released John. "You pledged your allegiance to me if I gave you revenge against those who did this to Rab. John is one. Give me the others who helped him and I will see them punished."

"They followed orders," Hew said in their defense.

"Then it is you who deserves the punishment."

Hew stood speechless for a moment and Rhys could see that he was weighing his options of which there were none. He had no choice but to submit to the Dragon, but Rhys had learned through the years that few men made wise choices.

"I will suffer no punishment for protecting my daughter, nor will my men for following orders."

"You renege on our agreement?" Rhys snapped and did not give Hew a chance to respond. "Listen well, McDolan, you gave me your word and I will see that you keep it. When I summons you, you will not hesitate to come to me and do as I command." He was quick to silence Hew when he went to speak, his strong voice resonating throughout the camp. "Not a word. I am not finished."

Hew felt the fiery anger that spewed from the Dragon's mouth and a tremble ran through him.

"You and your warriors will do as I order, Hew McDolan, or I will send my ghost warriors after you and only you. You will not see them coming, though you will feel the blade as one warrior slices your throat. Your clan will then be mine to rule."

Hew had no choice but to say, "I gave my word and I shall keep it."

"Wise decision."

"Will you see that my daughter is returned to me?"

"You struck a bargain and gave your word on it. Your daughter now belongs to me."

"But you are already wed. What will you do with her?"

"Whatever I wish," Rhys said and walked away from the man.

"But—"

"But what?" Rhys shouted as he swerved around to face Hew again. "Do you think me a fool?

I return your daughter and you wed her to a powerful chieftain who could prove troublesome to me. I think not. She is mine now. You gave her to me. I will decide her fate. I would suggest you make a more permanent camp between here and Macinnes land, for once Greer McLaud finds out you had his brother killed...you will need protection."

"How will he find out unless told?" Hew said with an accusing tone.

"The Highlands see and hear everything. Greer will eventually hear and seek his revenge." Rhys shrugged. "If you prefer to face Greer with your warriors alone, so be it."

"I will make camp where you say." Hew nodded firmly, several of his warriors nodding along with him. "What of Rab?"

"You killed him; you bury him, for if Greer ever sees what you did to him, he will do far worse to you than you did to Rab. We are done here." With those words, Rhys' warriors disappeared and he and Pitt went to their horses.

Hew called out to Rhys once he and Pitt had mounted their horses. "I will send word of where and when I settle camp."

"It is not necessary. I will know your every move." Rhys turned his horse and rode out of camp, Pitt riding alongside him.

~~~
~~~

"Lass," Henry called to the Nessa as he stood. "You are right, Lady Heather needs to rest in her chambers. I am sure the Dragon would not object."

"Finally, you have some sense," Nessa said, hurrying over to the table.

Henry did not argue with the insolent lass, he was too concerned with Lady Heather. She had not budged since resting her head on her arms.

Nessa laid a gentle hand on Heather's shoulder. "My lady, you will rest more comfortably in your bed." Nessa grew upset when she got no response. She shook Heather's shoulder gently. "My lady."

Rhys entered the Great Hall just then and seeing the scene in front of him, shouted out, "Henry what goes on here?"

It was Nessa who answered. "I will tell you what goes on here, my lord. Lady Heather was tired and he," —Nessa jabbed a finger in Henry's direction—"would not let her go to her chamber to rest."

"Henry was obeying my order," Rhys snapped.

"We were about to get Lady Heather to her bedchambers, but she does not want to wake up," Henry said.

Fear, something that rarely touched Rhys, rose up to grip at his gut and without hesitation he scooped his wife up into his arms as he loudly called her name, "Heather!"

Heather winced. "Why do you shout my name?"

"Because you refuse to wake up," Rhys said pleased to see she was not pale or could not speak. Still, though, she had not opened her eyes.

"I am resting."

"You will rest in our chambers," Rhys said as he walked out of the room.

"Why do you carry me?"

"You have yet to open your eyes and your body is limp in my arms. Do you honestly believe you could manage the stairs on your own?" He could not keep the annoyance out of his voice, though it was meant for him not his wife. He should have made her remain in bed today, but he had been selfish. He had wanted to spend time with her, and then he had allowed her to help birth a babe. This was his fault.

"I just need a bit more rest," she said, finding his arms ever so comfortable.

"And rest you will get, for you will not be leaving our bed for the remainder of the day."

"A couple of hours sleep will do me fine," she said.

Rhys did not bother to respond. He would tuck her in bed and assign another trusted warrior to stand guard, though he would not be far. He would continue his search for the secret room inside the keep.

She barely budged when he placed her on the bed, took off her boots, and tucked the blanket around her. She also did not stir when he kissed her cheek. She was beyond tired and needed a solid rest. He left her reluctantly and when he stepped outside the room, he found Henry and Nessa standing there.

"I will stand guard, my lord," Henry said.

"You will until I send someone to replace you. It will do your leg wound no good to remain standing for possibly hours."

Henry reluctantly accepted the Dragon's orders. He had little choice since he knew full well not to question them.

"Nessa, you will check on Lady Heather from time to time and when she wakes you will let Pitt know."

Nessa bobbed her head in compliance.

Rhys walked off relieved that rest was what his wife needed, though he was concerned with all that was going on. He had hoped to see the dispute between Macinnes and McLaud settled without battle, but with what McDolan had done to Rab McLaud, he doubted that would be possible. Then there was his old enemy. He needed to see that finished once and for all.

Chapter Seventeen

Heather woke, her sleep disturbed by a strange noise. She listened and heard nothing, which had her wondering if the noise had been from a dream, though she could recall none. Curiosity had her getting out of bed with a roll of her shoulder. No pain disturbed her head and she actually felt very well-rested. The nap had done her good.

She slipped on her boots and went to the door and when she opened it she was surprised to find no guard there. She wondered how long she had slept as she made her way down the stairs and into the Great Hall. It was empty and not a servant lurked about. She glanced at the windows and saw it was dark. Had she slept well into the night?

She stepped outside, walking down the steps to see if anyone was about and it was eerily silent. The village looked asleep for the night, but if it was that late where was her husband?

"My lady?"

Heather jumped, her hand going to her chest.

"I am sorry, my lady, I did not mean to frighten you. I but wondered what you were doing out here so late."

Heather turned to see Seamus and did not think it would be proper to explain that she searched for her husband when he should be in bed with her at this hour. "I should ask the same of you."

"When sleep refuses to come to me, I walk in the shadows of the village in hopes of finding out its secrets."

"What secrets?" Heather asked.

"To watch and see if more old people will be taken away and by whom? Who sneaks about for a late night visit? And sometimes I watch the Dark Dragon prowl the village."

She spoke her thought before she could stop herself. "Why ever would he do that?"

"I do not know, but he stops, watches, and listens and sometimes he will simply sit on the steps of the keep and stare into the darkness almost as if he is waiting for something to emerge from it."

A sound turned both of them silent and with gentle, slow steps they went in search of it. The two quickly moved into the shadows when they heard the sound again and watched as a cart meandered past them. They waited until the sound of it was a safe distance away, then followed, staying in the shadows.

"That is Aggie's cottage," Seamus whispered as the cart came to a stop in front of it. "She was old long before age got me. Glynnis always looked after her and she misses the lass terribly."

Heather and Seamus watched as the two men disappeared inside.

"The old ones are worthless to the Dragon. He is doing away with her, he is," Seamus said, choking back his tears. "Soon the cart will come for me in the middle of the night."

The cottage door opened and two men helped a crying Aggie out and into the cart.

"God bless her." Seamus sniffled back his tears. "She was a good woman."

The old woman's tears broke Heather's heart and without thought to her actions she stepped out of the shadows, demanding, "What goes on here?"

Seamus stayed where he was frightened if he showed himself that he too would be carted off, but his chest went out and a smile spread across his face, seeing how brave Lady Heather was to confront the men.

Both men stared at her as if they were seeing a ghost.

"I am Lady Heather, you will answer me," she demanded.

"They answer only to me," —Rhys stepped out of the shadows— "as do you."

The darkness seemed to cling to him as he walked toward her, making him appear as if giant wings extended from his sides. The two men stepped around the cart, keeping it between them and the Dragon.

"What are you doing out here this late and how did you get passed the guard this time?"

Anger was strong in his voice, though Heather was not sure if he was angry with her or the guard that evidently left his post. "I did not know the lateness of the hour when I came in search of you and there was no guard at my door to stop me."

"No guard?" he asked as if he had not heard her correctly.

She shook her head and repeated, "No guard."

He stepped closer to her, his arm going around her as if shielding her and he looked to the old woman. "It will not be long now." He nodded to the men. "Take her."

Heather went to ask him where the men were taking the crying woman, but he called out to Seamus before she could.

"Show yourself, Seamus."

The old man did as he was told.

"You will breathe not a word of this, Seamus, or I will no longer allow you to walk the village at night."

Seamus's eyes turned wide.

"You think I do not see you watching me, do not hear you? Do you think my men do not watch you? Go to your daughter, Seamus, before I change my mind and have you taken away with Aggie."

Seamus hurried off and she could see by his expression that the old man liked the Dragon even less now. And for a moment, she wondered if she could be wrong about his true identity. Quinn would never be so unkind to an old warrior.

She could not stop herself from saying, "It would be better if you befriended him than frightened him."

"There is no room for friendship when you lead."

"Pitt is your friend."

"And Pitt knows my leadership comes before our friendship, but enough questions."

Rhys kept her close against him as he hurried her inside the keep and straight to his solar.

Heather looked at Rhys as he filled a goblet with wine. Who truly was this man she wed? She thought she knew him, but did she? He handed her the goblet and she took it, eager to ask him questions, yet she remained silent. She drifted to one of the chairs near the hearth and sat.

Pitt entered, the door having been left open.

"Find out what happened to the guard at the door," Rhys ordered and Pitt closed the door behind him as he took his leave.

"Feeling better?" Rhys asked, standing near the hearth.

"Much, but then I should feel well-rested, having slept most of the night away."

"Sunrise is less than an hour away."

"It is no wonder I feel so refreshed, but what of you? Have you slept at all?" she asked, though looking at him he did not appear a man who lacked sleep. No heaviness marred his eyes nor did his body appear fatigued. He stood tall, his shoulders broad, his chest fit and his eyes as alert as ever. The one thing different about him was his dark hair. It was not drawn back. It fell to just above his shoulders, one side tucked behind his ear...the way Quinn had worn his. While it gave a familiar tug to her heart, she could not help but think of the changes in him.

"I slept well enough."

"But not alongside me," she said, recalling that she had not caught the scent of him on the bed linens when she woke.

"You needed rest."

"I rest quite well with you beside me," she assured him.

"I do not, for it is not rest I think of when lying beside you."

"What do you think of?" Heather said and found herself waiting for a reply while Rhys rested his hand to his chin and ran is thumb across his lips, paused in thought. Her eyes remained fixed on his lips and the way his thumb caressed them and she felt a small flutter in her stomach.

He stopped suddenly and with a brief step, hunched down in front of her. "I think of touching you in the most intimate of places."

Heather gasped lightly when his hands slipped under her skirt to caress her legs. His touch was gentle, running from her ankles up along her legs slowly as if he did not want to miss touching any part of her. And as he did, the flutter in her stomach grew and took flight, settling between her legs and growing ever stronger as his hands slipped over her knees and down between her legs to stroke the inner flesh.

Rhys watched her eyes flutter and her mouth dropped open slightly as he gently spread her legs apart. He had grown hard with his first touch of her, soft yet firm, and the further he explored the harder he grew. One yank forward and he could...he groaned with the thought of swiftly impaling her. Instead, he slipped his finger slowly inside her.

Heather gasped, her hands grabbing his shoulders and digging into his flesh as his thumb settled on the direct spot that throbbed unmercifully. She moaned, then sighed, then moaned again.

She grew so wet that Rhys could slip easily inside her without causing her much pain, but he would not take her here and now like a common wench. He would make love to her properly in their bed. For now, he would simply bring her pleasure, let her grow accustomed to his touch, and watch as she climaxed for the first time.

Heather inched forward in the chair, needing him to go deeper inside her and the slight plunge of his fingers drew a louder moan from her as she dropped her brow to rest on his.

"Kiss me."

It was a demand, not a request, and Heather complied most willingly. His tongue penetrated her mouth the same time his fingers plunged deeper. This time her gasp was caught in his mouth as his kiss turned more powerful and pleasing than she ever thought possible.

She moaned in disappointment when he tore his lips away from hers to whisper in her ear, "Come for me, I want to feel you come."

He teased her nub until she thought she would go mad and she dropped her head back and moaned so loud she thought all in the keep would think the Dragon tortured her, but then he did, though most pleasurably.

She cried out his name as she felt the overwhelming sensation continue to grow and as it did, she dug her fingers deeper into his shoulders. His name became a litany on her lips until finally...she felt an explosion of the most glorious sensation and let herself be swept away in it.

Rhys watched as the climax hit and took hold of her and seeing the pleasure she was getting from it almost had him coming himself. But the years of learning to stay in control took hold and besides, when he came it would be inside her.

As her climax subsided, she brought her head down to rest on her husband's shoulder.

"That and more is what I think of doing to you," he whispered in her ear.

If her breathing was not so labored, she would tell him that he could do that and more to her as often as he liked. Actually, she would not mind if they went to their bedchamber right now, for she had waited far too long to make love with the man she loved. For now, she just let herself enjoy all the little sensations that continued to linger in her body.

Rhys loved feeling the last of her climax ripple through her and that she rested her head on his shoulder without thought as if it was most natural. He wanted her at ease with him, wanted her to enjoy his touch, to look forward to it.

He closed his eyes against the thought that he refused to admit and constantly haunted him—he wanted her to love him. The problem was— could he give her the love she deserved?

Her stomach rumbled, interrupting both their thoughts.

"You are hungry," Rhys said, easing her back in the chair.

Her stomach may have grumbled, but it was the hunger that had lain dormant for so long that needed feeding. And she was not quite sure how much it would take to satisfy it.

Rhys stood and held his hand out to her. "The kitchen should be stirring by now. I will have them prepare something for us."

Heather was pleased that her husband would share the morning meal with her and took his hand to walk with him to the Great Hall. She not only wanted to spend more time with him, she was looking forward to the next time they would be intimate. And if she could hasten that moment, she happily would.

Sunrise broke just a few moments after they were seated in the Great Hall and food soon found its way to their table. They just began their meal when Pitt approached, a frown on his handsome face, though when his eye caught sight of Nessa he smiled at her. Nessa turned away, ignoring him and Pitt's frown returned.

"Sit, and eat," Rhys ordered.

Pitt shook his head. "We found the guard. He took a knot to the back of his head and was trussed up tightly. He remembers nothing, though he has been questioned endlessly. There is another problem."

"When is there ever not a problem?" Rhys said, sounding as if he had expected it.

"It seems the body that was to be disposed of is gone," Pitt said.

Heather felt her stomach clench and she suddenly felt her appetite wane, though not her courage. She looked to her husband. "Tell me the body you speak of is not Aggie."

"Though it does not concern you, wife, it is not Aggie we speak of."

"Then who?" Heather asked.

"Again, it is not your concern."

Heather thought to argue, but it would serve no purpose. Her husband would not tell her, but one way or another she would find out.

Fife hurried into the hall, his eyes darting to Nessa and wide smiles were exchanged between them before he solemnly faced the Dragon. The young warrior's eyes went to Heather and back at the Dragon's several times.

Rhys stood and walked around the dais and over to the large stone hearth, Pitt and Fife following. The three men talked in whispers.

When Rhys walked back to the dais, he said, "Remain in the keep while I see to this." He turned and walked out of the room, expecting her to obey.

Fife followed, though slowed his steps as he neared Nessa. He took a moment to stop and speak with her before hurrying after the Dragon.

Nessa in turn hurried to Heather. "Fife says something has been found in the barn, but he claims it is too gruesome to tell me what it is. I wonder if the wolf has struck again."

Knowing a wolf had not been responsible for the death of the two warriors got Heather wondering what had happened. "The wolf has not been caught yet?" she asked.

"There has been no word of his capture. If there was, my lady, there would be a celebration. And now with this," —Nessa shook her head— "everyone will make sure their loved ones are accounted for while wondering what secret the barn holds this time."

Nessa took off to attend to her duties and Heather sat alone at the dais with much on her mind. She wished her sisters were here so she could talk with them. She missed the many times they would sit and talk for hours. They never lacked for conversation, for there was always something for them to share. She would have liked to confide her suspicions about the Dragon to them. They would keep her secret, even advise her on what to do. They would not think her foolish or laugh at her; they would be happy for her.

Tears tickled at her eyes and she sniffled as she brushed them away with her hand. She would see her sisters soon. At least she hoped she would.

Two warriors entered the room, the taller warrior leading the red-haired warrior to the hearth to be seated. The taller warrior gave the other warrior's shoulder a squeeze as he gave a shout for a servant to bring food and drink. He left once the food was brought and the warrior who remained ate sparingly, his hand going often to the back of his head.

Heather rose and walked over to him. "May I join you?"

He went to jump up and winced, his hand rushing to the back of his head.

"Please stay seated," she said with a gentle smile and touched the back of her head in empathy. "I know how you are feeling and sudden moves can be painful." She sat, asking as she did, "What is your name."

"Edward and I am so sorry, my lady."

"Whatever for?"

"I failed to protect you," he said as if it was the worst thing possible.

"It happens. You were caught unaware."

"A ghost warrior is never caught unaware and if he is?" Edward shook his head slowly. "He has failed himself, his fellow warriors, and worst of all, the Dragon."

"Perhaps the one who struck you was simply more skilled at not being heard or seen."

"I have given that possibility thought, for I had remained alert the whole time I was outside your door and I heard or saw nothing."

"I heard something," she said and his eyes brightened. "It was a thud and now when I think on it, I believe what followed was you being dragged away."

"I do not know where the culprit could have come from, though there are many shadows that haunt that area." He rubbed the side of his head. "I remember hearing a sound overhead and I looked up and listened. I could not tell where the sound came from, then it stopped, but I continued to listen and that was the last I remember."

"You did well, Edward. You have nothing to be sorry for and I would have you guard me again without any concern."

"Thank you, my lady, you are most kind."

"Now you must eat, rest, and heal so you may resume your duties as my guard."

"I would like that, but I do not think the Dragon will permit it."

"We shall see, Edward," she said with a smile and left him to his meal.

Heather did not listen for footfalls following her up the stairs, but she did watch to see if any shadows followed her. She had learned a few of the ghost warriors' skills after being abducted and held by them until her escape. She had also learned to tread more lightly, having watched how the ghost warriors walked without making a sound. Their steps were precise and light and barely left a footprint in their wake.

Her husband's skills, though, far surpassed his warriors. She never heard him approach and she never saw anyone who could blend with the darkness as if he was born to it like he could. She wondered where he had learned such skills, but most of all she wondered why it had taken him so long to return to her.

She reached the upper floor without realizing it and that was one thing she needed to learn—not to let her mind wander, but to remain focused on her surroundings. Now that she was here, she might as well explore, but perhaps that had been her intentions all along.

With light steps, she approached the room that had been Mary's solar, the door ajar. She pushed at the door and it squeaked as it yawned open, appearing like a giant mouth ready to swallow her. She intended to look for the secret passage here, though in all honesty it was her mum that brought her here. After Seamus had told her that her mum had spent time here with Mary McComb, she wanted to come here and sit where her mum had once sat and see if the sound of her mum's soft voice or her sweet scent would return to her. Through the years the few memories she had of her mum had faded and it felt as if she had lost her all over again. She wanted those memories back and she hoped to regain them in this room.

Heather stepped into the room and shadows seemed to reach out to her, beckoning her forward. Darkness never appealed to her, though she was never afraid of it, but this room had been left to the darkness too long. She skirted her way around the chairs, tables, and chests to reach the tapestry that hung on the wall and when she yanked it back, she smiled.

She grabbed the edge of the large tapestry and gave it several hard yanks until she jumped back as it fell to the floor revealing a window that flooded the room with light. She turned with a flourish eager to inspect the room and stopped abruptly, her breath caught on a gasp that she forced silent, seeing a shadow slither past the open door.

Chapter Eighteen

Heather remained as she was, staring at the door. Had she seen a shadow or had it been her imagination? No one knew she had come up here. No guard had followed her, unless the shadow was a guard who had been following her all along. But if it was no guard, then who was it? The culprit who stalked the keep?

Look for anything you can use as a weapon.

Her sister Patience's voice rang loud in her head and she was relieved to be reminded of what her sister had once taught her and Emma. Heather quickly scanned the room.

Nothing large and cumbersome that can easily be taken away from you.

She kept her sister's advice in mind as her eyes continued to search. She smiled when she spotted the bone needle tucked in an unfinished piece of embroidery. It was small enough to conceal in her hand, but deadly enough when jabbed in someone's eye.

Heather approached the open door cautiously, wishing she had a torch or some type of light to illuminate the small area outside the door. The torch in the wall sconce did not burn bright enough to light the small area sufficiently, but if she could grab it and shine it on the shadows it would chase them away and reveal...what?

With her heart pounding hard in her chest and her hand trembling slightly, she reached the open door. She could do this. Had her sisters not complained of her quickness when chasing after them and catching them when they were young and unruly?

She could do this. She would reach the sconce and not only would it cast light on the darkness, but it would prove useful as another weapon if necessary.

Not letting her fear stop her, Heather rushed out of the room and grabbed the torch from the sconce and swung it around, chasing the darkness away to reveal... She released the breath she had not realized she had been holding. There was no one there. She was alone.

She smiled, though her heart continued to pound against her chest. She returned the torch to the wall sconce and turned to find the darkness laying claim to the area once again. She entered the room, satisfied that the shadows had played a trick on her.

She stopped a few feet in when she heard the squeak of the door closing behind her and a tremble rippled over her, but it was when the door shut and she heard the latch click that fear gripped her. She slipped the needle into place in her hand just as she felt a warm breath on the back of her neck.

Heather turned quickly, hoping to catch the culprit off guard and raised her hand ready to strike.

Rhys grabbed her hand, twisting it, forcing her to drop whatever it was she held, then yanked her up against him. "You could be in a dire situation right now, if it was someone other than me."

Heather gave her husband a hard shove, not that it did much good. He did not budge, so she took a few steps away from him. "How dare you frighten me like that?"

"How dare you disobey me *again*," Rhys snapped.

"I remained in the keep."

"I ordered you to remain where you were."

"That still does not give you cause to frighten me," she said, shaking her finger at him.

"Do not point your finger at me, wife," he ordered.

"Then do not give me cause to," she said, continuing to shake her finger at him the whole time.

Rhys was on her in less than a blink of an eye, his hand grabbing and consuming the offending finger in his grasp. "I am warning you, wife, tread lightly or you will—"

"Or what?" she shouted the anger that bubbled inside her now and then throughout the years suddenly erupting, spewing forth before she could contain it. "Punish me? Make me suffer? Do what you will, for I will not now or ever be an obedient wife."

Rhys rested his face close to hers. "And so your descent into darkness begins with anger displacing your sweet kindness."

Heather laughed softly. "The Dragon is blind, for where he sees anger, I see courage."

His dark eyes heated. "Watch your tongue, wife."

"Or what? Will you cut it out?"

"Never, for I want the pleasure of feeling your tongue lick my hard manhood until I spill my seed." His hand grabbed roughly between her legs. "And my tongue will be sure to return the favor."

Heather brought her lips close to his and whispered, "Promise?"

Her response shocked Rhys and he felt his loins turn hard. His hand shot up and grabbed the back of her neck and held her firm as his lips descended on hers.

There was no tenderness in his kiss and Heather did not care. She had hungered for it since he had made her come in the solar. And she wanted to come again only this time she wanted him inside her. She wanted what she had waited so long for...to make love with Quinn.

Rhys felt his need for her grow out of control. He did not even want to wait and strip her bare. He wanted to hike her skirt up and bury himself deep inside her until they both were breathless and spent.

He hoisted her up and she wrapped her legs around him and grabbed hold of his shoulders as he walked over to a waist-high chest and sat her on it while continuing to kiss her. He ripped at her blouse, freeing her breasts and squeezing one plump breast then the other, before teasing the nipples hard for him to enjoy.

She let out a soulful moan when his mouth left hers, but it soon turned to a pleasurable one when his tongue settled over her nipple to suckle it. Her passion soared and so did her need to touch him. She reached over his shoulders and grabbed his shirt, yanking it up and he lifted his head so that she could pull it off him.

His tongue returned to her nipple and her hands roamed down his back, feeling his muscles grow taut at her touch, and she grew impatient. She wanted him inside her.

She grabbed the sides of her skirt and yanked them up, spreading her legs as she did. She leaned down, her lips near his ear. "Please, I need you inside me now."

Rhys raised his head and took a step back, his fingers going to the ties at his waist to free himself when he suddenly realized what he was doing and stopped. This was not right, taking her for the first time here on top of a dusty chest. This was not what he wanted for her, not what he had planned, and not what he had waited for.

He stepped back, yanking her skirt down as he did.

Heather stared at him. What had happened? Had she done something wrong?

"This will wait until tonight," he said, stepping away from her.

"Why?"

"Because I command it," he snapped.

"I have waited long enough. I want you now," she demanded.

"No!" he shouted and walked to the door afraid he would lose control and take her like he would a common wench who wanted nothing more than a fast rutting. He stopped by the door. "We are leaving here. Now cover yourself."

Heather jumped off the chest, ignoring his command and leaving her breasts free. "You may be, but I am not."

"You will do as I say," he ordered sharply.

"Make me," she challenged her unrequited passion urging her on.

Rhys glared at her and seeing the flush to her face, her lips plump with passion, her nipples hard and her eyes hungry, he said, "Are you sure you want it this way?"

"Must the Dragon truly ask permission?'

Rhys felt the darkness awaken inside him and felt dangerous memories he fought to keep locked away begin to surface and inflame his loins. He walked toward her and when he reached her, he ripped her blouse and skirt off her, saying, "I will have you naked when I take you."

He lifted her and once again sat her on the dusty chest, then tore at the ties at his waist and freed himself, his manhood bursting free. He grabbed her about the waist and brought her forward to balance at the edge of the chest, but it was not his manhood that entered her, but his finger.

She protested while trying to squirm away. “I want you.”

“Challenge the Dragon, wife, and you pay the price.”

Heather gasped as he held her firm and his finger continued to tease her. But it was when his mouth descended between her legs to torment the sensitive bud with his tongue that her head fell back and she moaned so loudly it echoed off the stone walls.

She was going to come; she could feel the climax growing ever stronger. She shoved at his shoulders. “Please, Rhys, please, I want you inside me,” she begged.

He stopped, though his finger lingered inside her, teasing her ever so lightly, keeping her on the edge of climax. “You think to challenge me?”

Heather saw darkness like no other in his eyes. It swirled and gathered like a raging storm about to unleash its fury, and she knew she had foolishly stirred the Dragon from his dark nest.

She reached out, resting her hand gently against his cheek. “I do not wish to challenge you, husband. I wish for you to make love to me and finally make me your wife.”

Husband. The word sunk deep into Rhys and he shut his eyes for a moment, forcing the Dragon back down into the darkness, anger and passion—a dangerous combination— having awakened him. Only when he safely had returned the beast to his slumber, did Rhys open his eyes. "Never stir the Dragon again, for the beast has no soul and when fully unleashed he will not care what he does."

Rhys lifted her off the chest and retrieved his shirt from the floor, slipping it over Heather's head to cover her. He then took her hand and tugged her along behind him as he descended the stairs to their bedchamber.

"This time stay where I put you," he ordered curtly and left her there alone.

Heather sunk down on the floor, tears clouding her eyes. What had she done? She had been desperate to make love with Quinn, never realizing she would have to battle the Dragon to do so. A tear slipped down her cheek. Now what did she do?

She hugged herself, closed her eyes and took a deep breath. The scent of the Dragon drifted up off his shirt and wrapped around her possessively. It intoxicated her senses, just like his touch had, turning her vulnerable in his hands. Or was it her love for Quinn that had turned her vulnerable?

She stood and hugged the shirt to her, favoring the feel of it against her soft skin, for it felt like he was caressing her. She shook her head and striped the shirt off and as she tossed it aside, the door opened and her husband walked in.

Rhys stared at her for a moment, then turned his head to peer past the partially open door and said, "I will kill any man who disturbs me." He shut the door and dropped the latch, then shed his garments, and walked over to her.

His arms shot out, scooping her up so fast that she let out a gasp.

"Now, Heather, I make you my wife—my way."

He laid her on the bed, going down alongside her, and reaching out he let his fingers play across her soft skin ever so lightly, skimming her nipples that turned harder with each faint touch.

Gooseflesh ran over her when he grazed her nipples and she shivered when his fingers swept across the sensitive nub hidden in the triangle of blonde hair between her legs. He was laying claim to every inch of her and she did not mind, for she had surrendered her heart to him many years ago.

"Turn over," he said and she did.

His fingers continued to explore her, though this time his lips followed suit, kissing and nipping at the back of her neck, and along her shoulders as his fingers found their way down over her buttocks to squeeze it gently.

He did not ask her to turn over again, his arm went around her waist and with one swift turn he had her on her back.

She reached out, needing to do some of her own exploring and ran her fingers over his chest. He grabbed her hand when she moved to explore lower and stretched it above her head, then settled his lips on hers. His kiss was gentle and she responded in kind.

He released her hand and began to explore her again and her body responded, arching up demanding more from him. When his fingers finally teased between her legs, she felt her passion spark in anticipation, but again his touch remained tender.

She grew more eager as he slipped over her and spread her legs with his knee before settling between them.

"I mean you no pain," he whispered as his hard manhood probed between her legs.

Heather spread her legs wider, eager for him to plunge inside her and make her come harder than she had in his solar. But he did not plunge inside her. He entered her slowly and Heather felt her impatience mount. Finally with a sudden thrust, she arched her back, forcing him deep inside her.

She let out a small cry and he stopped all movement.

"Do not stop," she begged, wanting more from him...much more.

Rhys did as she asked, keeping his rhythm firm and steady and when her fingers dug into his arms and she cried out his name, he knew she was ready to come. He quickened his rhythm and no soon as he did, she cried out his name once again.

Heather felt the climax hit her and while it felt wonderful, it was not as strong as what she had experienced in his solar earlier. She continued to move against him as if she had not gotten enough, as if something was missing. She thought she felt Rhys come, his body tightening, but she could not be sure, for he made no sound.

He rolled off her soon after and as he lay beside her, she thought how lovely and how tender he had been with her just as she had imagined Quinn would be. She had imagined this moment often throughout the years.

She turned on her side and Rhys turned as well, tugging her against him and holding her firm as if he feared she would escape him. He spoke not a word to her and none came to her as well. She hoped sleep would claim her soon for her thoughts disturbed her. But sleep claimed Rhys first, avoiding her completely.

A single tear trickled from the corner of her eye. She loved Quinn. She had loved him from the first time she had laid eyes on him and he had once told her that he had felt the same. Nothing would ever change that love, then why was it that she wanted the Dragon in her bed?

Chapter Nineteen

Heather was relieved when she woke to an empty bed. She yawned and stretched, trying to chase the fatigue that still clung to her. Her endless thoughts had soon turned to worry that barely let her sleep last night. There was no denying that she had been disappointed in the moment she had dreamed about so often through the years. Worse though, was the thought that she could very well be slipping into the darkness with the Dragon, just as he had warned she might do.

While Quinn's touch was nice, it did not fire her soul like the Dragon's demanding touch.

She shook her head, trying to make sense of the fact that the Dragon and Quinn were one and yet they were different. What had happened to Quinn that had turned him into the Dragon? And why when Quinn had for a brief time broken free of the Dragon's hold and revealed his old self, did she prefer the Dragon?

She shook her head again. She did not want to descend into the Dragon's darkness, but she would go anywhere and do anything to save Quinn. She loved him beyond reason, which meant, she also loved the Dragon.

A knock sounded at the door and she called out for the person to enter, glad for a reprieve from her troubling thoughts.

Nessa bustled in with a serving tray and a smile. "It is nigh on noon, my lady."

Heather jumped out of bed. "I have never slept that long. I have lost half the day."

Nessa placed the tray on the small table and moved a chair over to it, holding it out for Heather to sit. "The Dragon said you had a restless night and that you were not to be disturbed, though I was to check on you from time to time."

He knew she had not slept well, but how? Had he not as well? If he had not, she had not known it, for he had barely moved the entire night.

"Did your head wound pain you, my lady?" Nessa asked, going to tend the bed after Heather was seated.

Before Heather could let Nessa know that her head was feeling much better, the bump fading in size and pain, she heard Nessa gasp. Heather was about to ask what was wrong when she realized it herself. There was proof on the bedding that the wedding vows had finally been sealed.

Nessa turned. "You are well, my lady?"

"Very well, Nessa."

"I will see to washing these myself," Nessa said, gathering up the bedding and went on talking. "There is much speculation of what is being kept hidden in the barn."

Heather's interest caught as fast as a flame did to a wick. She had completely forgotten about yesterday when her husband had abruptly left the Great Hall with Fife and Pitt. "Fife has said no more to you?"

"He insists it is too gruesome to discuss with me, though I have heard something, but I believe it more tale than truth."

"Tell me," Heather urged.

Nessa lowered her voice to a whisper. "I heard a severed head has been found, though no one is saying who it belongs to and since all ghost warriors are accounted for," —she shrugged—"who knows who it could be."

"That is awful." Heather shivered, feeling terrible for the poor soul and wondering how she could get into the barn and see the head for herself. "Is that where my husband is now?"

Nessa shook her head. "No, my lady. He spent the morning in his solar with Pitt, and then took to the practice field about an hour ago. He is usually there a couple of hours or more each day."

That would give her enough time to see if she could get into the barn. "Does the door remain guarded?"

"Aye, though the guard now remains hidden and eyes will remain on you wherever you go, so Fife tells me."

Heather smiled. "A romance brews with Fife?"

Nessa blushed. "I believe it does. He grows upset when he sees Pitt talking with me." She giggled. "I think he is jealous, though he has no reason to be, I have no interest in Pitt. I do wonder why Pitt bothers with me. I give him no cause to think I have any interest in him and yet it is as though he seeks me out." She smiled. "I must admit that he is interesting to talk with and easy to look upon and a woman could get lost in his deep blue eyes." She shook her head. "But he is not for the likes of me. One good poke and he would not look my way again." Nessa gasped. "I am sorry, my lady, I should not speak of such things with you."

"I am glad that you do," Heather said. "It reminds me of when I would talk with my sisters and helps me to miss them a little less. Now I should dress and be about, for I have wasted too much of the day already."

~~~

"What are you trying to do, kill them?" Pitt asked, handing Rhys a cloth.

Rhys took it and wiped the sweat from his face. He ignored the sweat that clung to his naked chest. He was not done yet; there was more fight left in him. "They will face a mighty foe and I want them prepared."

"Prepared is one thing, dead is another. If you do not go easy—"

"Easy? You think the enemy will go easy?" Rhys turned to the group of his warriors, looking ready to collapse. "Do you wish to live?"
~~~

All the men nodded vigorously.

"Then fight like you mean it or die cowards."

The men straightened and drew their shoulders back.

Rhys walked into the middle of the practice field, sword in hand. "You think your enemy will give you pause to rest, to catch a needed breath? The enemy will strike again and again and not stop striking until every one of you lies dead and the ground is soaked with your blood." He raised his sword. "The first one to leave a mark on me shall be generously rewarded."

The warriors lunged forward, attacking the Dragon.

In minutes, they all laid at the Dragon's feet.

Pitt shook his head as he handed Rhys the cloth once again. He kept his voice low when he said, "My words will stir your wrath, but better your wrath be stirred than you kill your men. Go to your wife and let the Dragon loose. He needs feeding."

Rhys turned a furious scowl on him.

It did not deter Pitt from continuing to speak. "That day you found me in that pit I was no longer the man I had once been. He had to die so that I could live and so that day Pitt was born. You did the same. The Dragon was born out of necessity. It is who you are now and who you will always be. You are being unkind to your wife to let her think otherwise." Pitt turned and went to help the fallen men to their feet and wake those still unconscious.

Rhys stood there, cloth in hand, Pitt's words leaving him to think on something he had not wanted to since he woke this morning. He had refused to let the Dragon loose last night, though God help him he had wanted to, but he feared the results. He would frighten his wife and forever keep her from their bed, and he did not want that. Yet he also did not want it to be the way it was last night between them. He had found no pleasure in making love to her and he could tell her pleasure was not what it had been in the solar when he made her come.

But the Dragon was a hungry one, having had two or three women in one night and had still been left hungry. He was also more demanding than gentle, but perhaps it had been because he was always trying to assuage his sexual hunger that never seemed to abate. He thought perhaps with Heather it might be different. The only difference was how disappointing it had been.

Pitt was right. He was not who he once was and never would be again and he was foolish to think he could somehow revisit the past and make it right.

Rhys turned. "Those who can still stand better be ready to fight me."

~~~
~~~

Heather left the keep, knowing eyes followed her every step. The question was...how could she avoid those eyes?

It was an overcast day with a light breeze in the air, making it feel more like early autumn than summer. The village was busy, women tending their gardens, children playing, and men making repairs on the few things still in need.

Heather smiled and returned greetings as she walked around the village, making certain she could see the barn from different angles. One guard stood at the front, the barn door closed, not that she could gain entrance that way. And there was no point in trying to gain entrance the way she had the last time. Her husband no doubt had had the loose board sealed.

How then did she get in there? Frustrated that she did not see a way, she continued to meander around the village.

"A storm approaches."

Heather glanced up at the sky and was surprised to see that gray clouds had gathered overhead and was about to agree with Seamus when she looked at him and saw that he leaned heavily on a walking stick. "Are you not feeling well, Seamus?"

"It is just an old injury that troubles me when storms brew and winter sets in and reminds me how old I am getting." He stepped closer. "Have you discovered where they took Aggie?"

"No, but I promise you I will."

His head drooped. "Before it is too late, I hope."

Heather placed her hand on Seamus's arm. "You have my word, Seamus, that I will find out what is happening to the old McComb villagers and I promise I will make sure that you remain here with your daughter and her family."

Tears came to the old man's eyes. "I never thought I would grow old. I thought a battle would get me before age would and I sometimes wish it had. I watch the Dragon and his men on the practice field and long for the days I was that young and spry. I do not like growing old."

"Daaaaaaaaaaaaa!"

"There she goes again, my Alaina," Seamus said with a shake of his head and a smile.

"She keeps a good watch on you. I believe she loves you very much."

"Aye, she looks after me. You should head back to the keep, my lady, soon now the sky will drop buckets of rain on us." He went to turn and stopped. "I remembered something Fane once told me that might help with finding the secret passage."

"Daaaaaaaaaaaaaa!"

"Bless her, she thinks my legs still move as fast as they once did. Quick now, let me tell you what I recall. Fane said that if there was ever an attack and the sword took him that I was to take Mary to her solar on the upper floor, and he told me to take my family with me."

"Daaaaaaaaaaaaaaa!"

"I must go, my lady, and I thank you for any help you can give me."

Heather watched him amble off, calling out to his daughter as he did and when he was a good distance away, she turned and hurried off, her destination Mary's solar.

She did not know if she was followed and did not care. She was determined to solve the mystery of the secret passage. If rain fell soon, it would drive her husband into the keep and he would no doubt search for her. She had little time to spare. She hurried up to the upper floor and grabbed the torch from the sconce. She entered Mary's solar and used the torch to light the logs in the small hearth. They caught quickly, the wood dry from having lingered there. She returned the torch to the sconce and when she stepped in the room again, she was pleased to see that the hearth's flames had cast sufficient light in the room.

In here was the secret passage and she intended to find it.

An hour later with dust covering a good bit of her and smudges of dirt dotting her face, Heather was no closer to finding the secret passage than she had been when she had first entered the room. Though, the room was much cleaner than before and much more inviting. She could understand why Mary McComb and her mum spent time here stitching and talking. The things they must have discussed, the hopes and sorrows they must have shared, just as she did with her sisters. She only wished her mum could have been there to share the years with them.

"What are you doing here?"

Heather jumped, her hand going to her chest. "Can you please announce your approach before you actually appear? You forever startle me."

"And you forever—"

"Disobey you—" she finished while the rest of what she intended to say abruptly died on her lips. She had seen her husband look formidable many times, but nothing like he did now. His muscles were swollen hard from exertion and sweat clung to his naked chest and arms, as if it refused to let go, and she could not blame it. She would love to be clinging to him right now and the wicked thought had, to her frustration, tingles nipping teasingly at the most intimate of places. She forced herself to finish what she had to say. "I know I forever disobey you and I see an unlikely chance of that ever changing."

Rhys battled his growing arousal, but then he had been battling it since last night. It was the reason he had left their bed before she woke this morning or else they probably would still be there. Now, seeing her covered in dust and dirt marring her lovely face made him want to dirtier her even more with his sweat-covered body. And damn if the thought did not turn him harder.

He slammed the door so hard behind him after stepping fully into the room that the whole keep must have heard it. "You will learn to obey me."

Heather had always found that kind words went far and could help avoid potentially difficult situations, but that was before passion took hold of her.

She walked over to him and leaned up to whisper in his ear, "Make me."

He grabbed the back of her neck tightly. "You are playing with fire."

God help her but she was, but she did not care. She needed to know the Dragon, taste him, and become part of him if she was ever going to truly be reunited with Quinn. "I do not fear getting burned."

"Then God help you, wife, for you are about to get scorched and the scars it leaves may be too deep for you to ever forget."

"I do not want to forget the moments I share with you. I want to always remember."

He reached out and with quick, rough hands stripped her bare, and then did the same to himself.

She reached out and ran her hand down his chest. "I love seeing you naked."

"Worry not, wife, for I will make certain you see me naked often."

"Promise?" she whispered, bringing her lips close to his.

He grabbed at the back of her hair and yanked her head back, bringing his mouth down near hers as he said, "You have the word of the Dragon. Now open your mouth for me."

This time she obeyed without question and was soon caught up in a kiss that had her lost in a haze of passion. He trailed the kiss down her neck, nipping as he went and sending gooseflesh racing over her before returning to her mouth.

She jolted when his hands grabbed at her waist and lifted her to slam against him. She wrapped her legs around his waist and her arms around his neck. And she startled again when he released her and her bottom slapped against the wood chest.

His mouth left hers to once again nip down her neck to her breast and when his teeth caught hold of her hard nipple, she almost leapt off the chest. Her desire soared and with it the urge to touch him, and her hand slipped down between his legs.

He felt like the finest wool, soft and smooth, though hard as metal and she enjoyed the feel of him in her hand.

His hand settled over hers, squeezing it and moving it up and down. "Grow me harder," he demanded and again she obeyed, though it was because she wanted to. She enjoyed the feel of him and the power of growing him large in her hand.

He suckled at her breasts while she did as he told her, a mistake on his part. He thought he would come then and there, his manhood responding enthusiastically to her innocent touch, but he would not allow himself to. The entire night lay ahead of them and the Dragon was too ravenous to be satisfied with simply one feeding.

While his mouth lingered at her breasts, his fingers drifted along her body, caressing as he went until he found that special spot in the triangle of hair between her legs and he began to tease it.

She dropped her head back with a moan and her hand fell off him to join the other in gripping the edge of the chest.

His hands cupped her hips and yanked her forward and as he did his own hips nudged her legs apart. Her eyes turned wide as she felt the tip of him ready to enter her, and she glanced down and gasped as she watched him drive into her swiftly. He sank deep inside her, then pulled out of her, though not completely.

"Wrap your legs around me," he demanded and when she did, his hands slipped beneath her backside, took firm hold, and lifted her enough so that he was able to move in and out of her with ease.

Soon his rhythm turned hard and fast, and after only a few minutes, she said, "I am going to come."

"Aye, you are, many times tonight," Rhys said and squeezed her backside as he yanked her hard against him.

She let out a cry, grabbing his shoulders as she felt her passion climb and climb and climb until she let out a scream as she suddenly plunged into a never-ending climax that completely devoured her. When she thought she was finally spent, her head fell to rest on her husband's chest.

"You are not done yet," he demanded as she fell against him. He pulled out of her, yanked her off the chest, and turned her around, bending her over to slip into her once more.

She gasped, though still wet, he seemed to feel larger inside her this way and when he began to pound against her, she once again braced her hands on the edge of the chest and was shocked to feel another climax begin to build inside her.

The slap of his body against hers with every thrust he delivered was like a strange enticing melody to her ears and fed her passion even more. So did the sharp, quick nips he delivered to the back of her neck with his teeth. But it was when his hand came around in front of her and his fingers began to work their magic on her nub that was beyond sensitive that she once again exploded in a climax and this time when she did, so did her husband.

Rhys rarely let out a moan when he climaxed and if he did, it was barely heard. This climax had him roaring out loud. Never had a climax felt as good as this one. He continued to pound against her, wanting to savor every last bit of it. And when it was done, he bent over her, bracing his hands beside hers, feeling more spent than he ever had from a climax.

They both remained like that for several minutes, neither wanting to move, neither wanting to separate. Finally and reluctantly, Rhys pulled out of her and turned her around to face him.

A tear trickled down her cheek.

"Did I hurt you?" he asked his stomach tightening at the thought as he wiped the tear away.

She shook her head, sniffling to keep more tears from falling.

"Then why do you cry?"

Another tear slipped out and she laid her head on his chest and wrapped her arms around his waist. How did she tell him that whether he was the Dragon or Quinn, it did not matter? She loved them both with all her heart and then some.

"Answer me, wife," he demanded.

She spoke from her heart. "I did not know how wonderful making love could feel."

A smile crept across his face, though his wife could not see it and he scooped her up in his arms. "I am not finished with you yet."

A grin quickly surfaced on her face as her arms went around his neck. "You just answered my prayer."

He held her tight against him as he walked down the stairs to their bedchamber. "You will tell me if you grow sore."

"And you will tell me if you grow tired." Heather was shocked to hear him burst out laughing at her remark and her smile grew. He was not pulling her down into the darkness; she was pulling him out of it.

Chapter Twenty

Heather winced as her husband pulled out of her.

"Damn it, Heather, I told you to tell me if you were sore," Rhys said, rolling off her to sit up beside her in bed. "How sore are you?" he asked, his hands reaching to spread her legs further apart

Heather quickly closed them tight.

Rhys looked down at her. "Do not tell me you are embarrassed for me to take a look when there is not a spot on you I have not seen, touched, or kissed."

"That was in the throes of lovemaking."

"You will obey me. Now spread your legs."

She shook her head.

"Am I to understand that you will only obey me when we make love?"

She smiled. "You are beginning to understand me."

"A pity that you have yet to understand me," he said and moved so fast that Heather let out a sharp cry when he spread her legs wide.

Rhys cringed when he took a look. "Damn it, Heather, you should have told me you were too sore to take me this morning."

"My desire for you outweighed my soreness," she said her cheeks blushing red.

"What can I do to ease your pain?"

"Stop looking between my legs."

He closed her legs gently. "Now tell me how I can tend you."

"I will see to it myself."

"I caused this and I will make it right," he insisted.

She laughed softly. "I did not force you to lay with me."

He laughed as well. "I could argue that, since you can be quite demanding in bed...or out of it."

Heather blushed again, recalling the places they had made love in the room. She had straddled him while he sat upon a chair, and the door shook when he took her against it. Her blush deepened when she just now realized the guard could have heard them. And what of her screams? She had been wickedly loud when he bent her over the table and also the bed. Her hand went to cover her mouth.

Rhys grabbed her hand. "Your deepening blush tells me your thoughts. I love the way you scream when I plunge deep inside you and I would order you never to stop," —he grinned— "but it is not necessary, for you will never be able to stop yourself from screaming out your pleasure."

"It is your fault," she argued.

"Aye, it is," he admitted, "as is this." He laid his hand gently at the apex of her legs. "Now let me tend you."

Heather rested her hand on his arm. "Please, let me see to it?"

"You ask like an obedient wife, so I will not refuse you, though know that I will not touch you again until I see for myself that you have healed."

"As you wish, husband," she said, smiling.

"I mean it, Heather," he said sternly and his arm was quick to scoop her around the waist and bring her along with him to settle on his lap once he sat braced against his pillows. "Now tell me what you were doing on the upper floor last night."

She moved to settle more comfortably on his lap and recounted what Seamus had told her. "So, that is what took me there, though to no avail, for I found no secret passage."

"We will search the room together later when I am finished with things that require my attention."

Heather tucked a strand of his dark hair behind his ear, then ran her finger down along his jaw to his chin. She searched his face for the young man she loved, but it was the Dark Dragon she kept seeing. Had he devoured Quinn completely or had Quinn had no choice but to surrender to him.

"Who was the man who made love to me for the first time in this bed? He touched and kissed me, but he was never truly here."

"A man trying to be someone other than who he is."

"Who is he?"

"He is a man more used to harshness than to kindness. A man more used to roughness than to gentleness when taking a woman. A man more used to hatred than to love.

Heather sat up straight. She ached to tell him that she had always loved him and always would, but she answered as she thought best for now. "I do believe I am falling in love with the Dark Dragon."

He took hold of her chin. "Do not waste your love on me, wife, for you will be sorely disappointed."

~~~

Heather stared at the sizeable wood chest two men had placed in the room under the window. The rain had stopped in the middle of the night, but the skies had remained overcast, so it was a gray light that filtered through the windows and over the chest.

Rhys had told her that he was having it brought to her, explaining that perhaps she would find some garments in it that she could wear or perhaps stitch to fit her size.

She had just finished tending herself with cool cloths and a light salve she had found worked well on the women in her clan who had suffered such a problem. Now she wanted to dress and get outside before rain fell again and forced her to remain inside. She opened the lid of the chest eager to find something to wear and be on her way.

Her mouth fell open in shock. The chest was filled to the brim with women's garments and as she rifled through them she wondered where her husband had gotten them all. Surprisingly, most
~~~

looked as though they would fit her and the few that did not would need only a tuck or two. None appeared too small or too large.

She chose a pale green garment that cinched at the waist and shoulders with ties, fitting her nicely. The sleeves fell just passed her elbows and it rode high on her chest. She did not want to waste time searching through all the garments, but she did dig her hands through the mound, hoping to find boots or shoes, and she was elated when she yanked out a pair of boots that strapped around the ankles. She was also delighted to find a pair of sandals, better left to use another day.

With her hair neatly plaited, she hurried out of the keep, grateful to Nessa for having brought food to her after Rhys had left. She walked around the small village, calling out greetings, stopping to speak with those she knew and getting acquainted with those she did not know. Now and then she would cast a glance toward the barn, though she did not make it obvious. A guard sat in front of the door, so that not even a quick-footed person could get passed him. Still, she was determined to find a way in there.

She walked along the edge of the woods talking with Belle until the woman excused herself to tend to her chores. Heather kept walking. She had thought she heard an odd noise when Belle had been there. Now she listened and was sure she heard something.

An animal was in distress. Ever since she was young she could sense when animals needed help and they seemed to sense that she could help them. She never told anyone about it, though she often thought her father knew. He made mention time and again how her mum had a special way with animals.

Heather stopped and listened and the sound broke her heart. She could not ignore the animal's cries of distress. She knew ghost warriors had to be watching her, but she could be fast on her feet when necessary. She only hoped that she was faster than the warriors who would chase after her.

She listened for a few more minutes, pretending she found something interesting on the ground and poked at it with her foot. Then all of a sudden she took off into the woods. She was relieved that it did not take long to reach the animal and that no one yet followed.

Her breath caught as she came face to face with the beast. It was a wolf, a large black one.

If the warriors saw him, they would surely kill him.

Heather stopped a few feet from the wolf and waited a moment before she began to approach him slowly and speak to him softly. "I am here to help, but I fear we have little time. So, I have no time to win your trust." She hunched down and held out her hand to him. "May I help you?"

The wolf seemed to sense her gentleness and urgency and approached her with quick steps.

Heather saw how he hobbled to her and once he was close, she laid a gentle hand at his side and continued speaking softly to him as she ran her hand down along his leg. She heard the soft rumble of a growl in his throat and it took a moment for her to realize that he warned her that soon they would not be alone.

"I must hurry," she said and lifted his paw to see that a sliver of wood had somehow embedded itself between the pads of his paw. It was red and sore, but if she could extract it, she was sure he would see to the rest.

She heard rushing footfalls drawing closer and while she stroked the wolf gently with one hand, she plucked the sliver of wood out with the other. "You must run," she whispered to him.

"Step away slowly, Lady Heather."

She almost sighed with relief when she heard it was Pitt and not her husband. She turned, keeping herself close to the wolf so that the warriors would not take a chance of releasing their arrows in fear of hitting her.

"He was injured. I saw to his wound. He means you no harm," she called out.

"Step aside," Pitt ordered again.

"I will not let you harm him." She realized then that more men were gathering around and they would be on the wolf as soon as he took off. She had no choice. She would not see the beautiful creature die. She had to run with him so that the warriors would not pelt him with arrows.

"The Dragon will be here soon, Lady Heather. He will not be happy about this."

That was enough to have her turn to the wolf and say, "Run!"

She followed right behind him, pleased that her frequent runs in the meadow with her sisters had served a purpose after all. She kept pace with the wolf or perhaps he had sensed her intentions and kept a pace she could follow.

The footfalls behind her were growing closer and she called out to the wolf, "Keep going. No matter what keep going."

The wolf picked up speed and she followed as best she could and when he jumped atop a formation of rocks and disappeared behind it, she sensed he was safe. She stopped abruptly and just as abruptly was grabbed from behind and swung around to face her husband.

Anything she was about to say died on her lips as soon as she saw his face. There was no doubt the Dragon stood before her. His dark eyes blazed with fury, his nostrils flared, and it would be fiery words he unleashed on her.

His hand tightened on her arm like an iron shackle. She was not going anywhere.

"We hurry back," Rhys shouted to his men.

She was surprised that the warriors did not follow after the wolf, but instead surrounded her and Rhys, providing a thick safety barrier around them. She wondered what kind of danger lurked in the woods that such precautions were taken.

When they were a few feet in the village, the warriors dispersed, while a few remained on the edge of the woods. Rhys kept walking, pulling her along with him, his pace barely slowing. People stared and whispers circled as they watched their leader practically drag his wife through the village. Heather almost tripped over her own feet twice, but Rhys was quick to right her.

Heather was shocked when he brought her to the barn. The guard upon seeing them approach, hurried to his feet and moved the bench away from the door just as Rhys reached out for the handle.

He yanked her inside, ordering the guard to shut the door behind him. He rushed her along, stopping at the stall where she had last seen the two dead ghost warriors. Nothing was there but a partially filled grain sack sitting atop a barrel.

His heated tone flamed his words. "I give orders for a reason—to protect my clan. You endangered not only your life, but the lives of my men by disobeying me. Evil lurks in those woods." He shoved her toward the barrel. "See it for yourself and perhaps then you will obey me."

A tingle of fear rushed over Heather as she took a step toward the barrel. If the sack held no grain, what did it hold? She cautiously undid the tie on the sack and pulled the edges down around whatever was in it.

Heather's hands froze when it revealed the severed head of a man that had been beaten beyond reason, his eyes gorged out of his head like the other warrior. Maggots feasted on what was left of the flesh and other bugs began to crawl out of the holes and what was left of his nose. His mouth hung agape as if in a perpetual scream when suddenly a spider crawled out of it.

She jumped back, her stomach revolting at the sickening sight and she turned to her husband, stretching her hand out to him.

Rhys grabbed her around the waist and hurried her away from the disgusting sight. He quickly bent her at the waist, saying, "Take deep breathes."

She did as he said and while doing so she heard someone enter the barn. The next thing she knew, Rhys was placing a wet cloth to her face. The coolness chased away the last of the protesting rumbles in her stomach and she straightened, though dropped back to lean against her husband.

Rhys had been too angry with his wife to care or give thought to how she would react when she saw the severed head. Now he regretted it and regrets were rare for him.

She turned in his arms, resting her head against his chest, wishing she could erase the atrocious sight from her memory.

Rhys wrapped his arm around her and gently eased her along toward the door.

Pitt stood there and opened it as they approached and Heather realized he had been the one to enter the barn before, but then he was always there when Rhys needed him.

Rhys watched the faces of his people as they looked at his wife as he escorted her through the village. Tongues would wag, speculating over what she saw that left her ghostly pale and trembling in his arms. The servants in the keep stepped away as Rhys walked through the Great Hall with her.

Nessa was the only one with courage enough to approach him. “Is there anything I can do for my lady?”

“Bring more wine to my solar,” Rhys ordered as he hurried Heather out of the room. He sat her in the chair by the fire after entering his solar and when he went to release her hand, she grabbed it.

“Do not leave me.”

Her actions had him recalling a similar reaction right here in the solar after she had seen the bodies of the two dead warriors. She had seen too much evil of late, but this time it had been his fault. Rhys took tight hold of her hand. “I am not going anywhere. I just want to add more logs to the fire. You feel chilled.”

“I am,” she said and reluctantly let him go.

Rhys bid Nessa to enter when he heard a knock and as soon as she did, he said, “Leave it. I will see to it.”

Nessa cast a worried look at Heather. She was palc and shivered even with the fire stoked and she wondered what had happened to her. She hated leaving her, but she had no choice. She closed the door quietly behind her.

Rhys filled a goblet and handed it to Heather.

Her hands shook so badly when she took it that Rhys cupped his around hers and helped her drink from it. Afterwards he took it from her and set it on the small table beside her chair.

Rhys did not like that no color had returned to her cheeks and that she continued to tremble. He leaned over and lifted her up into his arms, then sat in the chair, drawing her legs up and tucking her firmly against him.

After a several minutes of stroking her back, she looked up at him and said, "Who would do such a monstrous thing?

"The man I was a slave to for seven years."

"A slave?" Heather repeated almost choking on the word.

"Aye, a slave, forced to do an evil man's bidding."

Fear gripped Heather. "You escaped and now he comes for you?"

"No," Rhys said, shaking his head. "I won my freedom."

"Then what does he want from you?"

"What I took from him when I left."

When he remained silent for several minutes, she asked, "What did you take from him?"

"His wife."

Chapter Twenty-one

Rhys had not planned on telling his wife, at least not yet. But he had foolishly let his anger rule, something he had not done in years, and this was the results and a good reason not to let it happen again. He did wonder, though, if his inquisitive wife would make that impossible.

She had yet to respond; she simply stared at him out of shock or disbelief, he was not certain.

So many thoughts rushed through Heather's head, but only one word spilled from her lips. "Why?"

"She asked me to."

"Why?"

"Her life was in danger." Before Heather could ask why again, Rhys pressed his finger to her lips. "I was taken to a land with vastly different customs than Scotland. There, slaves obeyed their masters or suffered horribly for it. Wives suffered much worse fates."

"Wives?" Heather asked.

"Aye, wives. Masters had multiple wives, all generously provided for unless a wife did not please her Master."

"What happened?"

"It depended on the situation. Some simply disappeared, sent away to be provided for elsewhere if the wife had not displeased him. Those who displeased him suffered greatly."

"This wife who you took from him, did she displease him?" Heather asked his story sounding more like a tale than truth, yet it would explain much about what had happened to change Quinn so drastically. And her heart ached for him.

"Not yet, though she feared that she would. You see Haidar, the master, had five children from five different wives and they were all daughters. He wanted a son, demanded a son, and he proclaimed that any daughter born before he was given a son would be killed. So the next wife who got pregnant and gave him a daughter—" Rhys stopped abruptly the horrendous memory not one he wanted his wife to have. "So I agreed to take her and when I bid Haidar farewell, he never knew that his wife was safely concealed in one of the gifts he had bestowed on me."

"How very brave of you. You saved this woman and her child. Did she have a son?"

"I do not know and she did not want me to know or know her destination once I left her on her own. We both knew what would happen if Haidar came for us. No one could withstand his brutal torture."

"How long ago was this?" she asked.

"Three years."

His time spent as a slave plus three years made it ten years, the exact number of years Quinn had been gone. She tucked the thought away and asked, "Why wait three years to come after you?"

"The woman was wise and left a trail that would make him believe that she had run away but had remained in his country. And he would have never thought I had been involved with her disappearance."

"Why?"

"I have told you enough," Rhys said abruptly. "Now you see why it is imperative that you obey me. He seeks not only word of his wife and child, but revenge for me betraying him. His attack on us that day, his brutal killing of my two warriors, the culprit in our bedchamber, and now this severed head, is all to show me that I cannot stop him. He will have what he wants."

She cringed as she spoke. "He reminds you again with the gorged out eyes in the severed head that you will not see him coming. Do you know who the head belongs to and why the head was only left? And where was the head found?"

"Enough dreadful talk for one day," Rhys snapped. He reached for the goblet of wine and handed it to her.

Her trembling gone and feeling much improved, Heather took the goblet, but did not drink. "If the head was found on your land, then how did the person get passed your men without being seen?"

"Enough!" Rhys ordered. "Now you will tell me why you went into the woods and why you were running after a wolf."

Heather did not let his shout or demand bother her. She was so very pleased that he had shared some of his past with her, since it helped her to understand how the Dark Dragon came to be born.

She smiled and kissed his lips gently. "Thank you for trusting me enough to share part of your past."

"Do not think to distract me with kisses," he said, though the kiss certainly had brought attention to his manhood. "Tell me of the wolf."

Heather took a sip of the wine and handed the goblet to Rhys and he took a sip as she said, "I was not running after him. I ran behind him to protect him from your warriors. I knew they would not dare draw their bows with me so close to him."

"A wise conclusion for a foolish action."

"Not to me," Heather said in defense of herself. "The wolf needed my help."

"And you knew this how?"

Heather took the goblet from her husband and sipped slowly.

"Delaying in answering me will not help," he advised and slipped the goblet out of her hand to place on the table.

"It will delay having you think me a fool."

He caressed her lower lip with his thumb, not trusting his lips after her gentle kiss had stirred his hunger for her. "Never would I think you a fool, wife—foolish perhaps—but never a fool."

His response brought a smile to her face and his touch brought flutters to her stomach. Good lord, but she loved this man beyond reason. "Since I was young I had a certain way with animals. They came to me for comfort, help, and love, and I gave it most willingly."

"Are you saying the wolf came to you for help?"

"I believe he did, for I heard his distress quite clearly, though I had little time to make certain of his trust since your warriors were on my trail so fast."

"I am glad to hear that."

"By the time I removed the sliver of wood from his paw, your warriors were there. I tried to warn them away, telling Pitt that the wolf meant them no harm, but to no avail. I had little choice but to protect the innocent animal."

Rhys took hold of her chin. "You will stay out of the woods and never again let me find you tending a wolf." The purse of her lips and the tilt of her head alerted him to his mistake. "Let me clarify that. Never again will you tend a wolf whether I see you doing it or not, and I will have your word on it."

"I will give you my word that I will not go into the woods until this problem is resolved." She shook her head. "But I cannot give you my word that I will not tend a wolf, if it should prove necessary."

"Are you forcing my hand, wife?" he asked, giving her chin a squeeze.

"No," she whispered and placed her hand over his and eased it off her chin, cupping it in her hands. "I do not force you nor can I stop you from the decisions you make. I say again, I wish for truth and trust between us."

"Truth often times creates problems."

"Trust often times helps to avoid or solve them."

Bringing his lips close to hers, he whispered, "Do you trust me, wife?"

"With my life," she answered without hesitation.

His words whispered across her lips with a hint of a challenge. "You place your life in the hands of the Dark Dragon?"

"I place my life in the hands of the man I love." She pressed her lips to his before he could move away in anger, knowing once their lips touched there would be no separating them.

Rhys let the kiss go only so far, his passion flaming much too hot, far too quickly, and he could sense hers had done the same.

He tugged her head gently back by her hair. "You are still sore?"

Heather's hesitated to answer.

His hand dipped under the hem of her dress. "I can find out for myself or you can tell me the truth, since is it not truth that you want between us?"

Heather sighed. "It is, and I have yet to heal completely."

Rhys removed his hand from under her dress. "There is something I wish to be truthful with you about."

Heather smiled, pleased that he should do so.

Rhys ran his fingers down along her braid that rested on her chest. "The necklace you wore the other night, it was not me who left it for you." Her smile faded as Rhys continued. "Haidar gave that necklace to his wife when he found out she was pregnant, certain she would give him a son, since her mother had given her father four sons."

Heather rubbed her chest, feeling as if it was not the necklace that had touched her skin, but Haidar's hands.

Rhys took her hand in his aware of what his wife was thinking. "Haidar will never touch you; I will make certain of it."

Heather smiled and pressed his hand to her chest. "No one will ever touch me but you."

"You are right about that, for I will kill any man that even dares it."

Heather wrinkled her brow.

"What is wrong?"

"I think Seamus is right."

"Right about what?"

"Seamus made mention that one of your own warriors could have turned against you for a price, and with someone having gained access to our bedchamber twice now without being caught I would venture to guess he may be right."

"Your curiosity combined with your intelligence may prove—"

"Helpful," she finished with a soft laugh.

Her laughter brought a smile to his face something that had become more frequent with his wife around. And he wondered, or perhaps he more hoped, that she actually had the power to chase away the darkness that had been his constant companion for far too long.

She poked him in the chest. "Tell me you have not considered that one of your men may have betrayed you?"

"He has not betrayed me," he admitted. "He is loyal to his master Haidar and doing what he was sent to do."

Heather gasped. "Do you know who it is?"

Rhys shook his head. "I have yet to discover his identity. I have instructed Pitt to engage more with Nessa since she sees much of what goes on in the keep than any other."

"So that is why he has been seeking her out and talking with her." Heather shook her head. "I believe it might prove difficult for Pitt, since Nessa does not find him as appealing as she does Fife. I will talk with her if you would like and free Pitt of the chore."

"No doubt she will speak more openly with you, though lately I do not think that Pitt considers it a chore." Rhys eased her off his lap and onto her feet, then stood. "I have matters that need my attention. You will remain in the keep until I return." He held his finger up when she looked ready to protest. "That is light punishment for such flagrant disobedience. I must calm the many tongues you sent wagging with your actions and make sure they know you do not go unpunished."

Heather did not argue. She had made her choice, knowing there would be consequences to face and she would do it again.

His hand slipped around the back of her neck and with a quick tug he brought her up against him to kiss her. "Hurry and heal," he said when the kiss was done and he quickly left the room.

Heather sat, before her legs would hold her no more. She thought her desire for him would abate after how many times they had made love last night, but it had not. If anything, it had multiplied tenfold. And his words proved that he felt the same.

She reached for the goblet of wine and drank, wondering what could keep her busy while waiting for his return.

Mary McComb's solar.

The thought had her hurrying out of the chair and out of the room. Rhys would not mind if she started the search without him since it would confine her to the keep. With no reason to rush, she slowed her pace as she reached the stairs and with each step she took, she thought of what Rhys had confided to her.

She sat after entering Mary's solar, trying to comprehend what Quinn had suffered all these years. The awful things he must have gone through and what price he must have been forced to pay for his freedom.

Guilt nudged at her, remembering how she had grown angry through the years, thinking he had stopped loving her, thinking he had died, when all the while, he was fighting his way back to her. A tear trickled from the corner of her eye. Her heart had broken and she had thought her suffering unbearable when it had been nothing compared to what he had endured.

She wished that just once she could call him Quinn, let him know that she loved him, had always loved him and always would. She gave herself a few more minutes to cry for what they had lost, then she brushed her tears away. She would not linger in the past. They were here together now and that was what mattered most. She turned her attention on searching for the secret passage.

After an hour or more of examining every part of the room, she sat in the chair again and looked through the few pieces of embroidery in the basket. Picking up piece after piece, she wondered if her mum had helped Mary McComb stitch any of them and the thought of her mum suddenly had her missing her father and sisters.

The day she had been abducted had changed all their lives and in a strange way for the better. Emma and Patience both had found love and their father's health had improved. She smiled, thinking how thrilled he would be when he discovered that unknowingly he had given her what she wanted most...Quinn.

She sat a few moments more, several yawns attacking her and decided to return to her bedchamber and have a bit of rest. Her eyes caught on the room across the narrow hall as she stepped out of the solar and a thought struck her. What if she was searching the wrong room?

Grabbing the torch from the sconce, she opened the door and entered the room. A musty odor whipped around her and the shadows scurried away from the light as she made her way deeper into the room. She had to step around the many pieces of furniture that had been haphazardly placed in there.

A breeze brushed against her face as she stopped by the lone window. She drew back the heavy tapestry that covered it, surprised to see part of the window broken. Could that be how someone was gaining access to the upper floor, though the height would make it an impossible wall to scale or was it?

She would tell Rhys about it as soon as she saw him. The more she explored the more she realized it would be truly impossible to search this room. There was just too much in the way to do a thorough search. She would ask Rhys to have it cleaned out so they could explore every inch of it.

Disappointed she began to make her way back toward the door when a sudden gust of wind not only blew the torch out with the strength of a giant's breath, but it also slammed the door shut, leaving her in complete darkness.

Heather warned herself to remain calm. The dark could intimidate now and then, but now was not the time to let it. All she had to do was make her way to the window and yank the tapestry off and she would have light.

She placed the extinguished torch on top of something in front of her and turned, reaching out in search of the wall. She found it easier than she expected and was pleased by her quick progress. She took hold of the corner of the tapestry and gave it a hard yank.

Nothing happened and after what seemed like endless yanking, she stopped, frustrated. The skies had grayed again, but the light from the window would be sufficient to see her way around if she could get the tapestry down. A few more tries and she gave up. She pulled it back and did not release it until she made a mental trail to the door. Once in the dark again, she followed the trail in her mind, bumping her leg now and then before reaching the door.

She felt along the frame until she came to the latch and gasped...it was gone. She felt around the whole door—nothing. There was no way for her to get out of the room.

Chapter Twenty-two

Rhys stood near the edge of the woods with his arms crossed. Haidar waited somewhere out there for him and, knowing him as well as Rhys did, he knew there would be no avoiding a confrontation. But then the day he had agreed to help Anala, he knew this time would come. He could have been free, Haidar forever out of his life, but he had given his word to Anala.

He thought about the lie he told to his wife, but he had given his word and his word was something that he always kept. He had been with Anala when she gave birth. Sadly, she died, though the babe had survived, and he had given her his word that he would never tell anyone about the child and he would make certain the child was kept safe. She also left a message to be given to Haidar, if given the chance, and Rhys was eager to give it to him.

It took Haidar longer to find him than he had expected, but that had worked to his advantage. He had his ghost warriors and a massive army at his disposal, though he would not dismiss Haidar's ability to defeat him. What he needed to remember was that Haidar did the unexpected, upsetting his enemies and proving victorious more times than not.

Rhys had known full well this day would come. He had waited for it, prepared for it, was eager for it. His one regret when he had won his freedom was that he would not see Haidar dead. Taking his wife gave Rhys the chance to satisfy that regret.

Rhys heard the footfalls behind him and waited for Pitt to reach his side. "Still no luck in finding the rest of Rab's body?"

"No a sign of it," Pitt confirmed.

"And not one of the warriors who were keeping watch on McDolan saw anything?"

"He was snatched right out from under everyone." Pitt shook his head. "Perhaps the head was sufficient for his message and he disposed of the rest of the body."

"No, the head was a message for me. Haidar lets me know that he will severe me from all I hold close. The body will surface elsewhere on purpose." Rhys cast an eye up at the graying clouds. "Have you made any progress with Nessa?"

"She spares me barely a moment, while she gives freely of her time to Fife."

Rhys turned his head and a slight grin surfaced. "She prefers Fife over you."

"I cannot believe it myself, though I think I am making some small progress. She spoke with me a bit longer than she usually does the last two times I engaged with her."

"So what you are telling me is that you have learned nothing as of yet."

"Only that Fife brings her flowers far too often and I have heard him tell her just as often how beautiful she is—he is definitely right about that—and she is even more beautiful when she smiles."

Rhys's grin grew.

Pitt threw his hands up. "And he follows her around like a lovesick pup. I do not think there is a place she goes that he does not follow."

Rhys' smile vanished and Pitt's eyes widened.

"It has been right there in front of me this whole time," Pitt said with an angry snarl for not seeing it sooner.

"He also was the one who found the severed head," Rhys reminded.

"I should have seen it," Pitt said, growing angrier with himself.

"We both should have seen it, but Fife has been with us about a year, enough time for him to prove himself worthy of becoming a ghost warrior and for us to accept and trust him."

"What do you want done with him?"

"Watch him. Put only our most trusted and skilled men on him and when the time is right...he will be mine to deal with."

"What of Nessa?"

"You know you can say nothing to her."

"I do not want to see her hurt. She has a generous heart."

"Then set doubt in her mind as to how she feels about him," Rhys said.

"I think her mind is firm on him."

"Not if she lingered the last few times to speak with you."

"You think?"

Rhys laughed. "I never thought I would see you doubt yourself with a woman."

"And I never thought I would ever see you laugh."

"The right woman can do that to a man...make him do what he did not think possible."

Pitt stepped back, a look of horror on his face. "Bite your tongue. I am not falling in love with Nessa."

"I never said you were," Rhys said and laughed again, "now come with me.

"It is a ridiculous thought," Pitt said, keeping pace beside him and repeatedly refuting Rhys' claim with each step he took.

~~~

Heather leaned her shoulder against the door. She had pounded on it and shouted for help until her throat was dry. It was just a matter of time before Rhys discovered her missing and searched for her. She simply had to be patient. As far as the dark, not knowing what was in it caused more fear than the darkness itself. But there was nothing in this room that could harm her and she very much doubted the secret passage was in here, allowing someone to sneak up on her. There was no telling
~~~

when this door would be opened or closed. So if the culprit made his way in from outside, he could find himself unable to enter the keep.

At least she had eliminated one room where the secret passage could be hidden.

She turned her head suddenly, thinking she heard a sound and smiled when she heard footfalls and voices growing closer.

Pitt stepped off the top step after Rhys. "First Rab McLaud gets beaten to death by his father-in-law, Hew McDolan, then Haidar steals his body from McDolan, severs his head, and sends it to you. I wonder what is going to happen to the rest of him."

Heather's shout never reached her lips. She could not believe what she had just heard and she would hear more before she let them know of her presence.

Rhys stopped, realizing no torch flickered, though a modicum of light came from the open door of the one room. He spoke to Pitt as he went to see what happened with the torch. "Make no mistake he will make use of the rest of Rab's body. He may leave it on Macinnes land to fuel the winds of war between McLaud and Macinnes, making sure my warriors are busy elsewhere or he may deliver it directly to Greer McLaud and tell him that he saw the Macinnes chop off his brother's head and cast it to the animals. Whatever he chooses to do will benefit his plans."

"Shall I have a message sent to the Macinnes alerting them of the situation?"

"Not yet," Rhys said as he saw that there was no torch in the sconce.

His response had Heather pounding on the door and shouting. "Let me out! Let me out now!"

Rhys hurried to the door upon hearing his wife's anxious pleas.

As soon as it opened, Heather stepped out and stepped right in front of her husband. All the things she intended to say died on her lips. They did not seem as important as the words that spilled out instead. "You do not trust me enough to tell me the truth." Her hand went to her chest. "I thought, I truly thought..." She shook her head and went to rush past Pitt when she was grabbed. She was jerked to a stop and she turned to see and feel her husband's fingers close strongly around her arm.

Pitt took his leave without being told to do so.

No tears came to her eyes, though her heart ached. Then like cold water being thrown in her face, sensibility returned to her. She berated herself silently. How could she have thought of herself before her family? Their safety was more important than her worrying that Rhys did not trust her.

"My family needs to know about this," she said.

"They will know when I am ready to tell them."

"They could be in danger," she argued.

"They could be in more danger if I told them."

She tried to pull away from him, but he held her much too tight.

"I do trust you, wife," Rhys said

Heather was too angry to hear the sincerity in his words and so she lashed out, "But not enough to confide the truth."

"Some things are better left unspoken," he said.

"Not between husband and wife."

"You need to trust me on this," he said sternly.

"And you need to trust me."

~~~

Heather sat in the chair by the fire with her legs drawn up and her arms wrapped around them. She had not seen her husband since he had deposited her there a couple of hours ago and ordered her to stay put.

She had no want to go wandering about. She was too upset. He wanted her to trust him, yet he did not trust her, though he said he did and thinking on it he had sounded sincere. Could his reason for not telling her about Rab be a vital one?

All these years, she had the unwavering support of her family while Rhys had suffered as a slave to an evil man. How could she expect him to trust her as easily as she trusted him?
~~~

A flame jumped and shot a spark out, the tiny ember dying slowly on the hearth stone. Had it been like that for Quinn, a slow death until Rhys was forced to be born? And what was it he had said.

I know only hate not love.

She could not imagine living without love. The love of her father, her sisters, friends, the clan and even her mum's love, though she had died those many years ago. So somewhere deep inside him, he must have remembered the love she had for him. Why else had he returned here and wed her?

She realized then that she was expecting him to be as he was before and that man was no more. She had to be patient like she often warned her sister to be. It would take time and trust, whether he gave the same to her or not.

A light tap sounded at the door and Heather went and opened it to find Nessa standing there, looking upset.

"I am so sorry to bother you, my lady, but Fife is not feeling well. His wound is troubling him and though he told me I was not to bother you, it breaks my heart to see him suffer."

"I will have a look at him," Heather said, "though it does trouble me that his wound has not healed as it should."

"It is because he does not follow what you tell him. He waits outside by the kitchen garden, thinking I am bringing him a special treat, which of course I will once you are done tending him."

"And do I get a special treat for tending him?" Heather asked with a smile as they walked to the stairs.

"I am so sorry, my lady, I spoke out of turn, but there are times you seem more a friend than mistress of this keep."

"I am glad of that. It reminds me more of home."

"It was the same with your mum. I remember your mum visiting our cottage when I was very young. She sat and spoke with my mum as if they were great friends." Nessa stopped when they reached the bottom of the stairs. "Word spreads about your dealing with the wolf. Some whisper that you are a witch, others who knew your mum say that you have a special touch with animals just as she once did."

"It is nice to know I am like my mum."

"You are in more ways than you know."

Heather remarked on how delicious the kitchen smelled as she walked through it and outside to the garden along with Nessa.

Fife jumped up off the bench, an angry scowl on his face as she and Heather approached him. "You should not have disturbed Lady Heather."

"You should have told me that your wound still troubles you," Heather said as they drew closer.

The attack came fast, the warrior, his face smeared with dirt, lunging and barely catching Fife on the arm as he reached to draw a dagger from the attacker's waist. It was a quick scuffle more than a fight, the two men falling to the ground one after the other.

Nessa screamed and ran to Fife.

Pitt seemed to come out of nowhere and grabbed her around the waist, pulling her away from Fife.

Nessa struggled to free herself. "No, no let me go to him."

Heather, seeing Fife writhe in agony on the ground, went to help him when she was grabbed around the waist and flung away from him before her hands could touch him, her feet dangling above the ground as her husband held her against him.

Rhys moved a few feet away from the two writhing men and yelled out, "No one touch them."

Fife never looked Nessa's way. He kept his eyes on the Dragon and just before he took his last breath, he choked out, "Victory for Haidar."

The other man said the same before he died.

Rhys called out again. "Do not touch their bodies; they have been poisoned and if you touch them you will die."

Nessa looked up at Pitt, his arms still firm around her. "I do not understand." She shook her head, growing more confused when she heard Rhys issue orders to his warriors that circled Fife's body.

"Let no one, not even animals get near them. The poison will dissipate shortly, and then the bodies can be seen to."

Pitt walked Nessa away from the scene as Rhys continued to talk with the guards.

"I do not understand," Nessa said again when Pitt brought them to a stop away from the crowd that had gathered and was now being dispersed.

Pitt released her, though kept a supportive arm lightly around her. "Fife was a traitor. He was loyal to the man who is after the Dragon."

All color drained from her face and her legs got so weak that she reached out to grab hold of Pitt, but he had already tightened his arm around her and she leaned against him. "He used me, cared nothing for me, and like a fool I believed him."

"Why would you doubt him?" Pitt asked, tucking her closer to him. "None of us did. He played his role well."

Nessa stared at Pitt a moment and as she did tears began to fall once again until she was sobbing uncontrollably. Pitt gathered her up against him and placed his hand to her head, gently resting it on his chest. Then he held her tight and let her cry, feeling her pain far more deeply than he ever felt for any woman.

~~~

"Did I hurt you?" Rhys asked as he distanced them from the crowd that was dispersing and set her feet on the ground, easing his arm from around her.
~~~

Heather stood staring at him a moment, then simply threw her arms around him and buried her face in his shoulder. His arms circled her and held her tight. Her heart thudded in her chest and her stomach roiled not only for what had just happened but for what was to come.

She finally lifted her head and looked at her husband. "I do not want to lose you." She did not say *again*, though she thought it.

"Nor I you," he said.

His words sent her heart beating faster and she looked in his eyes and felt her stomach catch, for just a brief moment she had thought she had seen Quinn in them. Good God, there was no way she could lose him again, never ever again. Fear gripped her as she said, "There is no stopping him. He will come for you."

"He is hungry for revenge. Pitt and I had discovered only a short time ago that Fife was the one spying for Haidar. Plans were being made to watch Fife at all times to see what we could learn. Pitt was keeping an eye on him while waiting for the warrior assigned the first watch."

Heather shook her head. "Why did Fife jump in front of the attacker and save me?"

"You were not the target."

Heather tilted her head in question. "Who was the target?"

"Fife," Rhys said and went on to explain. "It was a suicide mission for both men, though it was probably planned to look as if Fife tried to save

Nessa from an attack. Haidar meant for all to be aware that the Dragon could not protect them from a superior foe. He also knows I am no fool and it was only a matter of time before I realized he had planted a spy amongst my warriors and discovered his identity."

"That was why Fife looked so angry with Nessa when he saw me with her."

"Aye, he would be very angry, for he could not let you die. If he did, he would have failed Haidar."

"I do not understand."

"Haidar will not come for me. He will come for you."

Chapter Twenty-three

Heather could feel herself pale, though his words made perfect sense. She should have realized it sooner herself. Of course, Haidar would want to take from Rhys what he had taken from Haidar. And with all that had been happening lately she had to admit there was a chance he might succeed.

She could not help but smile as an unlikely response tumbled from her lips. "I guess I should stay put when you tell me to."

He tugged her up against him. "He will never get his hands on you."

"I want to believe that, but I have learned in life that *never* is a word *never* to trust."

Thunder rumbled as if in agreement and a splatter of rain hit her cheek.

Rhys's arm dropped off her, though he quickly took hold of her hand. He walked over to the warriors guarding the bodies. "Let the rain soak them, then tie rope around their ankles and drag them into the barn. The poison should be gone by then, but just to be certain, try not to touch their skin."

More rain fell as Rhys hurried his wife along to the keep. He walked her over by the large fireplace in the Great Hall where a fire was burning, the rain having brought a chill with it.

She sat on a bench facing the hearth eager for the heat from the flames, cold having suddenly settled deep in her bones.

Rhys sat beside her after summoning a servant and instructing her to bring wine and ale. He took her hands and feeling the sudden chill, rubbed them between his two. “You are cold.”

She turned her head and said, “My family should be notified of all that is happening.”

“At the moment, they hold no interest for Haidar and I would prefer it remain that way.”

“How can you be sure?”

“Because he has seen that I care not what happens to your family. So he will not waste his time and resources on something that serves no purpose.”

This time when she looked into his eyes, she saw the cold, heartless Dragon staring back at her.

“Your family also does not need to be worrying about you when their concern should be with Greer McLaud. He will soon be upon them, demanding to know of his wife and Saundra. And I have yet to hear if he is aware of his brother’s death, though when he learns of it, I am sure he will blame the Macinnes.” Rhys poured wine for each of them, handing her a tankard. “Drink, it will chase the chill.”

Heather drank, wanting it to also chase her worries.

“You need to trust me, Heather,” he said.

"I do," she said, placing the tankard on the table and turned toward him. "I truly do trust you, Rhys, but I fear that sometimes fate has a way of stepping in and changing things no matter how often we say *never*."

He ran a finger slowly down the side of her face. "Know this now, wife, for I give you my word on it. If anyone was ever to take you away from me, nothing—absolutely nothing—would stop me from getting you back."

Heather smiled. "Then I have nothing to fear, for I know you will keep your word." *Just as you did all those years ago.* Perhaps one day she would finally be able to say it aloud to him.

"I am reluctant to leave you, but I must see to this," Rhys said and took hold of her chin. "I will have your word that you will stay in the keep." Rhys scowled when Heather hesitated to answer. "What is it?"

"I would like to see how Nessa is faring."

Before Rhys could tell her that he would have Pitt bring Nessa to her, Pitt entered the Great Hall, Nessa wrapped around him as if she would never let go.

Pitt approached them. "I cannot leave her alone while I see to my duties."

Heather hurried off the bench, slipping her arm around Nessa to ease her out of Pitt's arms.

Nessa looked at Pitt with such fright that he was leaving her, it tore at his heart.

"Come Nessa," Heather coaxed, "we will have some wine and talk."

Nessa looked at Heather and latched onto her. "I thought Fife cared for me."

Rhys had to grab Pitt by the arm and almost drag him out of the room, he was so reluctant to leave.

Heather sat Nessa on the bench beside her so that the fire's heat could warm her. She was more chilled than Heather had been and she remained much too pale.

"Drink," Heather urged, placing a tankard of wine to her lips and Nessa obeyed without question.

Nessa finally wrapped her hands around the tankard and raised it repeatedly to her own lips. She turned to Heather, tears clouding her eyes. "Forgive me, my lady, I foolishly gave my heart and trust to Fife because I believed he loved me. He followed me around the keep, claiming he missed me and had to be with me as much as possible and being blindly in love I believed him." A tear slipped down her pale cheek. "The Dragon will surely punish me for this."

"The Dragon will not punish you, Nessa. You have my word on that."

After Nessa finished her tankard of wine, she stood. "I must return to my chores."

Heather stood as well. "Not today, Nessa."

"I must," Nessa insisted, "or I will think of nothing else and only grow more upset with myself."

"I have an idea that will help us both, since it is impossible for me to sit and do nothing myself. I will have a couple of Rhys' warriors help us clean out the room on the upper floor stuffed with furniture. They should be only too glad to help since they must watch over me anyway. I can also have the latch repaired so that no one can get locked inside like I did."

"But the Dragon forbids anyone to go up there."

Heather smiled. "The Dragon will be pleased that I am keeping myself occupied in the keep. And I have no doubt that he will quickly be made aware of my intentions and I will learn fast enough if he objects. Besides, I am the lady of the keep and you must follow my order."

"As you say, my lady," Nessa said with a bob of her head and a slight smile.

Heather called out to the two warriors sitting nearby. "I require your help."

They both looked at each other and stood with some reluctance.

"I am not going to run off on you and cause you trouble with the Dragon. Since you both have been tasked with guarding me, I am going to put you to work. I want you to assist me in cleaning out the one room on the upper floor."

They both looked at each other again, before the one turned and spoke. "No one is permitted up there."

"I think the Dragon will permit it since it will keep me tucked safely away in the keep. One of you, go and ask him, while the other will come along with me and Nessa?"

They both shook their heads and the one who spoke before, spoke again. "The Dragon will have our heads if we leave our post."

With a pleasant smile and a gentle tone, she said, "Then I would suggest that you send another warrior to deliver the message, since I am going up there with or without you."

The one warrior went running and the other followed behind Heather and Nessa as they walked to the stairs. The other warrior returned shortly and by the time they reached the upper floor a third warrior appeared.

"My lady," he said with a nod and turned to the two warriors. "The Dragon gives Lady Heather permission to do as she wishes in the room and you are both to help her with whatever tasks she sets for you. I am to stand guard over you all."

"Wonderful," Heather said and grabbed the torch from the sconce and stepped just inside the room. "Your names?" she asked the two warriors who followed her.

"Duff," the shorter of the two said.

"Tam," the other said.

"Well, Duff and Tam, I think we will start with that heavy tapestry on the window." She raised the torch some so they could see it. "I need you both to take it down off the window so that we have some light."

The two men set to the task and with a few sharp tugs the tapestry fell to the floor, flooding the room with what light the stormy sky allowed.

Heather continued instructing the warriors and Nessa, and joined in to help as well, though the three protested. After a while they stopped, realizing their protests were useless, Lady Heather would do as she wished.

Pieces of furniture that were rotting from age were used to start a fire, in the small fireplace and chase the damp chill from the room.

Heather was making her way toward the corner of the room, having spotted a planked coffer chest she thought she could put to use when she saw Nessa pick up the cradle that had caught Heather's eye when she had first gazed upon this space. "Place the cradle aside, Nessa. I think it will serve as a good gift for Bea and Douglas for when their babe is born."

"That is generous of you, Lady Heather," Nessa said and handed it over to Duff.

Heavy chairs scarred with age seemed to stand as sentinels, keeping her from getting to the coffer. Tam was quick to come to her aid and began clearing the way.

Heather was relieved to see Nessa's cheeks full of color and tears no longer clouding her eyes. This task kept her too busy to think of Fife and how he had shattered her heart and trust. She knew it would take time for Nessa to recover from this horrible ordeal.

As soon as Tam moved the last chair out of her way, Heather approached the coffer with a smile. It was just what she needed to hold the many garments that overflowed the small chest in her bedchamber.

She reached out as she took another step closer and the next thing she knew the floor gave way beneath her and she plummeted down with it.

"Oh my God, Lady Heather," Nessa screamed as she disappeared before Nessa's eyes.

The two warriors ran to the hole in the floor and when the warrior who stood guard outside the door ran in, Duff shouted, "Get the Dragon!"

"Lady Heather, are you all right? Can you hear me?" Tam called down into the hole.

"I can hear you," Heather called back. "I am fine." At least she thought she was, since she felt no true pain.

"I am coming down there to get you out," Tam yelled.

"No," she yelled back. "Get me the torch." She almost shouted with excitement, believing she discovered the secret passage, but bit her tongue. Rhys did not want anyone to know about it.

"I will bring the torch down to you," Tam said.

"No, that is not advisable. The boards are soft beneath my feet and if you drop down onto them, I fear we may go straight through."

"The Dragon will see that Duff and I suffer more than a fall if we leave you down there alone, and he will be here soon."

"Nessa," she shouted and the next thing she knew the torch was falling down the hole, and Heather was quick to snatch it up.

"Are you a fool, woman?" Duff shouted.

"Lady Heather gave an order and I obeyed."

"You better have had good reason to do so," Rhys said sharply as he entered the room with the force of a swirling storm. When he saw Tam and Duff bent over the hole in the floor, his stomach clenched and he shouted, "Heather!"

"I am down here, Rhys," she called out.

Rhys rushed to the hole, the sight of him in all black, his brow narrowed, and his eyes blazing, caused the two warriors to hurry out of his way.

Rhys peered over the edge and relief ran through him when he saw her standing there, with the torch held over her head. Her face was smudged with dirt as were her garments, but she looked to be unharmed.

"Stand back. I am coming down to fetch you out of there."

"Lady Heather says the boards are too soft beneath her feet or we would have had her fetched out already," Tam explained.

"It is good you explained that. Now I will not have to punish you for leaving my wife down in a dark hole."

"Tam and Duff have been very helpful and quick to want to get me out of here. Please do not be angry with them."

Rhys looked down at his wife again and ignoring her plea, said, "Move to the side."

"So you can fall through the boards? I think not."

"What did you say to me?"

Duff and Tam stepped further away from the Dragon and Nessa stepped closer to the door.

"I am not moving," Heather shouted the glare from the torch making it difficult to see his face clearly, but that did not matter. She was familiar with the look of the fire-breathing Dragon.

"Move! Now!" Rhys's voice rumbled with anger.

"I will not see you hurt," she shouted back.

Rhys was about to let her know that was not for her to decide when he heard a noise. "What was that?" he called down to her.

Before his wife could answer him, he heard it again and knew. It was the sound of the boards cracking. "Move, Heather!" he yelled.

The boards gave out before she could flee and suddenly his wife was gone and all he saw was the torch flickering as it spiraled downward in the dark and her scream raced up at him.

"RHYS!"

The Dragon did not hesitate. He dropped down in the hole after his wife.

Chapter Twenty-four

Rhys twisted so that his body would take the impact of the fall rather than his legs and he was surprised when he landed on something softer than he expected. Though there was a jolt to his body, it did not stop him from hurrying to his feet and looking around for his wife.

He spotted the torch a short distance away and was grateful it still held its flame. He hurried over and snatched it off the floor, seeing that he stood on thick wood planking. He swung the torch up above his head to cast a wider light so that he could find his wife and when he spotted her prone body face down, fear gripped at his heart and he let out a slew of curses as he hurried over to her.

His arm brushed across something in the stone wall as he reached her. It was a metal sconce and he rested the torch in it before dropping down beside his wife. He had stopped praying a long time ago, so it was not a prayer that rushed to his lips but a warning that if anything happened to her, he would rage war on the heavens.

With a gentle touch, he turned her over on her back and was relieved to see her stir. “Heather,” he said forcefully, and then more sternly, “Heather, open your eyes.” For once, she listened to him and opened her eyes.

A smile slowly surfaced, seeing Quinn staring at her, his dark eyes full of concern and anger. *Anger*? Quinn rarely grew angry. She was about to ask him what was wrong, when he snapped at her.

"Do not dare move until I see if you suffered any harm."

"Rhys," she said softly, recalling what had happened and not surprised to see him there. "You followed me down the hole."

He leaned closer to her. "I would follow you to hell if necessary, though I do not believe they would want you there, since you would not obey the devil himself."

"I obeyed you; I remained in the keep."

"And when I told you to move?"

"I did not want you to get hurt," she said and attempted to sit up. Pain shot through her shoulder and she let out a moan.

Rhys let out another slew of curses beneath his breath for arguing with her when he should be tending her, and he snapped, "Do not move!" And when he saw a tear gather in the corner of her one eye, he silently cursed himself again and went against his own command. He gently slipped his arms under her and lifted her onto his lap to sit back against the stone wall and cradle her in his arms.

She rested her head on his chest with a sigh.

"You are in pain?" he asked.

"Only my shoulder," she said, wincing as she gave the shoulder not tucked against him a lift.

"Do not move it," he ordered.

"It probably took the brunt of my fall and is already bruising."

Rhys brought his hand up to rest on her shoulder, then caressed it slowly to see if he could feel anything.

Heather almost sighed aloud with how pleasurable his tender touch felt until he touched one particular spot. Pain shot through it, and she bit back the gasp that hurried to rush out. She did not want Rhys to know. He would forbid her to do anything but rest and she wanted to do anything but that.

"I do not feel anything. Nothing else pains you?"

"Nothing, but what of you?" she asked concerned that he had suffered an injury in the fall.

"I am fine," he insisted and moved his hand off her shoulder to rest at her waist. He wanted nothing more than to simply sit there and hold her and know she was unharmed.

"Are you certain?"

He squeezed at her waist. "I will let you run your hands all over my naked body and see for yourself as soon as we get out of here."

The image of her doing just that had her saying, "We should hurry and leave here."

"First, we must determine where *here* is."

Heather brought her head up off his chest and looked around. "Is this the secret passage?"

"I am assuming it is, though the lack of care and age has taken a toll on it."

Heather got to her feet with some help from her husband and they both stood and looked around. Their fall had been cushioned by a pile of blankets and a variety of garments. Heather yanked one out, holding up a cloak and seeing it had been a feast for rodents with its many holes. She tossed it back on the pile.

After taking in all of the small space, Rhys said, "From the looks of it, this is a spot where the family could wait out a siege in relative safety and take their leave if it should prove necessary. Time, dampness, and lack of care took its toll on the wood."

Heather dropped her head back to look up through the hole. "How far do you think we dropped?"

"Most times you find thicker wood planks closer to the bottom of the keep than the top, so I would say we are somewhere nearer the bottom."

"Rhys!" The strong shout echoed down the hole.

It was Pitt and Rhys shouted back to him. "We are good and looking for the way out."

"I will wait, though not long," Pitt yelled to him.

"He will send men?" Heather asked.

"If it takes too long for us to find our way out of here, then warriors will start dropping through the hole."

"Then we should hurry and save them the fall. Besides I need to touch every inch of you to make certain you are unharmed."

Damn if he did not grow aroused at the thought of her doing just that and he reached out and grabbed her arm just as she took a step away. She gasped and shut her eyes against the pain and he got angry at himself and her. "You are not being truthful with me. Your shoulder suffered worse than you told me."

"It truly is not that bad. It is the thought of you ordering me to rest that proves more painful and has me holding my tongue."

Rhys stepped closer to her and dusted dirt from her braid, his fingertips grazing her breasts which of course stirred his arousal even more and flared his annoyance.

Heather laid a hand on his chest and hurried to speak before he could. "Believe me, Rhys, I am fine. I would not lie to you about that."

He placed his hand over hers. "I will have your word on that, wife."

"You have my word."

He gave her a quick kiss, not trusting himself to linger. "Good, then let us find our way out of here so you can find out for yourself if I suffered any wounds." She smiled and he took her hand, then grabbed thc torch from the sconce. "Follow close behind me."

They made their way along a brief narrow passage that led out of the room to wood stairs.

Rhys turned to Heather and said, “Wait here until I see if the stairs hold.”

Heather waited and watched as her husband took the stairs slowly and disappeared beyond the curve, leaving her in complete darkness. It was not long before light filtered around the curve and Rhys returned.

“One of the steps not far from the bottom has rotted away and a few creak loudly so be careful, tread lightly.”

Heather followed behind him, his pace slow and cautious.

“Wait here,” he said just before he came to a stop and she did as he said. He extended his leg, clearing three steps at once, then he placed the torch in a sconce on the stone wall. He turned and reached his hands out to her. “Jump.”

She did not hesitate; she jumped into his arms. He caught her around the waist, holding her firm as he swung her away from the steps and lowered her to her feet. Her hands rested on his forearms and she gave them a squeeze and she did not know why, but she felt the urge to tell him, “I love you, Rhys.”

He stilled, suddenly unable to move.

“Whether you ever love me or not, does not matter. I will love you always,” she said and kissed his cheek softly.

“Why?”

“Why not?”

“That is not an answer,” he argued.

"But it is. Why would I not love you? There is nothing to stop me from loving you." She squeezed his arms again. "And there is nothing to stop you from loving me."

"You ask too—"

She hurried to press her fingers to his lips, forcing him silent. "I ask nothing of you. Simply give whatever you wish to me as I will to you. I love you and nothing is ever going to change that."

He brushed her hand aside. "We will see."

He turned and reminded, "Stay close."

One day. One day, she thought as she followed along, *he will tell me he loves me.*

After several twists and turns and jumps into Rhys' arms, they came to a dark tunnel. The entrance yawned like a giant's mouth in front of them.

Rhys held the torch high. "Dirt walls and wood beams."

"Will this take us away from the castle?" Heather asked, peering around his shoulder.

"We shall find out." He turned his head toward her. "The tunnel appears narrow and may get narrower. Keep your hand on my back at all times, so I know you are there behind me and in case we lose the light."

The scent of earth grew stronger and stronger as the passageway grew so narrow that Rhys's shoulders brushed the dirt walls, sending some of the dirt flying into her face.

Try as she might to ignore that the walls seemed to be closing in on her, she was not able to and with fear in her voice, she called out, "Rhys!"

He stopped and eased himself sideways and she immediately tucked herself under the crook of his arm, planted her head against his chest and wrapped her arms around his waist, and there she stayed.

Rhys felt her body tremble and knew her fear. He had experienced the same gripping fear himself the first time he had entered a similar narrow passage. But there was little room to console her here and little time to linger.

"How can you walk this barely passable corridor with no fear?" she asked, fighting the fear that any minute the walls would collapse around them and bury them alive.

"Fear was forced out of me through the years."

"I cannot believe that fear does not touch you in this confined space," she said and shivered.

He ran his hand down her arm and covered her hand that hugged at his waist. "I was forced to stand in a corridor such as this one with a line of men in front of me and behind me for endless days, shortly after I was sold to Haidar. Scraps of food and drink were passed down the line once a day. If you were lucky, some of it reached you. Those who seemed to lose their minds as the days went on were quickly disposed of by the person in front of him or the person behind him, sometimes both. The body would be kicked down the line beneath everyone's bare feet until it reached the opening where it was removed. Those who survived began training to be one of Haidar's infamous slave warriors. I was one of the unlucky ones—I survived."

"Do not say that," Heather scolded, easing away from him with tears glistening in her eyes at the horror he had endured. "Never, ever say that."

He reached out and wiped at the tears that were yet to spill. "I prayed for courage, then I prayed for death, then I stopped praying, but now that I am with you...I am glad I survived."

"We must hurry and get you out of here," she said, giving him a slight push.

"Me?" he asked with a slight smile.

"Aye, you do not need to relive such a horrible ordeal. We must get you out of here. Now hurry along," she said with a wave of her hand.

"Stay close," he reminded again as he turned slowly away from her.

"Always," she said and latched on to the hem of his leather armor.

After a few more feet, the corridor narrowed to the point that Rhys was forced to walk sideways and her heart went out to him when he looked at her with concern.

"Can you manage this?"

"If you can, so can I," she said and eased herself sideways.

He slipped his hand in hers and they made their way slowly along the corridor until suddenly the passage widened and brought them out into a small area. The walls in there were constructed of wood planking, though much of it had rotted. A ladder was braced against one wall and it lead up to what appeared to be a trap door.

Rhys turned to Heather. “You need to stay down here while I go see what is up there. If for any reason I do not return after a short time, you are to go back the way we came and wait for my warriors, though you will probably meet them on the way.” His voice turned stern. “I mean it, Heather, give me your word or I will pull the ladder up after me.”

“I will not come up after you,” she said, of course that did not include going up the ladder with the purpose of finding a way out, but she did not tell him that.

Rhys climbed the ladder and eased the latched door open slowly, then quickly disappeared up through it.

Heather waited in the dark, thinking about what Rhys had told her. She could not imagine standing in a confined corridor for days in the dark with no way out. She did not know how he had not gone mad. There did not seem to be an end to this Haidar’s cruelty, and she prayed she would never meet him.

“Heather!”

Rhys’ shout brought a smile to her face and she looked up at him peering down through the opening. “Climb up.”

She eagerly climbed each rung, grabbing onto a rope that dangled from a hook by the ceiling beam to help hoist herself further up the rungs. It struck her as she climbed that he had not mentioned if it was safe and before she neared the top, she whispered, "Is it safe?"

Rhys was impressed that she should ask. "At the moment it is, though I do not know for how long, so we must hurry."

Heather did just that, taking the last few rungs as quickly as possible, Rhys taking hold of her hand and helping her through the opening. She took a look around and saw that it was a single-room cottage that had fallen into disrepair. Dark gray clouds drifted by the gaping hole in the thatched roof, though thankfully no rain fell.

Rhys kept his voice low when he spoke. "I ran across this cottage when I first explored this land. We are a distance into the woods that runs along the side of the keep. Once the warriors who are posted in this area spot us they will hurry to guard us. We must move fast, the closer to the keep, the more guards."

"If you think danger awaits us, why not wait here for your warriors?"

"Fife died a short time after I learned that he was a loyal servant to Haidar, which means Haidar has watchful eyes on us at all times. If he learns of what is going on, there is no telling what he may do. And while we wait here for the warriors who follow us, we could be greeted by an unstoppable force of

Haidar's warriors when we finally do leave. It is better we make haste now." He dropped the torch down the opening. "My warriors will know to follow." He took her hand. "You will stay in front of me at all times and if by chance we are separated, you are to run screaming as fast and as loud as you can so my warriors will hear you."

Heather nodded.

Rhys took hold of her chin. "I can see in your eyes that you have no intentions of leaving me no matter what happens. There are times we must do what we do not want to. This is one of those times. You will leave me if necessary."

"And will you leave me if necessary? And do not bother to tell me that that is different, for if you will not leave me, then I will not leave you."

"We have no time to argue this."

"Then we best leave now and be done with it."

Rhys shook his head. "When I get you back to the keep—"

"Do not remind me, for I grow wet just thinking about how I am going to touch every inch of you," she said and headed to the door that hung half open.

He hurried over to her to let her know it would be quite different if he got his hands on her first when he heard it and so did Heather.

"It is too silent," Heather whispered, just realizing how eerily silent it had suddenly got. "No animals run or birds sing. Something disturbs them."

"They sense something evil lies in wait," he said.

"Then we best hurry and make haste."

Rhys' brow narrowed. "It is too late. Haidar is here."

Chapter Twenty-five

Rhys blocked the partially open door with his body.

"I am not leaving you," Heather said, though her blood ran cold with fear, knowing how evil Haidar could be.

There was no time to argue with her. Rhys scooped her up, carried her to the hole and dropped her down into it, hoping the fall caused her no harm. He then quickly snatched the ladder up out of the hole and shut the trap door. Then he went to face his nemesis.

Heather recalled the dangling rope just in time and swung her hand out hoping to grab hold of it, and she did. Pain ripped through her shoulder, but she did her best to ignore it. She swung around so that she could brace her feet against the wood plank wall as she pulled herself, with some difficulty, higher up along the rope. She lowered her feet once her hand touched the trap door. She let herself hang there a moment, regaining her strength, and then she used her shoulder, gratefully not the sore one, to push open the door.

It was a struggle once the door was open to work her way through it and when she finally did, she lay on the floor breathless, though not for long. She forced herself to her feet, remaining crouched down as best she could so as not to be seen and took a moment to shove the ladder back down the hole in hopes that Rhys' warriors would soon arrive.

Remaining crouched down, she worked her way to a hole in the wall behind the partially open door and peered through it.

She was able to see her husband and the man he faced. While Rhys stood alone, his enemy did not and fear gripped her heart when she saw the many warriors standing behind Haidar. He was nothing like Heather expected. But then what was a man who was capable of such horrifying evil and enslaving so many supposed to look like? He was a head shorter than Rhys and his body was thick in the waist. His hair was dark and long and drawn back and he wore a full beard. His features were not unattractive, but then neither were they memorable. He wore dark garments with a sash around his tunic and he held himself in a regal manner.

It was when she focused on his dark eyes and heard him speak, his accent foreign to her that a shiver ran through her. It was as if the devil himself spoke and this time Heather quivered with fear.

"You disappoint me, Rhys," Haidar said. "And you know how I repay those who disappoint me."

"You no longer rule over me, Haidar, so have your say and take your leave."

Haidar's voice took on a threatening tone that would shiver the bravest of men. "Not until I get what I have come to this barbaric country for...revenge for taking my wife and unborn child.

And please do not bother to deny it. It took some time, but imagine my disappointment, my pain, and my anger when I discovered that you had taken Anala. I do not think you want to know how I felt when I learned that she died giving birth," —he paused— "to my only son and that he died along with her."

Rhys continued to remain silent.

Haidar smiled. "I remember well how often I made you fornicate with the slave women and how often I took pleasure in watching you do so. Two, three, you even did four slaves for me in one night. I imagine you take your wife that often, which means she will be with child soon." His smile faded. "I am going to take what you took from me—your pregnant wife. And if she has a daughter I will see the child dead, but if she has a son, I will raise him as a fine slave. Then I will see that she gives me many sons, if not...I will see her die a slow death."

"I am going to kill you," Rhys said.

Haidar laughed. "That is not possible."

"I believe that is what you told me when I asked what I must do to win my freedom."

Haidar's smile faded. "Your wife will be mine. Your child will be mine. And perhaps if your wife pleases me enough—you have taught her to take you in her mouth, have you not? If not I will give her daily lessons. As I was saying, if she satisfies me—in various way—I will spare you a slow, agonizing death and kill you quickly in front of her."

"Your death will be fast, though more painful than you ever imagined," Rhys said.

"You do not have the courage it would take to kill me."

Rhys took a step toward him. "I have something more powerful than courage—I have hate!"

Haidar smiled. "That is what I am counting on."

He signaled his men and they soon were gone, leaving Rhys' warriors to find him standing alone when they burst out of the cottage one after the other until several circled him. More of his warriors suddenly spilled out of the woods, forming another protective barrier around him.

Rhys did not question how they got up through the trap door with the ladder gone. They had been trained to escape from various difficult places and situations. He was more concerned with his wife, having dropped her down the hole, the fall a far better fate than being taken by Haidar. And when his warriors had come across her, they would have seen that she remained there until he gave orders otherwise.

He was however, eager to know that she had not been harmed in the fall. He turned to one of his warriors and asked, "Lady Heather waits unharmed beneath the cottage?"

"Lady Heather was not there," the warrior said.

With a sharp order for his men to move, they parted quickly, clearing a path for him to hurry along and into the cottage. Rhys gave a quick look around and got no response when he called out her name. How could she have gotten up here if he had taken the ladder away? He shook his head. His wife was a resourceful woman, so if she did make it back to this room where would she be and why not answer him?

He turned his head and looked at the partially open door. If she had been hiding behind it this whole time, then she had heard every word between him and Haidar. He stepped around the door and there in the shadows of the corner, crouched down, her arms hugging herself tightly, and her face paler than he had ever seen it...was his wife.

Rhys bent over and scooped her up into his arms and before pressing her tightly against him, her arms eagerly went around his neck, then she buried her face against his chest as if she was attempting to hide away.

One step out of the cottage and his men once again circled him, and it was not until they reached the keep's stairs that his warriors dispersed, though they lingered close by.

Pitt burst out of the keep as Rhys took the stairs up two at a time.

"Seal that passageway so that it can never be entered at either end ever again," Rhys ordered as Pitt yanked the door open for him. "Haidar made himself known. We will talk later."

"Anything you need?" Pitt asked as they walked through the Great Hall.

"Time alone with my wife."

"I will see that you are not disturbed," Pitt said and went to do the Dragon's bidding.

Once inside their bedchamber, Rhys sat on the bed, continuing to hold his wife. He said nothing; he simply held her. She had heard things she should have never heard and learned things about him she should have never learned. And the worse part was that she would never forget what she heard, it would forever haunt her.

"I am so sorry, Quinn" she whispered against his chest.

He drew back, forcing her to raise her head and look at him. "What did you say?"

"Quinn. I realized who you were a short time after arriving here," she said. "The more I learn about your horrible ordeal, the more I realize why you have kept the truth from me. But it is not necessary any longer, I love you. I have always loved you and will always love you, no matter what."

He set her on her feet and walked away from her. "I am not Quinn."

"There is no reason to hide who you are from me."

He turned to her, anger and sorrow filling his eyes. "Quinn died, I buried him myself."

"No, you are my Quinn. It breaks my heart to know you were enslaved and suffered so horribly and I am so very grateful that you have returned to me."

"I am not Quinn. He tried to survive. His heart ached to see you again and his love for you never wavered. He was desperate to get back to you, but he was not strong enough. It was my word I gave him the night he lay dying that brought me here."

Heather shook her head. "No, you are my Quinn, I know you are."

"Quinn is dead. He is never coming back."

Tears ran down her cheeks as she rushed over to him and pounded his chest repeatedly with her small fists. "No! No! You are lying. You are Quinn! Quinn! Quinn! Please God—tell me you are Quinn!"

Rhys let her pound at him and when she stopped, her sobs nearly robbing her of breath, he lifted her up into his arms and carried her to the bed. He laid her down and climbed in beside her, easing her on her side to rest back against him. He wrapped his arm around her and rested his leg over her two, keeping her as tightly pressed against him as he could, and then he listened to her cry herself to sleep.

~~~
~~~

Heather woke with a wince and rolled off her sore shoulder. She jumped when a crack of thunder sounded. Rain tapped at the window and gray skies lingered. The dreary weather matched her thoughts and she pulled the blanket tighter around her.

She was relieved to find herself alone. She was far too confused and upset to see or speak to anyone, especially her husband. She had been so sure that Rhys was Quinn. Had she been so upset about being wed to the Dark Dragon that she saw something that was never there? Had she wanted Quinn so badly to return to her that she imagined she saw him in Rhys? Or could she be right?

I buried him myself.

The words stung her heart. Could it be true? Was Quinn dead and buried in a foreign land? She fought back her tears.

Shed your tears for the dead and be done with it. Life is for the living.

An old woman at her mum's burial had said that to her and she had done just that that day. But then she had had her two sisters and father to look after and a keep to run. There had been no time for tears. She had however shed tears for Quinn throughout the years, for she had not known if he was alive or dead.

Was it time to be done with Quinn and get on living? She got out of bed, the wood planks cool against her bare feet and went and retrieved the ring she had hidden when she first arrived here. She cupped it in her hand and went to stoop down by the hearth's flames to look at it. Quinn had made it for her and slipped it on her finger just before he left.

This ring is a symbol of my love for you and a promise that I will return and make you my wife.

He had said those words to her when he slipped the ring on her finger. She had worn the ring on her finger every day since then, until her betrothal to Rogan. She had removed it and strung it on the blue ribbon to wear around her neck.

She stared at the plain metal band that had held such promise and meant so much to her through the years.

The door opened and Rhys entered. Heather did not try to hide the ring from him as he walked over to her.

His dark eyes went to her cupped hand and he crouched down beside her. He snatched the ring from her hand, stared at it for several moments, then tossed it in the flames.

Heather went to grab for it, but his hand quickly closed around her wrist.

"You need it no more," he said and yanked her to her feet prepared to face her anger. He did not expect to be met with silence or the gentle look in her lovely green eyes. And the more she remained standing there silent, the more he ached to kiss her.

As if she knew his need, she rose up on her toes and with a brush of her lips across his, whispered, "Make me yours?"

"It is the Dragon you get and no other," he warned, growing harder by the second.

"It is the Dragon I want," she said and stepped away from him to stripe off her garments.

He watched her every move, his lips thirsting for her rosy nipples as her breasts fell free and as her garment slipped further down over her curved hips to reveal the triangle of blonde hair between her legs, he lost what little control he had.

He tore off his garments, reached out, and snagged her around the waist to lift her in his arms and carry her to the bed. He dropped her down on it and spread her legs, burying his face between them.

Heather gasped when his tongue began to tease her senseless. Her passion soared with every lick and stroke of his tongue, and she grasped the bedding, squeezing it tight as she dropped her head back and moaned aloud. Her moan grew when his hand slipped along her stomach to her breast to play with her nipple, rolling it between his fingers and squeezing lightly before giving it a sharp pinch that set her whole body quivering.

"Rhys!" she cried out.

He rose up on his knees and slipped his arms under her legs and pulled her toward him, sliding into her easily. And as he plunged deeper inside her, he said, "You are mine, Heather. You will always be mine."

It did not take her long to scream as she climaxed hard and fast.

"No!" she cried out, feeling on the verge of another climax as Rhys pulled out of her.

She cried out again when he grabbed her around the waist and pulled her off the bed and sat on the edge, for her to straddle him. She gasped as he sheathed himself inside her and planted his hands on her backside.

"Ride me," he ordered as he squeezed her bottom and set her to riding him hard.

Having been near to climaxing for a second time, it did not take long before she felt herself on the verge of doing so again. And just as it drew nearer and nearer, Rhys' fingers moved between her legs and stroked in just the right spot. She burst so hard in climax that she thought for a moment she would faint. She dropped her brow to his, her breathing rapid as tingles of pleasures raced through her over and over and over while Rhys squeezed her bottom and continued slamming her against him again and again, making her climax last.

She sighed and took his face in her hands and kissed him with what strength she had left. Then with her brow still resting against his said, "You have yet to come."

"One time will not be enough," he said and nipped gently at her bottom lip.

Her body shuddered. "I am yours Rhys, do as you wish."

"That is a dangerous thing to say to me, wife."

"Will you hurt me?"

"Never," he snapped.

"Then I have nothing to fear, but much to enjoy."

With his hands firm on her backside, he stood and she instinctively wrapped her legs around him and her arms went around his back. He kept her tight against him and walked to brace her back against the wall. Then he drove into her hard and fast and after a few minutes he buried his face in her chest and groaned long and hard as he climaxed.

Heather gripped the back of his neck with one hand, holding herself against him as his groan seemed to go on forever. His body finally stilled and his groan faded. She remained as she was, letting him linger in the pleasure of his climax and fearing if she moved he would know he had sparked her passion again.

She wondered if she was wicked wanting him as much as she did or enjoying him as much as she did.

He walked to the bed and to her regret pulled out of her before lowering her down and dropping down on his side next to her. His hand went to her breast to give it a gentle squeeze, then his finger began to slowly trace circles around her nipple.

"Passion still sparks in you."

"Is that wrong?" she asked anxiously

He smiled. “No, wife, it is not wrong. It is a good thing.” His finger moved to trace her lips. “Never keep it from me. Never be afraid to let me know you want me.”

She took hold of his finger. “You will do the same? You will let me know when you want me.”

Laughter rumbled along with his words. “I want you all the time.”

“I feel the same,” she said, releasing his finger, to trace her own over his chest. She stopped suddenly and stared questioningly at him.

Rhys dropped on his back. “What does your curiosity want to know that you are not sure if you should ask?”

Heather turned on her side to face him. “You are getting to know me well.”

“Very well.” He smiled and poked her gently between her legs.

“How many women have you been forced to be with?”

“Too many. I knew none before I was enslaved. I was one of the stronger slaves so I was given a chance to become one of Haidar’s slave warriors, not that I had a choice. I learned that Haidar expected his warriors to be exceptional in all things. So he made certain we trained hours on end. Once my training was done and I was part of Haidar’s elite slave warriors, I thought the forced performances were all behind me. But they were just beginning.”

“How did you finally win your freedom?”

"There was only one way...complete the task Haidar set. It was an impossible one, since he had no intentions of freeing any of his slave warriors, especially those who served him well."

"And you served him well?"

"Too well."

Heather heard the regret in his voice and she could not imagine the hell he must have suffered.

"Haidar set the difficult task." —he turned silent for a moment— "I accomplished it. He had no choice but to free me since he gave his word."

"What was the task?"

Rhys turned on his side. "That my wife, I will never tell you. And with your curiosity settled we will never speak of these things again."

She poked him in the chest, smiling. "Remember what I told you about *never*."

"And remember I told you that my word is law."

She let her hand drift over his chest and down along his stomach as she spoke, "And I am to obey."

He laughed. "Something you have yet to succeed at." His laugh faded when her hand slipped further down to take hold of him. He shut his eyes when she kissed his chest while her hand brought him to life.

Hc lovcd thc fccl of her lips on him and the way she squeezed him tight and tugged on him, growing him ever harder. Her kisses turned to nips and fueled his need for her even more.

It was when he watched her face dip between his legs that he reacted. He grabbed her and yanked her up against his chest. "You will not take me in your mouth."

"Why?"

"I will not have you learning that skill...yet."

"Because of what Haidar said to you about teaching it to me?" She shook her head. "I will know the taste of you and you alone and I will not let that evil man stop me from loving my husband." He looked ready to deny her and she quickly kissed him. "Please, Rhys, let me do this. Do not let him take this from us."

He kissed her gently and nodded, and she smiled. It was not long after that the Dragon let loose a tremendous roar.

They spent the rest of the day in bed, had supper brought to their chamber and the Dragon fell asleep long before his wife. When she was sure he slept soundly, she eased herself out of bed.

With light footfalls, she went to the fireplace, grabbed a slim piece of kindling from the basket and poked at the ashes with it. It took a few minutes to find what she searched for and she glanced now and then at the bed to make sure her husband slept.

Finally, she found it and used the kindling stick to drag it out from the embers. She let the ring sit on the hearth stone to cool before picking it up and wiping it off. She knew it would not burn; it was not meant to.

She looked over at her sleeping husband. He had not asked her about the ring when he saw it. Why? He had no way of knowing who had given her that ring. It could have belonged to her mother. He knew the ring when he saw it or else he would not have told her that she needed it no more.

She slipped it back into its hiding spot and walked over to the bed and looked down at her husband sleeping soundly, and whispered, "Quinn."

Chapter Twenty-six

Rhys sat by the hearth in the Great Hall alone. He had woken and not been able to return to sleep and so he had left his bed not wanting to disturb his wife. Sunrise was a couple of hours away so not a soul stirred in the keep, except for those guards he had posted that no one could see.

For the moment his wife was safe, but not for long. Haidar was bent on revenge, nothing would stop him. Rhys had known this time would come, though he had planned differently for it. Haidar would have been seen to before he wed Heather, so that Haidar could not use her against him, but her betrothal to Rogan MacClennan had forced him to change his plan. Her abduction had been necessary to prevent her from wedding MacClennan, and the unrest between the McLauds and Macinnes also altered his plans even more.

The time would come that he would see Haidar dead. His concern was that the evil man would find a way to capture his wife and it might take Rhys time to reach her. Minutes mattered with Haidar, for Rhys knew far too well the hell the evil man could put someone through in a very short time. And he could not bear to think of what he would do to Heather.

Rhys shook his head as a smile surfaced. Only Heather could break through his dark thoughts and make him smile, something he never thought he would do again. But the one thing she did that had truly surprised him was that she had awakened his heart. And damn if he was not feeling what it was like to love again.

He leaned forward on the bench, bracing his elbows on the tops of his bent knees and locking his fingers to rest his chin on. Truths could be painful and he did not want to hurt her, but he could not let her continue to believe that Quinn was alive.

It was in a dark, dank cell, the groans of dying men surrounding him and the stench so bad it made you want to die that Quinn took his last breath. He was gone; he would never return to Heather.

It was the Dragon who would protect her, make love to her, give her many children...love her. She had penetrated his darkness and to his surprise had infused it with light and love, an impossible feat and yet she had managed to do it.

The sound of footfalls entering the room broke through his thoughts and he waited as they approached him quietly. He listened to her every movement and when she was close enough, he turned, his arm stretching out to snag his wife around the waist and hoist her over the table and onto his lap.

Heather laughed softly. "I thought for sure you had not heard me."

"I will always hear you." He kissed her briefly, though with strength that left her wanting more.

"You think that a kiss?" she chastised with a twinkle in her eyes. "Or perhaps the Dragon's wife exhausted him last night and he is just not *up* to it."

"I think my wife needs to be taught a lesson," he said and flipped her over his knees so fast that she had no time to even gasp in shock.

She slipped out of his grasp just before his hand met her backside and she laughed as she danced away from him. "I will not let you take your hand to me."

He laughed as well. "You think you can stop me?"

"I am swift on my feet."

"Not swift enough to escape the Dragon." He jumped toward her and she ran form the Great Hall laughing. He laughed himself, for no matter how swiftly she ran, he would always catch her.

He went after her and reached her when she got to the top of the stairs to their bedchamber and scooped her up, tossing her over his shoulder.

She squealed with laughter and playfully pounded his back. His hand came down on her backside, but much too softly and Heather smiled. It turned to a gasp when his hand found its way under her nightdress to caress her backside.

"You do not play fair," she said.

"You are right, I do not play fair."

This time it was a groan that hurried past her lips when he ran his finger down between her buttocks, to dip in between her legs and tease her with his finger.

Once inside their bedchamber, the door closed, he dropped her on her stomach on the bed and before she could turn over, he stretched out on top of her. He nipped playfully at the back of her neck, his teeth taking sharps bites that sent shivers through her.

"Stay as you are wife, I am not done punishing you." He felt her soft laughter ripple through her body, though he soon changed it to a shiver as he ripped her nightdress off her. He kissed and nipped along every inch of her naked back and when he started to do the same to her backside, the shiver changed to a moan.

She was a delectable morsel and he could taste her forever, but he was hard and aching and he wanted inside her. He stripped off his garments before yanking her up on her hands and knees and entered her with such a hard thrust that her whole body jolted.

He thought he had hurt her and it was the last thing he wanted to do. He was about to ease out of her when she pushed back against him, forcing him deeper inside her. He smiled. She was as hungry for this as he was, and hc slammed against her.

He kept a firm hold on her backside as he plunged in and out of her, their bodies pounding against each other, their groans filling the room, and their climaxes building rapidly.

They climaxed together, Heather calling out his name and Rhys biting his tongue so the words would not spill out.

Good God, Heather but I love you!

When they were both spent, Rhys took her in his arms and they lay wrapped around each other. In minutes, Heather fell asleep and Rhys followed soon after. And surprisingly, he felt a tingle of something he had not felt in a very long time...fear. He feared losing his wife and her love, and he swore to himself he would never ever let that happen.

~~~

"What do you mean you do not know where Lady Heather is?" Rhys asked, bolting out of his chair and Pitt doing the same beside him.

Duff took a step back. "Lady Heather was right here in the Great Hall a minute ago. The warriors guarding the door did not see her. She did not pass Tam standing guard by the stairs. I took a look in the kitchen and she is not there. She just disappeared."

Rhys slapped his hands down on the dais table. "People simple do not disappear."

Pitt shook his head at the young warrior in warning. He knew exactly what he was going to say and it was the wrong thing at the wrong time. Rhys
~~~

would not want to hear his warrior remind him that the Dragon was adapt at doing just that, being there one minute and gone the next.

"Nessa!" Rhys shouted and the servant lass jumped and hurried over to the Dragon. "Have you seen Lady Heather?"

"No, my lord, the last time I saw Lady Heather she was here in the Great Hall."

"A room full of ghost warriors and my wife vanishes in front of them all." Rhys shouted.

"That would include you too," Pitt said with a smile.

"Perhaps I should have a pit dug just so I can toss you back into one."

Pitt sobered his expression, though a smile still threatened to break free and he took a step closer to Rhys. "It seems your wife has done what others could not...she has touched your heart," he said for Rhys' ears alone. "Scowl if you will, but you cannot deny the truth." He did not wait for a response, he turned and called out. "Find Lady Heather now, she could not have gone far."

Pitt walked around the dais to Nessa. "A thought on where she might be?"

Nessa felt more uncomfortable than ever around Pitt ever since the incident with Fife a few days ago. She had made certain to avoid him as much as possible, but it had bccn difficult since he was around more often than not. She had been grateful for his consoling embrace, but she also felt foolish for having been such a fool.

"She has been keeping close to the keep since the day she mistakenly found the secret passage. So, I do not believe she wandered off. She would stay close by."

A servant entered with a tray of sweet cakes and followed behind Rhys as he went to speak with one of his warriors. "My lord," he called out.

Rhys turned sharply and the young servant cringed and stumbled back away from him.

"What do you want?" Rhys snapped.

The servant kept his head bowed as he extended the tray out to him. "Lady Heather instructed me to see that you got a sweet cake or two."

"Where is she?" Rhys snapped again.

"Lady Heather stepped outside the kitchen to see the new pups born a few weeks now to the kitchen dog."

Rhys grabbed a sweet cake off the tray and said to Pitt as he passed, "Call the men back, I will get my wife."

Pitt nodded and called out to the men and as he did, he reached out and stopped Nessa from leaving with a gentle touch to her shoulder. "How are you doing, Nessa?"

"I am well, sir."

"Pitt. I have told you to call me Pitt.

She swallowed her pride and said, "Forgive me for not saying this sooner, but I am ever so grateful for your kindness to me the day—"

"Fife made himself known for the deceitful man he was? It was good that his reign of lies ended, and it is due to you that in the end we knew who he was or you and Lady Heather could have lost your lives."

Nessa shook her head. "Me?"

"Aye, I saw wherever you went so did Fife, and it troubled me that he seemed so taken with you, but he never attempted to kiss you. There had to be something wrong that he did not at least try to steal a kiss from a beautiful woman like you."

Nessa felt her cheeks heat.

"Perhaps later when all is quiet, we can enjoy some sweet cakes together and talk. I am sure there are things that still trouble you and I am a good listener."

Nessa felt too vulnerable to trust another man, especially one as handsome as Pitt.

Pitt held up his hand. "We will only talk; I will not try to kiss you," —he smiled—"not yet at least."

Nessa did not think her cheeks could get any hotter, but they felt on fire and embarrassment had her nodding and hurrying off, thinking of ways she could avoid the handsome warrior.

~~~

Rhys stood in the open doorway, finishing the sweet cake while he watched three little, black pups, except for one who had one white paw,
~~~

scamper and climb all over his laughing wife. She sat on the ground by a small shed that the dog no doubt had claimed for her home with the pups. One pup was nipping at her fingers another slept comfortably in her lap and the other slipped beneath the hem of her dress.

That did it for Rhys. That area was for him and him alone. He bent down, yanked the little pup out and dumped him on his bottom, ordering sharply, “Mine, stay out!”

The pup could not climb into Heather’s lap fast enough, stepping over the sleeping pup to plant himself as close to Heather as he could get. The other pup, the one with the white paw, sensing something was amiss, hurried to drop himself against her thigh and drop his head down so he would not be seen, or so he thought.

“A brave little batch you have there,” Rhys said and sat down beside his wife. “And what are you doing leaving the keep without telling me?”

“I am sorry. I was distracted when one of the pups wandered into the kitchen while I was getting the sweet cakes for you.”

It dawned on Rhys then that Heather had told him that she would go fetch sweet cakes for them, but he had been so busy speaking with Pitt that it had slipped his mind. Still, though, she had stepped outside the keep.

“Stay in sight of a guard at all times,” he said.

“I assumed a guard follows me at all times.”

"One follows that you can see, the other you do not see, but the two work together, so do not make it more difficult for them."

Her soothing strokes finally had the one pup settling down, nearly on top of the other pup in her lap.

"I was thinking," Heather said, reaching out to slip her hand around his. "This is foreign land to Haidar. How is it that he seems familiar with it?"

Rhys squeezed her hand. "I can understand why your father sought your counsel. You often see what others fail to see. I thought the same myself and dispatched one of my men to see what he can find out. The more likely answer would be that Haidar promised someone riches in exchange for his help, though the only thing the person will see is the end of Haidar's blade as he slices his throat."

"With Fife having been with you about a year, then that would mean Haidar had known all this time where you were. Why did he wait?"

"To see if I wed. It is important to him to repay me in kind. It makes his revenge that more satisfying and makes him more powerful in the eyes of his people. Besides, he would not want to take a chance of anything going wrong, so he would plan well."

She smiled and gave a slight tilt of her head as she said, "And you would do thc same...you would plan. You would leave nothing to chance."

He loved when she smiled. It was so natural, so heartwarming. "I am going to have to be careful with you, wife. I am not going to be able to keep secrets from you."

Her smile spread. "The more I learn about you, the more I see who you truly are."

The smile that had slowly worked its way to his mouth vanished. "Be very careful, wife, you may see something you do not like."

Heather's laughter drifted on the warm air, and she released his hand to rest hers between his legs. "I think I need to look more closely to know for sure."

His smile sprang free. "You have looked extremely close on several occasions, but do feel free to look as often as you would like."

"I will do that."

"And I encourage you to do so."

The pup with the one white paw raised his head and yapped, being too young for it to sound like a bark.

Rhys was impressed, for just after the yap he heard the hurried footfalls. He just may have to train the pup.

Pitt was suddenly in front of them and his intense look had Heather anxious.

"Word has arrived. Greer McLaud is not far from Macinnes keep. And besides Greer's wife's body being found on Macinnes land, a headless body has also been found there."

Chapter Twenty-seven

Heather paced in front of the window in Rhys' solar. Thankfully Rhys had included her when he and Pitt retired there to discuss the impending problem. She was worried for her family, for her clan. They were good, honest people and none deserved to suffer because of a man hungry for power and wealth.

"My family needs to know of this," Heather said worry filling her gentle green eyes.

"They have been kept apprised of Greer's movements," Rhys said.

Heather turned to glare at her husband. "And you did not think to tell me of this?"

"Until there was something to tell you, there was nothing for me to say," Rhys said and held his hand out to her.

Heather reached out and took it, easing into the folds of his tender embrace.

"Our union has its advantage. Is that not why you married me?" he asked.

"Aye, it is, but it is different now." Heather turned with a smile to Pitt. "Do you know that I love the Dragon with all my heart? And he loves me, though he does not realize it yet, but I am patient and will wait for however long it takes."

"The Dragon is a lucky man," Pitt said with a grin.

"That he is," Heather agreed. "And soon he will realize just how lucky, but for now...what do we do to help my people."

"We wait," Rhys said more pleased by his wife's remarks than he would have either of them know. "We see what Greer does. We see if he is aware that the Dark Dragon is now an ally of the Macinnes."

"With his wife and brother's body found on Macinnes land Greer will demand retribution and," —she stopped abruptly, her brow knitting—"why would Haidar dump the headless corpse on Macinnes land?"

"A question I was wondering myself," Rhys said, giving his wife's waist a gentle squeeze. "Greer is rash and unpredictable, dangerous traits in an enemy. It would be foolish for anyone to think him an ally. Greer would appear loyal, until it did not suit his need any longer."

"As he did with Hew McDolan," Pitt said.

Rhys nodded. "He turned a friend into an enemy when he allowed his brother Rab to send Saundra away with the intent of having her killed. Of course, if Saundra had not escaped, Hew could still be an ally of Greer's."

"It is good we kept watch over Saundra, though she did make it easy for us, escaping on her own," Pitt said.

"You followed her and made certain she stayed safe?" Heather asked with a curious stare.

"Aye, we did," Pitt confirmed.

Heather looked from Pitt to her husband, back to Pitt, and then to her husband again. She quickly moved out of his embrace to stand in front of the two and pointed her finger from one to the other as she said, "You let me escape!"

"Of course I did," Rhys admitted. "Did you not once question how you could escape my ghost warriors so easily?"

Heather sighed, shaking her head. "It was not until later that I gave it thought and wondered over it."

"It was time for you to return home," Rhys said. "Negotiations with your father had been completed. Once the documents were signed, you belonged to me." He gave a nod to Pitt and he quietly left the room. "If your father would have agreed when I first approached him requesting to wed you, it would not have been necessary for me to abduct you. It had not been part of my plan."

"You spoke with my father about marrying me before the marriage agreement had been made with Rogan MacClennan?"

Rhys nodded. "I had someone approach him. Unfortunately, he was not in favor of it. He was actually quite clear that he would never allow such a union to take place."

"So you abducted me and forced my father to agree."

"He left me little choice after he agreed to a marriage between you and Rogan, though it took some convincing since he was quite certain your sister Patience would be successful in finding you, and she did come close a couple of times. Your father understood that I would be denied for only so long, and with the unexpected threat of war with the McLauds, he realized refusal was no longer an option."

"His health as well was not good," she said, feeling guilty that he had shouldered this burden himself.

"Your father was not as ill as he made it seem."

"What do you mean?" she asked, though did not give him a chance to respond. "Are you suggesting my father faked his illness?"

"Aye, I am." Rhys stood and walked over to the side piece, filled a goblet and held it out to her.

She shook her head. "My father would never—"

"Your father knew it was past time his daughters wed and since the three of you showed no interest in it, he knew he had to do something. Feigning an illness, making the three of you think he was too weak to lead the clan would make you more agreeable to an arranged marriage. If anything, he knew the three of you were loyal to your clan and would do whatever was necessary to see it kept strong." Rhys raised his goblet of wine. "I toast your father, a very wise and brave man."

"This is complete nonsense. He sought my counsel on many things, why not this?" Heather asked more to herself than Rhys. She simply could not comprehend her father doing this.

"You and your sisters are very close. Would you have been supportive of an arranged marriage for either of them?"

She thought of both Patience and Emma. Patience would never have accepted an arranged marriage and when Rogan had turned down her father's proposal for such a union between him and Emma, saying he would only wed the beautiful sister, it had hurt Emma and made her adamant about never marrying.

Heather shook her head. "I could have never forced my sisters to wed against their will."

"Your father did what he had to do, not only for his daughters, but for his clan."

"How do you know all this? It is as if you have lived among us," —Heather's mouth dropped open and her eyes turned wide—"oh my God, you planted a spy in our clan."

"It was necessary," Rhys said, setting his goblet down and walking over to her.

She poked him in the chest when he got near. "Who? Who is the traitor? I will inform Patience and have him returned to you immediately."

"I do not think your father will agree to that," he said, brushing her poking finger aside.

"He most certainly will."

"Afraid not," Rhys said with a smile and wrapped his arms around her. "He has grown rather attached to the spy and I do not think he will surrender her."

It took Heather a minute to understand. "Maura?"

Rhys nodded.

"Does my father know she spies for you?"

Rhys nodded again. "Maura came to me when she learned that your father felt the same for her as she did for him. She asked permission to leave, not wanting to see your father hurt. I told her to tell him the truth and if he wanted her to leave then she had my permission to do so."

"My father did not want her to leave," Heather said, thinking how long it had been since her father had loved.

"Not at all," Rhys confirmed. "Your father is a wise man. He understood that Maura was not there to harm your clan, nor did she harbor any ill-will against it. She was more an emissary than a spy. Maura is a good woman and will make your father a good wife."

"He wants to wed her?" Heather shook her head and answered her own question. "Of course he does. It has been so long since he has loved, he would not want to lose her. You know this woman well? You can vouch for her good nature?"

"Aye, I can," Rhys said, "Maura is my aunt, my mother's sister."

A smile spread wide across Heather's face.

Rhys laughed. "I know what you are thinking. You think to ask her many questions about me, but she will answer none of them, unless I give her permission to do so. I would concern myself more of what Patience will think when she finds out. Emma, I think, will be sympathetic."

"You are right. Patience will grow angry whereas Emma will be happy for our da. You are getting to know my family well," she said, though wondered if it was because he already knew them well and cared for them. "My father would have wanted to know more about the man who would wed me. Does he know more about the Dragon than I do?"

"That was not part of the marriage agreement and your father had little negotiating power."

"Did you ever meet with my father personally?"

"He insisted on it and I respected him for it, so I met a couple of times with him."

"But he never saw your face?" she asked, curious to know if perhaps her father saw in Rhys what she did...that he was Quinn.

"He asked, but it was another thing that was not negotiable."

Heather eased out of his arms and he reluctantly let her go.

Silence settled between them for a few moments before Heather said, "Why did you let me escape? Why not just return me home?"

"I thought it best that you have a few days of freedom before you learned your fate."

"So when you let me go, I was already your wife."

"Aye, you were and I was impatient to claim you as such," Rhys said.

"I would have never thought that I would be glad that you did. And while the Dragon can breathe fire at times, he also can be a loving creature."

Rhys walked slowly over to her. "A creature you say, not a beast?"

"A beast strikes without cause or thought and cares naught for the consequence," she said, stretching her hand out to him.

He wrapped his hand around hers and pulled her up against him. "I have done just that often."

"When you were a slave warrior and it was forced upon you," she said her arms reaching up to wrap around his neck. "You are a slave no more. You are free to do as you wish. To love who you wish and to make love to whom you wish."

Rhys gave her a gentle kiss. "There is one woman that I want to make love to all the time."

Heather smiled. "She pleases you that much?"

Rhys kissed her gently again. "She pleases me in more ways than she will ever know."

"She must be very special to you." Heather pressed herself more tightly against him.

"Aye, that she is. She has done what no one else has been able to."

Heather tilted her head, curious. "And what is that?"

He brushed his lips across hers and whispered, "She has worked her way into my heart."

Heather brushed her lips across his and whispered, "And she intends to remain there forever."

"That is good, for I intend to keep her there forever."

He kissed her then, different from ever before since his words were the closest thing he had come to telling her that he loved her, and it pleased her beyond reason.

The kiss naturally aroused them both and it was some time before the Dragon and his wife left his solar.

~~~

Heather woke suddenly. She sat up and looked around the bedchamber. She was alone. Something was wrong, she could feel it. She hurried and dressed, wondering what took her husband from their bed. She was barely out the door when she heard the bell toll.

She hurried through the keep and out the door, halting for a moment at the top of the keep's stairs to stare in horror at the flames shooting into the air.

The barn was on fire.
~~~

Men, women, and children rushed out of their cottages, snatching up buckets as they went. Rhys' warriors came running, some from their posts, knowing if the fire was not contained quickly the whole village could be lost. Warriors raced into the barn to get out whatever animals were in there.

The fire was spreading rapidly, a night wind carrying some of the flames in the air and dangerously close to a few cottages. If they did not douse the fire soon, cottages would catch the flames.

Heather looked around for Rhys, but he was nowhere to be seen and neither was Pitt. The warriors needed no one to tell them what to do. They were quick in getting a brigade formed to the well and buckets filled and passed on to be dumped on a fire that would soon be raging out of control.

"Lady Heather, go to the keep and stay there," Henry ordered, rushing up beside her.

"I can help."

"No," Henry insisted. "All the warriors are needed here or we will lose the whole village. Go to the keep now and stay where you will be safe or the Dragon will have all our heads." He rushed off, calling out for another line to be formed.

Heather's first thought was to ignore Henry and join one of the brigades, but when two more warriors begged her to hurry to the keep, she realized her presence created more of a hindrance for them. She turned to leave, stopping abruptly when she spotted a dog barking at the side of the barn the flames had yet to reach. When she saw two little pups barking along with their mother, she realized the problem. The third pup was stuck in the burning barn.

She hurried over to the dog and as she got closer, she could hear the frantic yaps of the pup trapped inside. If she could somehow get in from this side...Heather did not hesitate. She ran to the side of the barn and near the corner found a loose plank. She squeezed behind it and slipped inside.

Flames were greedily consuming one wall of the barn and would soon be spreading to the other walls. Smoke filled the air and would shortly consume the whole area. Heather wasted no time in looking for the pup. Once she spotted him, she rushed over to him, crouching down as the smoke grew thicker and picked him up.

His small legs were tied together and as she quickly freed him, she realized what she had done. She had walked into a trap. She recalled her husband's warning.

He will find your weaknesses and use them.

Someone had purposely tied up the pup and left him there to lure her in. She had to get out and fast.

With the smoke growing heavier, she kept low and when she reached the loose plank she shoved the pup through first. She stood and went to squeeze between the planks when she was suddenly grabbed by the arm and yanked back in. A hand was quickly pressed to her mouth and in seconds she found herself shoved out the back of the barn where a plank had been removed, and carried off into the woods.

~~~

Rhys and Pitt saw the smoke as they approached the village and rushed forward. Rhys was off his horse in an instant, one of his warriors taking hold of the agitated animal and directing him away from the heat and flames of the fire.

Pitt hurried alongside Rhys as they made their way to the brigade of villagers passing bucket after bucket of water. Rhys could see that the barn could not be saved but the bucket brigade had managed to stop the flames from reaching other structures.

Henry hurried over to him.

"Where is my wife?" Rhys asked before Henry could say a word.

"I sent her to stay in the keep. We needed all hands to fight this thing or we would have lost the entire village and possibly the keep."

Rhys turned to Pitt. "Go make sure she is there."

Pitt hurried off.

"We need to keep on the flames until there is nothing left for them to claim," Henry said. "We got the animals out safely, so it is just the barn we lost."

"What happened?"
~~~

"I do not know," Henry said, shaking his head. "Most everyone was asleep. I have yet to find out who rang the bell and to alert us."

The little black pup with the one white paw ran toward Rhys at the same time Pitt did, but the pup reached him first and yapped repeatedly, too young yet for a full bark, while he jumped against his leg.

"She is not in the keep," Pitt yelled as he approached.

Rhys looked down at the pup that was now backing away from him as he continued to yap as loud as he could. "Where is she?"

The pup ran, then stopped to see if Rhys followed and when he saw that Rhys was right behind him, he kept running. The pup kept his distance from the burning barn as he led Rhys, Pitt, and Henry to the woods behind the back of the barn. He ran to a spot and grabbed something with his tiny teeth, though he could not keep hold of it as he tried to bring it to Rhys.

Rhys stopped as soon as he saw what the pup was trying to show him—his wife's boots.

He stared at them and fear like he had not felt in years rose up to nearly choke him. Then he did what he did years ago...he let the Dragon loose.

He snatched up her boots and shouted an order to Pitt, "Get my warriors; we ride into battle."

Chapter Twenty-eight

Show no fear. Rhys will come for you. Show no fear. Rhys will come for you. Show no fear. Rhys will come for you.

Heather kept repeating the words in her head, though the thought of what would happen to her before Rhys could reach her scared her to death. Haidar wanted revenge and she was the weapon he would use against Rhys to get it.

She cringed and stumbled as her one foot stepped on a rock hidden beneath leaves and she went down hard? How many times had she fallen? She had lost count after seven times. She had wanted to cry out when they yanked her boots off, knowing what lay ahead, just as she did now. She hurried to stand, not an easy chore with her feet paining her so badly and her wrists tied together. She had learned quickly that if she lay there she would get kicked until she stood.

She made it to her knees when the warrior that held her wrist rope kicked her in the thigh and she could not help but wince.

"Up! Up!" he ordered and kicked her again.

She got to her feet, though she did not know how and once again followed behind the warrior. He kept a fast pace and Heather feared she would not be able to keep up with him much longer.

Besides, the further away from the keep they got; the longer it would take Rhys to get to her.

Rhys had suffered far worse than what she was suffering and for far too many years. If he could do it for as long as he did, then she could survive until he came for her. And she had no doubt he would come.

She refused to linger on what she would have to endure until he found her. She would do whatever it took to survive, whatever it took to be with Rhys again, and whatever it took to see her family again.

She bit her tongue against the pain in her feet. They had to be cut and bleeding by now. If only it was morning. She could at least see where she stepped and could avoid the forest debris that stabbed at her feet with every step.

It seemed like they walked for hours. Any minute Heather expected, more so hoped, to see the sun rise, but it did not happen and she wondered if sunrise was further off than she thought. They walked until Heather could barely feel her feet and her legs felt as if they were on fire, her muscles burned so badly. Then suddenly the pace slowed and Heather noticed a flicker of light just up ahead.

They had reached a camp and she wanted to cry with relief.

After entering the campsite and being brought closer to the fire, the man holding her rope gave it a hard yank. Heather stumbled and fought to stay on her feet and as soon as she regained her balance, the man kicked her legs out from under her. She raised her arms to cushion her face from the fall, her body smacking the ground hard. This time the breath was knocked out of her.

Fear gripped her as she tried to remain calm and breathe, and she silently prayed for Rhys to hurry and come for her. She could not wait to feel his strong arms around her and the thought helped her finally breathe easy.

"Knees," the man ordered sharply.

She struggled to get to them, her legs ached so badly. When she finally did, the man slapped a strong hand on her shoulder, anchoring her to the spot and fear fluttered in her stomach.

"She is tired. This is good, she will not have the strength to do anything, but obey me."

Heather raised her head to look at Haidar, but he had stepped behind her.

He stepped in front of her again after only a few moments, smiling and nodding. "Good, she will not be able to walk with how badly her feet suffered." His smile grew as he stood staring at her. "Dirt does not even mar your beauty. I may keep you longer than I thought," —he sneered—"and make your husband suffer even longer."

Heather would have preferred to remain silent, worried if she said a word her fear would show. But if she could keep him talking, then it gave Rhys more time to reach her before Haidar could do anything to her.

She tossed her chin up. "My husband will come for me."

"Of course he will."

"He will kill you."

Haidar laughed. "He will never defeat me. I taught him what he knows. I made him bow to my will just as I will do to you. And it will be ever so enjoyable for me, but so terribly painful for your husband and not so pleasant for you, unless you learn to accept your fate and obey my every command, something it took your husband a while to learn."

"But he did, and won his freedom."

"So he told you about that," Haidar said, nodding. "It was, what I believed, an impossible task. I never expected him to succeed. I expected his tortured body to be returned to me, but instead I was quite surprised when he returned with my enemy's intended bride, the task complete."

Heather was shocked by the news. Rhys had enslaved another to free himself.

I promise I will return to you, nothing will stop me from coming back to you.

Quinn's departing words came back to her. His promise had come at a great cost.

"I took her as my bride that day. He left three months later with a great deal of wealth I bestowed on him for accomplishing the task, though he took something far greater with him than wealth...he took my wife, Anala, the woman he had captured for me."

Heather kept silent not able to speak if she wanted to, shocked by what she had just learned. But then having grown to know Rhys and knowing Quinn as she did, neither man would let a woman suffer if he could help it.

"It was not so much that he took Anala, but that he took my unborn child...a son who died before he could live. I stood at the shoreline and watched as everything I so generously gave him was loaded onto the vessel, never knowing Anala was among them, never thinking he would betray me in such a way." His eyes narrowed. "Now I will see him suffer greatly for his betrayal."

Heather could not help but think that at least Anala and her son were forever free of such an evil man.

Haidar began to unwrap the black sash around his waist. "We will leave a little something for your husband to see how much I enjoyed his wife, though I will make sure not to disturb the seed he has no doubt planted inside you. I have plans for his child. He nodded to the man who held her rope. "Strip her bare and leave the torn garments where they fall. That should be a clear enough message for him."

~~~

The Dark Dragon rode his stallion through the woods. He wore his leather armor but no
~~~

helmet. His warriors rode along on both sides of him, lighting the way with torches.

He cursed himself a hundred times over for leaving the keep, leaving Heather. He should have known something was about to happen when his contingent of warriors arrived from the west and told him that Haidar's warriors had not been spotted. He had moved them in preparation for this trap. The one good thing about that was that Haidar would not expect the size of the troop Rhys brought with him.

Many of his warriors at the McComb village insisted on joining with the warriors that had just arrived. They were eager to find Lady Heather and bring her home safely and once and for all be rid of the enemy that had continued to plague them. Other warriors remained behind to finish extinguishing the fire.

Rhys also had received a message from Innis. He had set a plan in motion after discovering important information and if all went as planned, Rhys would have Haidar exactly where he wanted him.

A halt was called from the lead warrior and Rhys did not question it. His men were superior warriors and knew well what they were doing.

Pitt rode up beside him. "A moment, they think they found something and want to be sure."

Rhys nodded and his stallion snorted, wanting to keep moving as anxiously as his master did.

"Patience Macinnes will ride as soon as she gets that message," Pitt said, waiting beside him on his horse.

"I expect her to; they need to be ready for what is to come."

"My lord," a voice called out.

Rhys dismounted as did Pitt and they followed a warrior who waited a few feet ahead. His warriors circled a small area and they parted when Rhys approached. The best tracker Rhys had was hunched down close to the ground in the middle of the circle. He looked up at Rhys and he could see the tracker did not want to tell him what he had found.

"Tell me," Rhys ordered.

"Lady Heather's feet were bleeding by the time she reached here and she took a hard fall here as well. You can still see where her body hit the ground."

Rhys looked to see where the tracker pointed. The size of the outline fit his wife and he could picture her taking the fall, her knees hitting the dirt and her arms going up in an attempt to protect her face as she went down hard and fast. He fisted his hands at his sides, his heart rammed against his chest, and rage filled his whole body. He knew exactly what his wife was going through and he hated knowing she would suffer even more before he reached her.

"They do not hide their tracks well. It is as if they leave a trail for us to follow," the tracker said.

"That is exactly what he is doing. Keep following and remember his men hide well."

The troop waited until Rhys mounted, and then they took off.

~~~

Heather had no way to defend herself and even if she could she barely had the strength to do so, but she did not let either stop her. She did something Patience had once taught her. She waited until the warrior got close and she used the only part of her body that had some strength left... her head.

As the warrior leaned down and tore her sleeve off her shoulder, she came up with her head fast and hard, catching him in the jaw and sending him sprawling to the ground. She quickly grabbed the rope away from him as he lay squirming in pain.

"I admire your courage, though I do not think it will last long," Haidar said and waved to two men to finish the task. His hand suddenly stilled, halting them. "What is that sound?"

The camp turned quiet and listened.

When nothing was heard Haidar raised his hand again and froze in place, his eyes turning wide.

From the darkness, dozens of glowing green eyes suddenly surrounded the camp. Growls started and grew as wolf after wolf slowly and cautiously entered the camp, their sharp teeth bared in warning
~~~

as they walked over to Heather and one by one circled her, creating a shield of wolves around her.

One warrior mistakenly placed his hand on the hilt of his sword. A wolf shot out from the darkness behind him and dragged him back into the dark depths of the woods, screaming.

Heather shut her eyes and cringed until his screams were no more.

Haidar said nothing and made no move, his hand still up in the air. The warriors did the same.

Heather forced herself to her feet, ignoring the pain as best she could.

Suddenly an arrow shot into the camp just missing one of the wolves and a pair of wolves jumped out of the darkness, lunging at a warrior. Their sharp fangs tore at him as they dragged him into the woods, his screams echoing in the night.

No arrows followed after that and from the look on Haidar's face, the warrior who shot it would suffer for his misdeed.

Heather started walking, the wolves keeping their circle tight around her. Her feet pained her badly with each step she took and her body ached all over, but she forced herself to keep going. The wolves had come for her and they would see her to safety and all she had to do was walk along with them. She called out no parting words to Haidar as she disappeared into the darkened woods. She would leave him to her husband.

Once out of sight, the wolves parted and she knew what they intended. She took off running with them. She told herself not to feel, not to think, just to run as free as the wolves.

Haidar stood not moving at all, his face contorted red with rage and his arm aching from holding it up so long. Wolves remained snarling and snapping if anyone dared to move, and then they began to leave until none were left, their growls and howls continuing to echo in the air.

"Find the fool who fired that arrow and kill him," Haidar ordered the man who stepped toward him as he brought his arm down painfully slow. "Then gather the men. Plans have changed."

~~~

The sun was rising when Rhys and his men neared the camp. A halt was called and Pitt hurried over to him.

"Dismount and come see this now," Pitt urged.

Rhys followed an anxious Pitt and found himself staring at what looked like more than a hundred wolf tracks. "No bodies?" he asked.

"I have the men searching now," Pitt said and went off when a warrior shouted out to him.

Rhys went and picked up a piece of rope off the ground. He was familiar with the purpose it served since he had worn one around his wrists for some time. Dare he hope—something he had not done much of in many years—that somehow Heather got free before the wolves attacked? Or had they attacked? He stared at the tracks and crouched
~~~

down to look more closely and saw a human track amongst the wolf tracks.

He stood and called out for Pitt, but he was already headed his way.

"Two bodies, or what are left of them," Pitt said, "and a third with his throat cut."

"Haidar's way of punishing those who fail him." Rhys shook his head. "I think the wolves may have rescued Heather."

"That would explain the foot tracks keeping pace with the wolf tracks," Pitt said.

"Then we follow," Rhys ordered.

"They set a fast pace and with the injuries to her feet, which probably have worsened the tracker does not believe Heather would make it far."

"Then she should be close." Rhys hurried and mounted his horse. "Which way do the tracks go?"

Pitt pointed as he mounted his horse. "Back toward McComb land."

Chapter Twenty-nine

Rhys stood alone, staring at his wife sprawled face down on the ground with at least half a dozen wolves keeping a tight circle around her. One large black wolf stood in front of the circle, his fangs bared and his growl deep.

When two of his men had come across the scene they had wisely backed away and had come to fetch him. Rhys had ordered his warriors to stay where they were and not approach the area. He had removed his leather armor and left all weapons behind against Pitt's strong objections.

He approached the wolves with his hands held out from his sides, showing he meant them no harm. The black wolf was not impressed; he continued to snarl

Rhys wanted to run over to his wife's prone body and see that it was only exhaustion that had her lying so lifeless, but the wolf would never let him pass. And if it was not sleep that had claimed her, he had to know and do what he could to help her.

He took a chance and called out, "Heather!"

His powerful voice annoyed the wolf and he lunged in warning, his snarl even more threatening.

Rhys did not back away, though he did change the tone of his voice. It sounded more caring, though it remained strong. "Heather, wake up. I have come to take you home."

The black wolf continued pacing in front of the circle, his snarl lessening.

"Heather it is me, wake up."

The more he called and the more she did not respond, the more his fear grew and he began to pace as well.

The Dragon and the wolf paced back and forth, their eyes never leaving each other.

Finally, Rhys stopped and called out, "Heather wake up, it is I...Quinn. I have come back to you. Please wake up. I have missed you terribly and I love you so very much."

Never had he felt such joy as he did when he saw her body move.

He called out again. "Wake up, Heather, I want to hold you again. Kiss you. Tell you over and over how much I love you."

She stirred even more and Rhys kept talking, urging her with his loving words.

Pain shot through Heather each time she moved, but she heard Quinn calling to her and she had to get to him. She stretched her arms out from her sides and moaned louder, but it was when she moved her legs and feet that she cried out the loudest in pain.

She let the pain subside before moving again and more slowly this time, Quinn's voice urging her to wake and sit up. When she finally got her eyes open, she was shocked to see the wolves surrounding her. The awful memory came back to her then. The wolves had saved her and protected her until Rhys could reach her. She was ever so grateful for their friendship.

She wondered though, it was Quinn who called to her. She was not mistaken about that since he was still calling out to her urging her to wake up and sit up and telling her how much he loved her.

A smile sparked her strength and she managed to push herself up to sit, though her body ached terribly and she cringed when she saw her feet. They were covered with dirt and caked with blood so she could not tell how bad her wounds were. She also could not see Rhys clearly with the wolves circled around her, so she attempted to stand.

A mistake. She fell to her side in pain.

"Do not try and stand," Rhys shouted and the black wolf lunged at him again in warning.

It took strength she feared she did not have to sit up again and remain that way. Once she did, she began speaking softly to the wolves, thanking them for their help and protection and telling them it was all right for them to leave her now. She was safe. The man here would not harm her. He had come to see her safely home.

The wolves began to drift off one by one until the black wolf was the only one remaining.

The wolf went to stand next to Heather and she slowly rested a gentle hand to the side of his face and whispered, "Thank you. I am forever grateful to you for your help and friendship."

Rhys approached Heather slowly seeing that though the wolf walked off, he stayed just far enough in the woods to watch and wait and make certain Rhys did not harm her. Once he reached her side Rhys did not hesitate, he scooped her up in his arms.

Pain rushed through her, but she fought against it and slipped her arms around his neck. "I knew you would come for me."

"Always," he said and kissed her brow gently, relieved he finally held her in his arms.

As he walked off with her, she said, "You are Quinn."

"We will discuss that later."

"No," she said with a gentle firmness, "you will tell me now once and for all. You are Quinn, are you not?"

He hesitated and he seemed to battle himself before finally saying, "I once was Quinn, but the young man you knew is no more."

She smiled, her heart filling with such tremendous joy that she thought she would burst. "Quinn, Rhys, Dark Dragon, you are all the same to me and I love you all equally and always will."

He stopped walking and pressed his brow to hers. "There were times I feared I would never be able to say this to you again. I love you, Heather, more now than I ever did and believe me when I tell you that the Dark Dragon loves you beyond reason."

She kissed him gently. "Take me home, husband."

~~~

The pain in her body seemed to keep rhythm with the horse's rapid pace. It pounded and pounded until it reached her head and she began to feel herself drift into darkness.

"Heather!"

Heather felt the heat on her face from the fiery roar of the Dragon.

"Heather!"

She struggled to get away from the burning heat of the Dragon's breath, but could not escape the shackles that bound her. She thrashed against the unbearable heat licking at her skin, but was forced to stop when the shackles tightened around her.

Heather almost cried out in relief when the pounding finally stopped, but her throat was too dry to speak and it sounded more like a muffled moan. She felt herself being carried and tried to beg for something to quench her unbearable thirst, but the words would not come.

"What did you do to her?"

Was that Patience's voice she heard?

"Damn you, what happened to my sister?"
~~~

"Get her to her bedchamber where I can look after her."

That was Emma, she would get her a drink. Heather tried to call out to her sister, but she barely got out a raspy moan.

"She needs something to drink."

A tear came to her eyes. Leave it to Emma to know what she needed.

Heather was ever so grateful when she was placed on a bed. She wanted to strip off her garments and sleep until she felt better, after she quenched her thirst.

"Get out and leave her to us," Patience ordered.

What was the matter with Patience talking to Quinn that way? She always loved him like a brother. Heather almost sighed with relief when she felt a strong hand lift her head and drop something cool against her lips. She opened her mouth hungry for more and the cool drink was a blessing to her parched throat.

"Get out, we will tend her."

"Patience, do not talk to Quinn that way," Heather struggled to say.

"She thinks you are Quinn," Emma said, choking on tears.

"Hot, so hot," Heather said, pulling at her dress.

"Leave us," Patience ordered, giving Rhys a shove.

Rhys grabbed her and Emma by the arms and rushed them over to their husbands. "Get them out of here now."

"I am not leaving my sister," Patience said, her husband Hunter fighting to keep her from going after the Dragon.

Emma's husband Rogan kept hold of her hand as she took a step toward the Dragon and said, "Please, she is burning with fever. I know what to do."

Rhys wanted to chase them all away, but he knew of Emma's healing skills and he relented. "You can stay and help."

"Then I stay too," Patience said.

"Only if you follow what I tell you and you do not argue with anyone," Emma ordered. "Your temper will not serve our sister well."

"Emma is right," Hunter said, releasing his wife.

"I will do whatever you say and save my temper for later," Patience said, letting the Dragon know she was not done with him.

"Hunter and I will be right outside the door if you need anything," Rogan said and went to the door with Hunter, though it opened before they reached it.

Nessa hurried in, tears in her eyes and a bucket of water in each hand. "My lord, what can I do to help Lady Heather?"

Rhys looked to Emma. "Tell her what you need." He turned and went to his wife, taking her hand. "I am here with you and I am not going anywhere. Your sisters are also here to help."

Heather licked at her lips and thankfully Rhys understood and lifted her head to give her more of the cool brew. "Do not leave me," she said as soon as she could.

"Never," he said and kissed her cheek, growing alarmed by how hot she felt. He turned to Emma. "She is burning."

"We need to get her out of her garments and get her cleaned so I can see how bad the wounds are. I also need some plants brewed."

"I will see to that, tell me what you need done," Patience said.

It did not take Rhys and Emma long to strip Heather, now unresponsive to their words or touch, and when they did, Emma started crying, seeing the many bruises on her sister's soft skin.

"I am sorry," Emma said, "I cry much too easily since I have gotten with child."

"Shed as many tears as you want," Rhys said, "and shed them for me as well for my anger will not let me shed any and my mind is too busy planning my revenge."

Rhys worked silently beside Emma washing the dirt off Heather's body, but when it came to her feet, Emma laid a gently hand on his. "Please let me see to her feet. I need to tend the wounds gently so they do not open and bleed again. It would help if you bathed her face, neck, and shoulders with a wet cloth to help get the fever down."

Rhys nodded and did as Emma said. He was so intent on seeing to his wife's care that he did not hear Patience return or the sisters whispering.

Heather suddenly stirred and called out, "Quinn."

Rhys was quick to answer, taking hold of her hand. "I am here, Heather, do not worry. I am not going to leave you, not ever again."

She settled, though did not let go of his hand.

Rhys finally looked to Emma to see if she was finished tending Heather's feet.

She, along with her sister, was staring at him.

He knew what they were thinking, but he was too concerned with his wife to discuss it with them now. "How are her feet?"

Emma answered quickly. "Some bruises and abrasions, though only one that could pose a problem since it shows signs of redness. I will soak the wound with a special brew I have and that should help ease the redness so that it does not turn putrid. We can take turns tending her if you would like?"

"We need to discuss what happened here and why your troops move in from the west and north." Patience said. "With Greer's wife's body being found on Macinnes land and Rab McLaud's headless body to contend with, war with the Clan McLaud seems inevitable."

It was time for everything to come together, though he had not planned on his wife being abducted, but he would not give Haidar a second chance at taking her away from him. The Dark Dragon would finally see it ended

"I will take the first watch," Emma said to Rhys. "I want to clean her wounds more and see that she gets enough of the special brew. And if she should ask for you, I will see that you are summoned immediately."

Rhys did not want to leave Heather, but he also needed to see her protected and safe and he would have to go to battle to see that done. "If anything should change—"

"I will fetch you immediately," Emma assured him.

Rhys kissed Heather's brow and thought it felt cooler to him, His lips drifted near her ear and he whispered, "I love you. Do not dare leave me." He stood and looked to Patience. "I have a plan."

~~~

Heather sighed as she opened her eyes. The soft light from a low burning fire in the hearth was the only light in the room. She looked to the window and saw that it was night. How long had she slept? And had she dreamed she heard Patience and Emma?

When she saw her husband sitting in a chair next to the bed, his head bent back, his mouth
~~~

opened slightly, and a slight snore coming from him, she smiled.

She sighed again. They were home and safe and—"

"Heather?"

She looked to her husband. "You woke."

"So did you?" Rhys moved to sit on the bed beside her, his hand reaching out to rest at her brow. "Thank goodness your fever is finally gone. It has been two days and— "

"Two days? I have been with fever two days?"

"Emma has tended you well."

"Emma is here?"

Rhys nodded. "Patience as well and her name truly suits her for she has tried my patience considerably."

Heather laughed and was pleased to feel only a slight ache. She reached out and took his hand. "Lie with me."

Rhys slipped out of his garments and into bed with her, something he had been aching to do these past two days. Emma had forbid him from sleeping with Heather until she was free of fever and so he had slept in the chair after placing it close to the bed. He missed having his wife in his arms and that is what he did now. He turned on his side and draped his arm over her waist tucking her close to him.

Heather sighed, his cool, naked body feeling so very good against her slightly warm one. She had endless questions to ask him and she started with the most obvious one. "How did you end up a slave in a foreign land?"

"My da and I were attacked on the road by a band of thieves. They killed him and I woke in chains on a ship, bound where I did not know. It was a hellish voyage or so I thought. It was nothing compared to the nightmare I was about to live. I was sold shortly after being taken off the ship. I never knew how cruel someone could be until I met Haidar. He bought most of the slaves and my training to become a slave warrior started almost immediately."

He kissed her gently. "I missed you so very much and I cried the night I knew Quinn had to die if I was to survive. And dying meant letting go of you and the love I had for you. In order to survive, I had to become as ruthless as Haidar and I could not let love stand in my way. I promised myself that night that whoever I became that that man would protect you and love you if he could."

"It hurts me to know how you suffered, especially having tasted just a small portion of Haidar's cruelty."

Rhys caressed her arm slowly. "He did not have a chance to touch you, did he?"

"No, I kept him talking for a while, hoping you would reach me before he could," —she could not bring herself to say what might have happened— "he seemed to want me to know why you deserved to be punished. He told me what you did to win your freedom."

"I never truly won my freedom. Anala won it for me. When I captured her, she could have screamed and alerted the guards. Instead, she told me that she could show me a secret way out and if she went with me willingly, then I would have to promise to one day free her. I did not hesitate to agree."

"So you remained where you were, making Haidar think you did not want to leave yet, gaining his trust while planning to abduct his new wife?"

"I gave Anala my word and if anything, I am true to my word, though we both knew what it would cost us eventually."

"You knew Haidar would find out and come for you one day," Heather said.

"I think I truly wanted him to, though I expected him sooner than this, but I should have known better. He would want to take from me what I took from him."

"He will try again," Heather said and shuddered at the thought.

Rhys felt her shiver against him and he held her close, wishing he could hold her even tighter but worried that he would cause her pain. "He can try and come for you, but you will not be here."

"What do you mean?" she asked anxiously.

"As soon as you are fit to travel, we will leave for your home."

"My home is where you are," she said on a yawn, then smiled.

"Then you will be home, for I will be with you. Now no more talk, you need to rest."

"One more thing."

Rhys agreed with a nod.

"What do you keep locked in the room on the upper floor?"

"Get well and I will show you."

Chapter Thirty

Heather let out a happy screech when her two sisters entered her bedchamber and she tried to scramble out of bed.

"No, No," Emma scolded, hurrying over to her. "You must stay abed at least for today." She settled Heather back in bed, and then gave her a huge hug.

Patience pushed her aside. "Let me get to her, and she looks fine to me. She should get up so we can take her home." She gave Heather a tight hug.

"Easy, she is still sore," Emma admonished.

Patience shook her finger at Emma, though looked at Heather. "Listen to her, telling me what to do. It has been like this since she has been with child."

Heather smiled, shaking her head at her sisters who were the same as ever. "I have missed you both so much. You are feeling well, Emma? "

The two sisters sat on either side of her on the bed.

"I am fine, we both have missed you and have worried terribly about you," Emma said.

"Has the Dragon treated you good," Patience asked.

Without hesitation or qualm and with a smile spreading across her face, she said, "I have fallen in love with him."

Patience scowled. "You barely know him."

"You do look happy," Emma said.

"Stop encouraging her," Patience scolded.

"Stop encouraging her to be happy?" Emma asked incredulously.

"He is the Dark Dragon," Patience said as if it was insane to even consider the thought of loving him.

"He is Quinn," Heather said and her sisters' heads turned in unison to stare at her in shock. "The Dark Dragon is Quinn."

"It is the fever," Patience said to Emma.

Heather laughed. "It is a long story and one I do not know if he wishes to share, but I give you my word...he is Quinn."

A tear fell down Emma's cheek. "He came back to you just like he promised he would."

"You are sure of this?" Patience asked. "He could be telling you a tale to get you to trust and love him."

"I discovered it myself and he refused to admit it until he had no choice and the truth came out. I have no doubt that he is Quinn."

The door opened then and Rhys walked in, Hunter and Rogan entering behind him.

Patience flew off the bed and punched Rhys in the shoulder. "So you are Quinn, are you?"

Rhys leaned his face close to Patience's. "Your punch has improved since you were little and so has mine and I will knock you on your arse just as I did when you were young, though a bit harder than I used to, if you hit me again."

"Damn, it is you," Patience said and punched his shoulder again. "What took you so long to come home?"

Rhys shook his head and turned to Hunter. "God bless you for marrying her."

"What do you mean God bless him?" Patience snapped. "He is blessed I let him marry me."

Emma was laughing and wiping tears from her eyes as she walked over to Rhys and gave him a hug. "It is so very good to see you again."

"You as well, Emma." He turned to Rogan. "You are a lucky man."

"That I am," Rogan said and reached out and drew Emma into his arms.

"The three of you are lucky to have each one of us," Patience said and her husband threw his arms around her in a tight hug.

"Do not think that will stop me from punching him again now that I know who he is," Patience warned.

"He is still the Dark Dragon," Hunter reminded.

Patience thought a moment. "Then he can teach me the skills of his ghost warriors."

Hunter rolled his eyes while everyone else laughed.

Heather tried to stop the yawn that surfaced, but all she could do was raise her hand to cover it.

Rhys walked over to his wife, sitting down on the bed beside her and slipping his arm around her. “You need to rest more.”

“He is right. You should nap,” Emma said, “we will see you later.”

Patience grumbled as Emma forced her out the door.

Rhys turned and pressed his chest to hers, to gently ease her down on the bed while he stole a tender kiss.

“I miss your breath-robbing kisses,” she said, wrapping her arms around his neck so he could not move away.

“Get better and I promise you more than breath-robbing kisses.” His hand roamed down along her side and slipped under her backside to give it a squeeze.

A knock sounded at the door and Rhys was glad for the intrusion. He had gone without making love to her for two days and it was two days too many. He wanted nothing more than to make love to her, but she was not well enough yet. So, he needed to stay a safe distance from her.

He bid the person to enter as he got off the bed.

"Excuse, my lord," Nessa said, "but Lady Emma said I should bring this to Lady Heather and make sure she drank it."

"Then I will leave you to the task," Rhys said and hurried past her to the door. He stopped and turned. "Drink it all, wife. I am eager for you to get well."

Heather smiled as the door closed behind him.

Nessa placed the tankard on the chest and went to help Heather sit up. "You look much better, my lady."

"I am feeling much better," Heather frowned. "But you do not look well, Nessa, is something wrong?"

Nessa retrieved the tankard and handed it to Heather.

"Sit and talk with me, Nessa, till I fall asleep."

Nessa sat, a tear stinging the corner of her eye until it finally fell down her cheek.

"Talk to me, Nessa," Heather encouraged.

"Everything changes, my lady," she said, sadness filling her face. "Two of the original McComb clan disappeared last night. Seamus, me, and his family are the last of the Clan McComb and Seamus is sure the Dragon plans to get rid of us." She wiped at her tears. "I spoke with Pitt, he talks with me often and I must say he is more thoughtful than I thought. He tells me not to worry that all will be fine, but how can I not worry when all who I know are disappearing?"

"As soon as I am well, we will be leaving for the Macinnes keep and I shall take you with me," Heather said. "I will not let anything happen to you."

"Truly, my lady?"

Heather reached out and Nessa quickly took her hand. "Truly, Nessa. When I arrived here, if it were not for your kindness and help, I do not know what I would have done."

"I would be only too pleased to serve you, my lady."

"Then after I rest you may return and start packing my chests and be sure to start gathering your belongings."

Heather fell asleep wondering what her husband had planned. Usually she would sneak around and try to find out, but now, she would simply ask him.

~~~

Rhys watched his wife sleep. It was growing late, not only the day but the time they had to leave here. Haidar would regroup and return with all his men and from what Rhys' men were reporting to him, Haidar was doing just that.

The last of the McCombs would be taken tonight, except for Nessa. Pitt, to his own surprise, had grown more than fond of her and with how
~~~

much his wife seemed to favor Nessa, he planned for her to come along with them to the Macinnes keep.

He could not wait any longer. The day after tomorrow they would leave. He would have a cart made ready to accommodate Heather and they would go, never to return here again.

He leaned over and kissed her brow. “Sleep well, we leave for home soon.”

~~~

Heather woke and to her dismay saw that it was night and that she was alone. She could not tolerate sleeping so much or lying abed for so long. If they were to leave soon then things needed to be done.

She swung her legs off the bed, the pain brief and tolerable. It was when she stood that she had the problem. Her feet were still a bit sore and her legs weak from spending far too much time in bed. She slowly made her way across the room, leaning on whatever she could along the way. She pulled a skirt and blouse from the chest and slower than she would have liked got dressed.

By the time she was done, she was feeling better from moving around, but when she went to put her boots on, the pain had her hesitating. Her feet were not ready for them. She sat feeling defeated, but only for a moment. She recalled seeing sandals in the chest Rhys had sent to the
~~~

room for her. She smiled with glee when she found them and slipped them on, tying them around her ankles and up along her legs.

Now she needed to find her sisters and have them help her.

Heather realized how late the hour when she entered the Great Hall and found it deserted. Not even the servants lingered about. She thought to go outside, but it would be foolish of her to do that. With it being so late and the night so quiet, there was always a chance of her being abducted again and that she did not want to happen.

A noise in the shadows had her stilling and looking around.

"Lady Heather."

Heather turned with a start, her hand going to her chest, her heart pounding so hard she thought it would burst, to see Seamus emerge from the shadows. "You frightened me, Seamus."

"They are coming, Lady Heather. I heard the cart rolling through the village. They have come to take me away, never to be seen again."

Tears started rolling down the old man's cheeks and Heather went to him, slipping her arm around him. "I will not let them take you, Seamus."

"You cannot stop them, my lady. Everyone in the village is preparing to leave. The word is that the Dragon intends to burn the whole village and the keep to the ground." He wiped at his tears. "It has been my home since birth and he is going to destroy it."

"It is your home no more and what are you doing out of bed, wife?" Rhys said, stepping out of the shadows.

Heather stepped in front of Seamus. "He is frightened, Rhys, having seen those he knows carted off in the middle of the night to God knows where, never to be seen again. I know you would not hurt the old people or anyone you had taken away. So please, for me, tell Seamus where he is being taken so he does not worry himself sick."

Rhys cast a stern glance at Seamus. "You are lucky to have Lady Heather as a friend. The cart takes those to their new home, though tonight Seamus and his family will join the other families, recently taken to a safe area on Macinnes land. There he and the others will remain until the winds of war die down."

"So you would like us to believe," Seamus said, his voice trembling. "The cart takes us to our doom. You get rid of those who cannot serve you. Otherwise you would be truthful with us and not sneak us off in the dark of night. And what of Glynnis? What happened to her?"

Rhys approached Seamus and he watched impressed as the old man tried to stand tall like the warrior he once was, but age refusing him the dignity. "I owe you no explanation, but I will give you the respect due a seasoned warrior and tell you that whatever I do, I do for the safety of my people. And as for Glynnis, she is safe and well. Now your family awaits you and you will go with them one way or another."

Heather turned to Seamus. "You know me and you know my family. Know that when I tell you that my husband is a good man that I speak the truth. He will not hurt you or your family. He will see you all kept safe."

Seamus's shoulders slumped. "The Macinnes I trust."

"You will see all will be well. I will visit with you when I arrive at Macinnes keep."

Rhys noticed she did not say home and it filled his heart with joy. He was home to her now and she truly believed it.

Henry stepped out of the shadows. "Come on, Seamus, your family waits."

Seamus looked to Heather. "I will see you soon."

"That you will Seamus," she assured him.

Once they were gone, Heather stepped close to her husband, wrapped her arm around his and whispered, "How many more of your warriors lurk in the shadows."

"Enough to stop anyone from taking you. Now what are you doing out of bed. It is the middle of the night and you need your rest."

"I did not know the time and I am tired of lying abed all day."

"It is night," he said and swiftly gathered her up in his arms, "and you belong in bed."

"You will join me," she said with an inviting smile.

"Are you trying to seduce me?" he asked, approaching the stairs.

Heather nuzzled at his neck with her lips.

"Stop that," he ordered sharply. "You have only been free of the fever two days. I will not make love to you until I am sure you are well enough."

"I am well enough," she insisted.

He gave her body a tight squeeze and a painful gasp slipped past her lips. "You are not well enough. You will rest until we leave." He did not dare tell her it would be the day after tomorrow or she would never rest. He was grateful her sisters were there to help.

"I will rest on one condition."

He eyed her skeptically. "And what might that be?"

"Show me what is in the locked room."

"Then you will rest?"

"Aye, I will rest."

Rhys carried her up the stairs to the upper floor and set her down easily on her feet.

Heather laughed lightly. "Do you know what those from the McComb clan believe you have locked away in there?"

"Women."

Her brow went up. "You knew?"

"Were you not warned when you first arrived here that I have eyes and ears everywhere? My men keep me apprised of all that goes on as well as servants who wish to win favor with me."

"Another question," Heather said.

"I thought you were eager to see what was in the room."

"I am, but as long as I am learning your various secrets tonight I might as well satisfy my curiosity about another one."

"And what one would that be?"

"What happened to Glynnis?"

"Now is not the time for that story."

"Please," she asked nicely.

"What I tell you is for you only."

She nodded.

"After the man Glynnis loved died, she attempted to take her life. I found her and saw that she was taken care of and when she healed and had a chance to think of what she had done, she felt ashamed. She did not know how she would face her clan. I offered her a new home where she could make a new start. She agreed and asked that Aggie be sent to join her once she fully healed. Glynnis and Aggie are both together now and doing well."

"You are a generous and loving man," Heather said a tear peeking from the corner of her eye.

Rhys kissed the single tea away. "Not many would agree with you." He reached up along the top of the wood door frame and pulled down a key. He unlocked the bolt and the door squeaked as he opened it.

"Wait here," he said and entered the room, getting swallowed up by darkness.

A light suddenly flickered and grew and Heather did not wait, she was too eager to see what was inside. She stopped and stared when she entered the room. The room was half full of chests with fine silks spilling out of some while other chests overflowed with fine garments. Gold statues and artfully painted urns sat side by side and large round pillows in bright colors were piled haphazardly on top of one another. Gold candlesticks almost as tall as she stood like sentinels near the window.

She walked amidst the items to stand in the middle and take in all she could, though she surely missed something, there was so much to see. Her eyes landed on her husband. "What is all this?"

"Things I collected in the three months I was a free man. Some I purchased myself with the coins I earned for winning my freedom, some were gifted to me for my bravery and some were gifts from Haidar." He walked over to her and took her in his arms. "These are all for you, though it is only half of what awaits you at home."

"They are all truly beautiful. I do not know what to look at first."

"Look to your heart's content and if you see anything that you want to look more closely at I will get it for you."

Heather drifted out of her husband's arms and walked around, stopping now and again to touch or look over the various items, until finally she said, "I found something that catches my eye and I want more than anything."

Rhys went to her side. "Show me it and it is yours."

Heather smiled and tapped his chest. "You, I want you. You are worth more to me than all the riches in the world."

Rhys took her face in his hands. "I do so love you, wife." He kissed her, intending it to be no more than a light, tender kiss.

Heather would not have it. She did not think nor did she care that she was still healing. She had missed her husband and the intimacy they shared, and she let him know it. She wrapped her arms around his neck, hanging on as if she would never let go, rubbed her body invitingly against his, feeling him grow in strength against her, and kissed him with a hunger that left no doubt what she wanted from him.

Rhys tried to fight it. She was still healing, he reminded himself. He had to get her back into bed, a thought that only fueled his rapidly mounting passion.

Push her away. Send her to her chambers. Take your hands off her. Stop kissing her.

Heather tore her mouth away from his. "Please, please," she begged, "make love to me."

"You need to rest," he argued.

"I need you more."

"You have not fully healed." Was he trying to convince her or himself?

"Your love will heal me."

He did not want to deny her or himself, but it was for her own good. He was about to tell her just that when she stepped away from him and stripped herself bare.

Chapter Thirty-one

Rhys had been trained to never lose control, to never to let anything rule him, to always be in command. At this moment, he was not in command...love for his wife had taken command.

He went to the door, shut it, then striped himself bare and as he walked over to his wife, he said, “We go slow and easy, for you are still bruised and sore.”

Heather smiled and ran at him, jumping just as she got to him.

Rhys caught her and her legs locked around his body, her arms around his neck and her lips took charge of his. So much for slow and easy, he thought.

It took only a few short minutes for him to lose all reason and surrender to not only her hunger, but his as well. He turned to carry her to the pillows.

“No! No!” she protested. “The door, brace me against the door and make me come hard and fast, then we can go to the pillows and you can make me come again.”

“Only twice?” he teased.

She turned a stricken expression on him. “Good lord, no! You have two days to make up for.” She smiled then and resumed kissing him.

Her teasing words turned him hard and raging passion took control and with quick strides he carried her to the door, braced her against it, lifted her bottom, and drove into her.

She dropped her head back against the door with a thud and moaned with pleasure before saying. "I have so missed the feel of you inside me."

Rhys settled his lips on her neck and in between playful nips said, "I have missed you, Heather, God how I have missed you."

Tears stung her eyes. He was not talking about the last two days, but the last ten years. She choked back her tears and lowered her head, to whisper in his ear. "Never again. We will never be separated again."

"Never," he agreed and he did as she asked, he took her hard and fast and when she climaxed, her screams of pleasure fading, he carried her to the pillows and stirred her again.

Rhys had not intended for them to make love as long as they did and by the time they finished, sunrise was not far off and Heather was sound asleep.

He dressed, then wrapped her in a strip of red silk he took from one of the chests and carried her down to their bedchamber and tucked her in bed and kissed her on the cheek before leaving her to sleep.

He found Pitt in the Great Hall talking with Rogan and Hunter and joined them.

"I am surprised, though relieved, to see that Patience is still abed," he said teasingly to Hunter.

Hunter laughed. “She is with your warrior Henry insisting he teach her some of his skills.”

Rhys shook his head, though had to laugh. “How do you manage being wed to her?”

“I have thought the same myself,” Rogan said with a grin.

Hunter raised his tankard. “With humor and passion.”

Nessa approached the table with another pitcher of ale.

“Nessa, go fetch Lady Heather’s garments from the room on the upper floor that is now unlocked and take them to her room, but do not wake her. She needs her rest.”

Pitt was quick to stand. “I will help you.” He placed his hand to her lower back and escorted her from the room.

“I do not think the task will be done soon,” Hunter said, grinning.

Rhys shook his head and told them about Fife and what he had done to Nessa. “I believe Pitt had feelings for Nessa before everything happened and afterwards when he was there to comfort and help her, he began to realize just how much he cared for her. Time will tell if Nessa feels the same.”

“Considering everything that has gone on here, your people seem content. No one protests leaving?” Rogan asked.

“It is not their choice; it is mine,” Rhys said. “And I do what must be done for their well-being.”

"My brother Greer cares for no one's well-being. He wants war with the Clan Macinnes. He has wanted war with them for some time. He has planned for war and has gathered allies that fear him too much to deny him," Hunter said.

Rhys shook his head. "Then his allies must be made to fear someone more than him. And I am sure you have something to say about that, Patience, so do join us."

"Damn, you heard me," Patience said, stepping out of the shadows and approaching the table. "I thought I might have gotten the hang of walking silently."

Hunter held his hand out to her. "I did not hear you."

"Neither did I," Rogan said.

Patience took her husband's hand and slipped her legs over the bench to sit beside him. "You two do not count." She looked to Rhys. "And the only person Greer's allies would fear more than him would be you. But it takes time for word to reach them that the Dark Dragon has wed a Macinnes and is now allied with the clan. And then there is your foe. Surely he would ally with Greer if it would benefit him."

"Haidar does not ally with anyone. He uses them until they are of no more use to him."

"I am curious," Patience said.

"A trait you share with your sister," Rhys said.

"I share many good traits with her and Emma," Patience said with a smile. "Why leave here when sizeable troops have arrived to protect you?"

"They are not here to protect me. They are here to prevent war."

Nessa rushed into the room. "Lady Patience, your sister Emma asks that you hurry to Lady Heather's room."

Patience sprang up off the bench, though not as quickly as Rhys.

"What is wrong?" Rhys demanded, walking toward Nessa with Patience hurrying alongside him.

Nessa bit at her lips and tears stung at her eyes. "I do not know."

Rhys hurried up the stairs, Patience trying unsuccessfully to get passed him. He threw open the door and Patience ducked under his arm and rushed in before him.

"What is wrong?" Patience asked anxiously.

"Nothing," Heather assured her sister with a yawn.

Rogan and Hunter entered the room and stood to the side.

Rhys looked at his wife and silently cursed himself. She looked exhausted, her face pale and her eyes drooping, as if they wished to close, and her shoulders slumped.

"I could not wake her," Emma said worry still clear in her voice. "And I found her wrapped in this red silk..." She did not finish the obvious. Heather was naked beneath the red silk.

"I woke in the middle of the night and could not sleep. I only fell asleep a short while ago," Heather explained her face flushing pink.

"You are feverish again and how do you explain what you are wrapped in?" Emma asked her hand going to Heather's brow.

Heather shoved her sister's hand away. "I have no fever. I am tired that is all."

Patience turned and marched over to Rhys and poked him in the chest. "You did this. You could not keep your hands off her."

Emma gasped. "Did you? I warned you against it."

Hunter and Rogan went to their wives.

Rogan slipped his arm around Emma. "This is best left to Rhys and Heather."

Hunter took hold of Patience. "Rogan is right."

Patience squirmed out of her husband's grip and poked Rhys again. "I thought you loved Heather."

"He does!" Heather said in a stern voice as she climbed out of bed, tucking the red silk that cocooned her to hold at her chest. She grimaced as she walked toward Patience.

Rhys moved to help her, but she stopped him with a raised hand and a stern look. She stopped beside Patience and Hunter wisely stepped away. "I do not interfere with you and Hunter. She looked over at Emma. "Or you and Rogan. I ask the same of you when it comes to my husband and me."

"I do not want to see you hurt," Patience said.

"Either does my husband," Heather said.

Emma fought back tears. "We have always looked after each other."

"And we always will," Heather assured her. "But things have changed since we wed." She turned to Patience. "You need to know that the Dark Dragon loves me and I love him just as I know Hunter loves you and you love him." She turned to Emma. "And Rogan loves you and you love him. You see, we are not the only ones who love us anymore."

"I do not want us to part," Emma said a tear running down her cheek as she walked over to her sisters.

"We will never part," Heather said, holding her arm out to embrace Emma.

Patience slipped under Heather's other arm.

Rhys nodded to Hunter and Rogan and the three men slipped quietly out of the room, leaving the sisters alone.

Heather kissed Emma's brow. "I will be there to deliver my niece or nephew." She turned to Patience and hugged her close. "And you will come spend time with Rhys and me so you can learn the ways of the ghost warriors. We will never part. We will always be sisters and we will always love one another."

The three hugged and tears were plentiful, but the Macinnes sisters knew without a doubt that love would always keep them together.

~~~

Rhys found his wife on the upper floor directing Nessa in the packing of Mary McComb's solar.

"You have not slept enough," he scolded as he walked over to her and took her in his arms.

"I could not return to sleep after speaking with my sisters," she said, resting her head to his welcoming chest. "And I want to make sure that everything I want goes with us since you have plans for us to leave tomorrow."

Rhys shook his head. "I need not ask how you know. You have friends here who would tell you."

"I do not see how we can be done by tomorrow," Heather said, "though your warriors have worked hard in emptying the room of all your treasures and loading them on to the enclosed wagons."

"Your sisters have been a great help and my people were aware that this was not a permanent home. I think most look forward to leaving and finally going home."

Heather kissed his cheek. "You will always be my home, Rhys."

That she continued to acknowledge him as Rhys, pleased him. He was Quinn no more and had not been for some time, and he was relieved that she understood that.

"I love you, wife," he said and hugged her close.
~~~

She smiled. "I will never grow tired of hearing you tell me that."

"And I will never grow tired of telling you," he said. "Now how can I help?"

~~~

Heather yawned and dropped down in the chair by the hearth. Tonight would be her last night here. It was the place where she had come to discover her love for the Dark Dragon and reclaim her love for Quinn. It would always hold a special spot in her heart.

Rhys came up behind her and rested a strong hand on her shoulder. "You need to sleep. It will not be an easy journey for you with those bruises that still pain you. I have a cart prepared for you to travel in."

Heather laughed. "I will ride in no cart. I left Macinnes keep in your arms and I will return there in your arms."

"You are a stubborn woman."

She laughed again. "I am a loving wife who does not wish to leave her husband's side."

Rhys stepped in front of her and lifted her out of the chair and up into his arms. "And by my side is where I always want you to be."

"There is something I wish you to do for me," Heather said.

"Anything," Rhys said.
~~~

Heather went and retrieved the ring she had saved from the fire and handed it to him.

"I looked for this, regretting I had thrown it in the flames."

"It sealed our love once and I wish it to seal our love again," she said. "It is a symbol of our everlasting love."

Rhys took her hand and slipped the ring on her finger. "I was surprised, though pleased to see that you still had it."

"I wore it the whole time you were gone, only taking it off when I thought I would wed and still I kept it close. I wore it on a ribbon around my neck. Now, it will forever remain on my finger."

Rhys kissed her gently as he lifted her into his arms and carried her to the bed. They would not only seal their love again this night, but they would make memories to live long in their hearts.

~~~

Sunrise brought with it a flurry of activity. The animals were the first to be led away, since it would take a bit more time to get them to Macinnes land. Wagons were piled with furnishings and food supplies and laughing children thought it a delight to ride upon them.

Emma joined Heather to see if anyone needed tending before it was time to leave. And afterwards it was her sisters' turn to leave. They hugged and
~~~

talked of how tonight they would celebrate at home, a family once more if only for a brief time.

The people went next, walking alongside their carts, talking and laughing and not at all upset that they were leaving, but then Rhys had said they would be going home soon and who would not want to go home?

Nessa smiled as she waved to Heather, looking happier than she had expected, but then Nessa was leaving unhappy memories behind.

Heather walked into the keep to have one last look. It was so silent and empty. Anything that had remotely made it a home had been removed. It was now an empty shell. She hurried outside, memories causing tears to run down her cheeks.

The small village was empty, not a sound was heard.

"It is time to leave," Rhys said, coming up behind her.

Heather turned and melted into his arms, letting her tears fall, knowing that she was leaving much behind, though taking so much more with her.

Rhys lifted her onto his horse and mounted behind her. He reached down and took something from one of the warriors that had been standing there.

"A gift for you," Rhys said.

Before Heather could tell him that she needed no more gifts from him, he dropped the black pup with the white paw in her lap. The little fellow scrambled up her chest to lick her tears away.

"He saved you and since he protected you once he will always do so. Name him what you will, he is yours."

Heather smiled and hugged the little pup close and, content with where he was, he curled up against her and went to sleep.

Rhys directed his stallion away from the village and once a short distance away, he turned his horse and raised his hand.

Soon cottage after cottage went up in flames and when flames poured from the keep's windows, tears rolled down Heather's cheeks.

"It was necessary," Rhys said, feeling her weep. "If I had not done it, when Haidar found it empty he would have. And it was not his to burn."

Rhys turned his stallion. "Now it is time to prevent a war."

Chapter Thirty-two

Heather had been at Macinnes keep for two days now and it was funny how it no longer felt like home to her. She had never thought the day would come when she would feel that way. But she had been wrong. While she still cared for the people here and loved her family, it was different now that she had Rhys. And more recently Finn, the name she had given the little pup who was entertaining himself by scampering through the garden, taking bites of different plants.

"You are happy, I can see it," her da said, joining her on the bench in the keep's large kitchen garden.

Heather was pleased to see her da looking so well. "More than I ever thought possible," she admitted to him and herself as well. "I must ask—did you know the Dark Dragon was Quinn?"

"I had strong suspicions. He materialized suddenly, requesting your hand in marriage and then demanding it. And he seemed to know so much about you. I had to rely on my instincts, though it seemed unlikely that Quinn should return after all these years, something told me otherwise. And so I took a chance. I wanted you to be happy. You deserved it."

Heather reached out for her father's hand. "I am so grateful that you did. Now, da, you need not worry about any of your daughters any more. We have each found good husbands. It is your turn to enjoy the woman you love."

His eyes turned wide.

Heather smiled. "Rhys told me of Maura and you and I think it is wonderful. I imagine Emma will too." She shrugged. "Patience I am not so sure of."

They laughed together.

Patience came running toward them. "Hurry, da, Greer has sent a message to you and waits not far from here with an army of warriors."

Donald hurried off and Heather scooped up Finn, the pup protesting with a small yap as she tucked him under her arm and carried him off to the keep.

~~~

Everyone waited anxiously in the Great Hall to learn what the message read that Greer McLaud had sent Donald Macinnes.

Donald shook his head as he finished reading and announced, "Greer declares war on Clan Macinnes for the murder of his wife and demands the release of his brother Rab and Saundra who he claims the Macinnes took as prisoners."

"So he does not know what happened to Rab," Hunter said, "yet he knows his wife is dead
~~~

and Saundra resides here. I would venture to guess that his assumption that we hold Rab prisoner gave him even more reason to wage war."

"He says we have until tomorrow at dawn to release Rab and Saundra or he will attack," Donald said. "I will invite him to come speak with us."

"You waste your breath," Rhys said his arm around his wife and the pup snarling and nipping at his boot. "He is not interested in talking. He plans to defeat you and claim your land. He thinks nothing will stop him."

"Rhys is right," Hunter said. "Nothing will stop him." Except a sword, Hunter thought, though would not say so since his mum sat at the table beside Ewan and was still grieving for the death of one son.

"Before dawn tomorrow, Hunter and I will go speak with Greer," Rhys said.

"Hunter and you can come if you want," Patience said, "but it will be me, a Macinnes, who rides out there to confront Greer."

"If your father permits it," Rhys said.

"I need no permission from my father," Patience snapped.

"He is still chieftain of Clan Macinnes and you do not go without his permission," Rhys warned.

Donald raised his hand and Patience wisely kept silent. "Patience is right. A Macinnes needs to ride with you and she will be the one to go."

"As you say," Rhys said with a nod. "Few words will be necessary to exchange with him since more of my troops wait on word from me. When he learns that the Dark Dragon is allied with the Clan Macinnes and that he cannot possibly see victory, let us hope he wisely surrenders."

"I will send a message to Greer, letting him know we wish to speak with him at sunrise," Donald said.

Ross, Ewan's youngest son, spoke up "What will happen to Saundra now?" He placed a hand on her shoulder, standing protectively behind where she sat at the table not too far from his father.

"By agreement with her father, Saundra belongs to me now. Her fate is mine," Rhys announced to startled cries and wide eyes.

Ross squared his shoulders and bravely said, "Then I request her hand in marriage."

Rhys looked from him to Saundra. "What say you Saundra?"

"I would like that and be ever so grateful if you would grant permission," Saundra said and turned a smile on Ross.

"Then so be it, I grant permission," Rhys said.

A much needed cheer rose in the room.

Talk and preparation for tomorrow continued and it was a somber supper that was shared.

Everyone retired early, wanting to be fit for battle tomorrow if necessary.

Rhys had learned that having a woman before battle drained a man's strength and not wanting to discuss with his wife how he had discovered that, he waited until he was certain she would be asleep before he joined her in bed.

Heather woke with a start, causing Rhys to do the same and causing Finn to rouse from his spot by the hearth and start howling, though it was not much of a howl for one so young.

"What is it?" he asked

"Something is wrong?" she said and jumped out of bed to hurry into her clothes.

Rhys did the same, slipping his leather armor on as well.

Heather scooped up Finn and followed Rhys out the door.

Patience and Hunter were dressed and already in the hall. Emma's door opened and she and Rogan stepped out dressed as well.

"Something is not right," Emma said.

The bell sounded its ominous toll.

They were being attacked.

They all rushed through the keep and when Rhys went to step outside, he quickly turned and pushed his wife back, shutting the door and reaching to drop the wood bar across it. Rogan and Hunter hurried to help him.

"Stay here, all of you," Rhys ordered. "These men fight like no other. My men will deal with them."

Pitt rushed in from another entrance. "Haidar's men are swarming in and behind them are Greer's men."

"Have our troops been alerted? Haidar will have made sure they did not see this coming."

"I have sent word with more than one warrior."

Donald Macinnes soon entered the Great Hall along with Maura. Ewan and Una soon followed, and Ross and Saundra were not far behind.

Without warning, Rhys jumped at Patience, giving her a hard shove and sending her stumbling just as a blade was about to slice her shoulder. He quickly sent his blade through the warrior who was covered in black and could barely be seen. Next, Rhys shoved Rogan out of the way and swung his sword again impaling another man that dove out of the shadows along the wall.

Pitt stopped another with his sword.

"Get the women out of here," Rhys yelled as more warriors suddenly emerged from the shadows.

"You know where to go," Donald yelled to his daughters, drawing his sword and seeing Patience do the same.

Heather grabbed Finn who was busy standing guard in front of her, yapping at anyone who came near her. She took Emma's arm and hurried her out of the Great Hall, Una, Maura, and Saundra keeping pace with them.

There was a small room just before you reached the kitchen that few ever noticed since it blended with the shadows and that was where Heather took the women. She held the door as one after the other rushed in and was about to step in right behind Una and close the door when she felt as if her arm was torn from her body, someone having grabbed and yanked so hard.

"Shut it! Shut it!" Heather screamed as she struggled to free herself. She heard Emma yelling *no*, and was relieved to see the door slam shut and hear the board fall into place. They were safe...for now.

The hand gripped her tight. She could not budge it. She dropped Finn, not able to hold him as she fought to break free. The little pup yapped and yapped at the warrior, and followed after Heather as she was dragged through the kitchen and out the door.

Anger and fear gripped her and she lashed out at the warrior determined not to be taken again. The warrior swerved around, his hand coming down on her cheek so hard that for a moment it stunned her and she could not see clearly. She heard Finn's repeated yaps, and then she heard him cry out in pain. Fury rose up in her that Finn could be hurt and she let her anger loose on the warrior with all the strength she could muster.

Suddenly, his hand fell off her and she was free.

"Run!"

She looked to see Seamus standing there, a sword in his hand, the blade dripping with blood.

"Run!" he yelled again and gave her a shove and went to follow her when a blade suddenly tore through his chest and he gasped. The blade disappeared as fast as it had appeared and he fell to his knees, his dying breath urging her, "Run!"

Heather turned, but it was too late. One of Haidar's warriors stood behind her and in front of her stood Haidar.

"This time you will not get away," Haidar sneered. "And you will never feel the soil of your homeland beneath your feet after this day is done."

"True, but it is you who will never feel the soil of your homeland beneath your feet again."

Heather turned to see the Dragon standing behind her, gripping the hilt of his sword, the blade covered in blood, Haidar's warrior dead at his feet and Finn standing on top of him, his little chest puffed out proudly and his head high. She scooped Finn up off the dead warrior, and ducked behind him.

"More of my warriors will come," Haidar warned.

"Your warriors are meeting their deaths at the hands of my men."

"That paltry group in the woods that await your word?" Haidar said with a laugh.

Rhys waited until his laughter died. "You taught me well. That troop was there for you to see what I wanted you to see. It is the massive army of warriors behind them that you failed to see and who now finish off your warriors one by one."

"You have learned nothing," Haidar challenged. "The warriors who wait on my ships will be here soon and I will see everyone dead, except you and your beautiful wife, of course."

Rhys wiped the blood from his sword on the body at his feet. "They will not becoming and your ships will not be sailing...my warriors made sure of that. As I said, you taught me well and now it is time for you to die." Rhys lunged at him with his sword.

Heather had seen what a skilled swordsman her husband was and now she saw why. Haidar handled a blade as if he was born with it in his hand. The Dragon had learned from a master and suddenly Heather feared for her husband's life.

Haidar seemed to toy with Rhys, deflecting every thrust and swing with ease as if he purposely prolonged the inevitable. The enjoyment Haidar was getting was apparent in his smile and confident movements.

Finally, Haidar seemed to tire of his actions and stepped away from Rhys, his smile replaced with angry scowl. "You rob me of burning your home and you rob me of taking you home with me and seeing you suffer for what you have done. But before I take your life know that your wife will suffer more than you ever did."

Rhys moved so fast that he was a blur to Heather and Haidar as well, and the next thing she saw was Haidar's sword arm sliced near to the bone, his sword dropping from his useless hand. But Rhys did not stop there. By the time he finished, Haidar was on his knees, blood running down from what was left of both his arms.

Haidar raised his head, fighting against the pain. "At least I die at the hands of a worthy opponent."

Rhys dropped his sword and pulled a dagger from his boot. "I promised Anala I would deliver a message to you before I killed you." He stepped behind Haidar, grabbed him by the hair, and yanked his head back, pressing the dagger's blade to his throat. He leaned down and whispered, "Anala told me to tell you that she gave you the only son that you would ever have and never live to see."

Haidar's eyes turned wide. "My son lives?"

"He does and good Scottish parents took him in, they love him, and call him their own, and he will never know any differently." Rhys drew the blade across Haidar's throat swiftly and as he bled to death he glared at Rhys with hate-filled eyes.

Rhys wiped the dagger clean on Haidar's shirt and snatched his sword up off the ground and looked to see his wife crouched over a body. He went over to her and dropped down beside her and saw that it was Seamus.

She turned tearful eyes on her husband. "He died trying to save me."

"Then I am forever grateful to him and pleased that he died a warrior's death, not a crippled old man, which I believe was his intention when he picked up his sword and joined the fight. I will see he has a warrior's burial and see that he is buried where he wished to stay—on McComb land, his home." He helped Heather to stand.

She glanced over at Haidar, and then back at her husband. "You are finally free."

"I was finally free when I first held you in my arms."

He went to kiss her when suddenly a warrior rounded the corner with his arm tight around Patience's throat and a dagger in his hand. He made a wide berth around Rhys and Heather.

Hunter came barreling around the corner and stopped when his eyes fell on his wife. "Let her go, Greer, this is between you and me."

"You ruined everything," Greer yelled.

Heather wondered why Patience did not do something. She had seen her sister get out of that type of hold many times. Then she saw the blood running down her arm. Patience was too weak to fight back. Instinctively, she stepped forward and felt a strong hand pull her back.

Heather looked at her husband. "She needs tending now."

"Wait," Rhys ordered.

Heather did not argue. She trusted her husband; he would not fail her sister.

"You did this yourself," Hunter said and cast a quick glance at Rhys who gave a slight nod to him.

"I should have killed you before I killed our father," Greer shouted. "You were always nothing but trouble to me."

"Then here is your chance. Fight me like a true warrior."

Greer looked from his brother to Rhys. "Once I kill you the Dragon will kill me."

"I give you my word that if you kill me no one will stop you. You will go free," Hunter said and gave a nod to the Dragon.

"I will see your word kept," Rhys said.

Greer let go of Patience and stepped away as she dropped to the ground.

Rhys went over and lifted her into his arms and brought her to his anxious wife.

"Leave us," Greer shouted.

Rhys turned after placing Patience on the ground, Heather already busy tending her. "If I leave and you live there will be no one to guarantee your safety. Now fight and be done with it, you fool."

"I will come back for you," Greer sneered.

Rhys laughed. "Ghosts do not frighten me."

Raging anger turned Greer's face bright red and like the fool he was, he charged at his brother.

Rhys was well aware of how skilled Hunter was with a sword, but it was his ability to focus and let nothing interfere when he wielded his sword that made Hunter an exceptional swordsman.

Greer thrashed about while Hunter delivered precise blows and Rhys could see that Hunter was delaying killing his brother, but then Greer deserved to suffer some before he died for having taken his own father's life.

"Kill the fool and be done with it!" Heather shouted.

Rhys turned, shocked by her words.

Hunter smiled, though it vanished as with two quick strokes he ended it, Greer's body dropping to the ground dead. Hunter hurried to his wife. When he saw her eyes closed and looking so lifeless, his eyes went anxiously to Heather.

"We need to get her inside and sear the wound before she loses more blood," Heather said. "And you must know it was Patience who insisted I shout that out to you."

"I knew the words were hers even if the voice was not," Hunter said, easing his wife up into his arms.

"She wanted you beside her that was why she urged you to be done with it," Heather said. "Whenever she got sick or frightened when she was young, she would not want me to leave her side. Now, as it should be, she wants you...her husband."

"I will not be leaving her side until she is well," Hunter said and carried her to the door.

"I never wager," Rhys called out, "but I wager you will be eating those words soon enough."

Chapter Thirty-three

One month later

The Macinnes sisters sat on a bench in the garden that had once been Heathers pride and joy, their hands clasped to one another.

"You will see that the garden is tended well," Heather said tears clouding her eyes.

"I will make certain of it," Patience said, sniffling back tears.

Tears rolled down Emma's cheeks. "I cannot wait until this babe is born so I will stop crying so much."

"What does Hunter have planned for the Clan McLaud now that he is chieftain?" Heather asked.

"We have talked, but he has made no decision yet. In time, he will know what to do."

"But you will not leave Macinnes land, will you?" Emma said, though she and Heather already knew the answer.

Patience shook her head. "Never, and Hunter is well aware of that." She squeezed her sisters' hands. "It is odd. I will miss not having you both here, but I look forward to life with my husband."

Heather smiled. “We will always be there for one another, always love one another, but it is time we start our own lives.”

“And we have three fantastic husbands to do that with,” Emma said.

Patience shook her head. “I still do not know about the Dragon. He can be a handful to deal with at times.”

Emma and Heather burst out laughing.

~~~

It had taken time and much work to recover from the battle. Haidar’s warriors had fought to the bitter end until not one of them was left. Greer’s warriors quickly surrendered to Hunter their new chieftain. The damage the village had suffered during battle was quickly repaired and the dead, friend and foe alike, were buried.

The time finally came for Heather to bid her family good-bye once again, but this time it was a much happier farewell. She had hugged and kissed her da and made him promise to come visit her. She made Maura promise to look after her da, though Heather had no doubt she would. The woman truly loved him. She had cheered along with everyone when Una and Ewan announced they would wed. And she shed tears of joy when she watched not only Una and Ewan exchange marriage vows in a simple ceremony, but Ross and Saundra as well. Rhys had insisted they wed before his departure so
~~~

that he knew Saundra was safe and well cared for. She had assured her sister Emma for the hundredth time that she would be there for the birth of her babe and wished her a safe trip, she and Rogan taking their leave shortly after her and Rhys.

Heather gave a final wave to all as she rode off tucked in front of her husband on his stallion and Finn curled comfortably asleep on her lap.

"Tell me what I can do to make this parting easier for you," Rhys said, kissing her brow.

"You have already made it easier."

"How have I done that?"

"You let loose the Dragon to love me."

He leaned his head down and whispered before kissing her, "The Dragon has always loved you and he always will."

THE END

Titles by Donna Fletcher

Single Titles

San Francisco Surrender
Rebellious Bride
The Buccaneer
Tame My Wild Touch
Playing Cupid
Whispers on the Wind

Series Books

Wyrrd Witch Series

The Wedding Spell
Magical Moments
Magical Memories
Remember the Magic

The Irish Devil
Irish Hope

Isle of Lies
Love Me Forever

Dark Warrior
Legendary Warrior

The Daring Twin
The Bewitching Twin

Taken By Storm

The Highlander's Bride

Sinclare Brothers' Series
Return of the Rogue
Under the Highlander's Spell
The Angel & The Highlander
Highlander's Forbidden Bride

Warrior King Series
Bound To A Warrior
Loved By A Warrior
A Warrior's Promise
Wed To A Highland Warrior

Highlander Trilogy
Highlander Unchained
Forbidden Highlander
Highlander's Captive

Rancheros Trilogy
Untamed Fire
Renegade Love
Third book yet to be titled

Sexual Appetites of Unearthly Creatures Novella
Sexual Appetites of Vampires

Macinnes Sisters Trilogy
The Highlander's Stolen Heart
Highlander's Rebellious Love
Highlander The Dark Dragon

About the Author

Donna Fletcher is a USA Today bestselling author of historical and paranormal romances. Her books are sold worldwide. You can find out more about Donna and, if you don't want to miss any of her new releases, you can subscribe to her Book Alerts at www.donnafletcher.com .

Printed in Poland
by Amazon Fulfillment
Poland Sp. z o.o., Wrocław